THE FOX PROWLS

The Fox Prowls

by

VALENTINE WILLIAMS

*Secret Service
Series*

New York
P. F. COLLIER & SON CORPORATION
PUBLISHERS

CONTENTS

I. R.43 STARTS IT   1

II. 'IN RE BOREANU, NÉE CELMAR, DECD.'   3

III. ENTER THE BARON DE BAHL   8

IV. A WANDERER COMES HOME   16

V. FIRST BLOOD   23

VI. RENDEZVOUS IN PIERCE STREET   31

VII. STEPHEN BLURTS OUT A SECRET   37

VIII. MELISSA MEETS THE BARON   47

IX. A KING IS DEAD   57

X. THE BARON PRESENTS HIS FRIENDS   67

XI. 'THE VOICE OF FATE'   75

XII. CASTLE ORGHINA   81

XIII. THE FIRST WARNING   88

XIV. BLOOD IN THE SNOW   94

XV. BOULTON BLOTS HIS COPYBOOK   103

XVI. MELISSA HAS A MIDNIGHT VISITOR   111

XVII. WHEN A NAIL IS NOT A NAIL   117

XVIII. THE LIGHT BEGINS TO BREAK   127

XIX. A SUMMONS FROM CHARLES   135

XX. IN THE MOSQUE   142

XXI. THE MAN ON THE BALCONY   150

XXII. THE DNIESTER SQUARES AN ACCOUNT   156

XXIII. STEPHEN HITS THE NAIL ON THE HEAD   166

XXIV. THE BARON HAS A PLAN   176

CONTENTS

XXV. THE FERRYMAN'S HOUSE 182

XXVI. 'NOT OF THE LION, BUT THE FOX' 189

XXVII. FRONTIER INCIDENT 197

XXVIII. THE POT BEGINS TO BOIL 205

XXIX. A TAP AT THE WINDOW 215

XXX. THE CAT'S NINTH LIFE 225

XXXI. MONEY TALKS 230

XXXII. A SHOT IN THE DARK 238

XXXIII. VON WAHLCZEK COMES BACK 247

XXXIV. MONSTERS OUT OF THE NIGHT 255

XXXV. UNDER THE BOYAR GATE 261

XXXVI. EPILOGUE IN THE FOG 267

THE FOX PROWLS

R.43 Starts It

FERDINAND VERMUIVEN, underpaid drudge in a Bucharest money-changer's office, started it. It was his somewhat grubby hand, protruding from under its paper cuff, that lit the fuse. Fizzing and spluttering it ran from Bucharest to Belgrade, from Belgrade back to Bucharest, and from Bucharest to London, where it detonated a bomb in a certain quiet suburban mansion.

If Ferdinand Vermuiven had not looked up from his desk that morning, the whole course of Don Boulton's life would have been changed.

Glancing casually through the plate-glass window at the seething traffic of the Calei Victorei, the clerk perceived a large, rather untidily dressed man sauntering along in the sunshine. He carried his hat in his hand and displayed a crop of crisp white hair. He was accompanied by a spruce individual with a black and restless eye which he flashed ardently at every woman they passed. It was upon the second of the two men that the clerk's gaze dwelt. An hour later, at the humble brasserie where he was wont to take his mid-day meal, he called for pen, ink and paper and wrote to one Peregrine Dyson, importer, at Belgrade:

Hon. Sir,
The undersigned has honour to report that Guido Miklas is back. I see same this A.M. in Victory Street with person un-

known. Description of said person, age circa 50, white complexion, ditto hair, respectably dressed. Regret that business prevented immediate pursuit of said Guido Miklas as per yr. esteemed instructions at our last meeting but on receipt your hon. orders will follow up prompt, habits of party concerned being familiar to yrs. truly but in latter event small advance for indispensable expenses humbly asked (by telegraph s.v.p.!)

Your oblige servant to command,
Hon. Sir,
Yours faithfully,
R.43.

Two days later Vermuiven had a companion when he left the office to pay his customary evening visit to the café. But instead of going to the obscure establishment he usually frequented, he took his friend to a noisy place with mirrors, potted palms and a gypsy orchestra, where a man with a shock of white hair sat with a jaunty individual with a restless eye. Thereafter, Vermuiven escorted his companion to the main telegraph office, after which they drove to the airport, where the clerk saw his charge onto the plane for Belgrade.

To London, into a restful suburban square, the fuse led hissing. Miss Hancock, the Chief's secretary, signed for the telegram: Breakspear in the Ciphers upstairs, across the landing from the Secret Inks, decoded it. Like a flame the news ran round the Cipher Room: Major Armitage, working in the Chief's outer office, knew it, even before the buzzer summoned him.

'You're for Bucharest, Geoffrey,' the Chief greeted him. '"The Fox" is on the prowl again.'

CHAPTER II

'In Re Boreanu, Née Celmar, Decd.'

WHEN old Countess Boreanu died at the age of eighty-eight in her shabby apartment at Bucharest and left Castle Orghina to Stephen Selmar by will, Selmar was crossing to Europe in the *Queen Mary*. It was the first real vacation he had had in Europe since his college days. His previous visits had consisted of a whirlwind round of the Selmar agents in Britain and on the Continent; but now that he had retired from business, he felt entitled to relax and enjoy himself. Moreover, he was planning to test out on a long motor trip through Switzerland and Italy the new Selmar model, which would not be on the market until the New York Automobile Show in the fall.

He had a very happy seven weeks loafing between the Alps and the heel of Italy, especially as the new car came up even to his highly critical standard of performance. His only regret was that Melissa had refused to accompany him. But Melissa was temporarily interested in a young man with a wave in his hair and a job in refrigeration and, having had him included in an invitation she had received to a camp in the Adirondacks, was spending the summer in America. Arguing that a millionaire's only child is privileged to indulge in such whimsies and reflecting that young Barnes was an improvement on the dubious Italian prince who had been Melissa's penultimate passion, Selmar bore his daughter's defection philosophically, relying on her promise to join him in Europe later on. He contented himself with sending her daily cables, mostly of a facetious order:

> ZERMATT TRY NOT THE PASS THE OLD MAN SAID STOP BALONEY TO THAT STOP THE SELMAR EIGHT FLIES THEM ALL STOP MISSING YOU LOVE STEVE
>
> VENICE THIS HOTEL LIKE AN OVEN STOP TELL BOY FRIEND GREAT OPENING FOR AIR-CONDITIONING HERE STOP WHY NOT BRING HIM OVER LOVINGLY STEVE

He liked Melissa to call him by his first name: it kept him young, he used to tell her.

October had come round before Maître Grigorescu's letter, mailed to Selmar at the works in Michigan, caught up with him in London. He found it at his bank there when, having reached Paris at the end of his trip and garaged the car, he flew across the Channel to visit tailor, hosier and shoemaker. Melissa was to join him later — he had a vague plan of spending the winter on the Riviera — but that would not be for another month at least. Already he was beginning to find time hang heavy on his hands, and the lawyer's letter came to him as an amusing diversion.

He read it as he sat, a big, bronzed figure in his holiday grey tweeds, in the chair at the manager's desk. The letter was in English. Written from a Bucharest address on paper headed 'Grigorescu & Sapiro,' it said:

In re the Countess Boreanu, née Celmar, decd.

Dear Sir,

We have the honour to inform you that our late client, the Countess Boreanu, deceased the 17th July last, has bequeathed to you under her will the family property situated on the River Dniester, in the province of Bessarabia, known as Castle Orghina...

'Well, I'll be hornswoggled!' ejaculated Selmar and turned the letter over, as though further elucidation were to be discovered on the other side. Finding nothing, he read on:

The passage in our client's will relative to the bequest, rendered into English, is as follows:

To Stephen Selmar, automobile manufacturer, of Lansing, Michigan, the only descendant of our ancient house who has accomplished anything useful in my lifetime, the historic family stronghold, Castle Orghina, which came back to the family with the expulsion of the Russians and the reunion of Bessarabia with Rumania in the Great War. The aforesaid Stephen Selmar may not be aware of his descent from the illustrious Stephen cel Mare, Moldavia's mighty hero of the fifteenth century and the founder of our line, but I regard him as a worthier representative of our famous ancestor than my useless grandnephews, Georges and Michel, whom I am delighted to disinherit utterly. If only through the excellent motor-car which bears our name (though, unfortunately, in the American spelling) and to whose qualities I can speak, having derived much enjoyment from my Selmar limousine in my declining years, he has revived the family lustre. To him, therefore, I deed Castle Orghina, built and held against the pagan hordes across the Dniester by our common ancestor upon whom Pope Sixtus IV conferred the title of 'Athlete of Christ.' I ask him to receive an old lady's blessing, coupled with the hope that he will spare from his millions the few thousand dollars required to preserve the family stronghold from total ruin...

'Crazy as a coot!' Selmar murmured, pushing back his hat with a bewildered air. The letter wound up by assuring him that his obedient servants, Grigorescu and Sapiro, were prepared to take his instructions, by letter or in person, at any time.

'Where's Bessarabia, Joe?' Selmar asked the bank manager. Mr. Harper wasn't very sure, but he'd send for the atlas. Meanwhile, Selmar read the letter through again.

He knew the family tradition, of course. The first Celmar to land in America had come from Vienna after receiving a bullet through the lungs with the Austrian infantry at Austerlitz, had gone back to soldiering in the War of 1812 against the British, and retired with a grant of land to the Ohio Valley, the name thereafter appearing alternately as 'Selmer' or 'Selmar.' Aunt Agatha, who dabbled in genealogy, had dug up the yarn about the family's descent from Stephen cel Mare: 'cel Mare' meant 'the Great' in Rumanian; but Stephen had not paid much attention to her — he was too busy building motor-cars.

Wilks, the office messenger, brought the atlas. Selmar and the manager pored over it together: Harper pointed to Bessarabia northeast of Bucharest, with Soviet Russia bordering it on the east. Selmar had grown thoughtful. 'How does one get to this place?' he demanded.

'Through Bucharest, I'd say,' replied the bank manager. 'Let's see, doesn't the Orient Express go to Bucharest, Miss Wheeler?'

His blonde secretary spoke up from her desk in the corner. 'That's right, Mr. Harper.'

'How about flying?' Selmar demanded.

'I guess you could fly if you wanted, Mr. Selmar,' said Harper. 'I'll have someone enquire about the services for you if you like.'

'Thanks, Joe. And they'd better book me by the first available plane. Can I give Miss Wheeler a cable?'

'Sure.' The stenographer came forward, pad in hand. 'To your daughter, is it, Mr. Selmar?'

'That's right. The same address.' He drew reflectively on his cigar and began to dictate.

GET OUT YOUR ATLAS   STOP   WE HAVE BEEN LEFT A CASTLE   STOP   IT'S IN BESSARABIA MAP REFERENCE RUMANIA   STOP   GOING DOWN TO LOOK IT OVER STOP   HOW DO YOU FANCY BEING A CHÂTELAINE   STOP LOVE   STEVE

The same evening the reply came back.

ARE YOU CRAZY OR ARE YOU CRAZY   STOP   WHO LEFT US CASTLE AND CAN YOU SEND IT BACK   STOP DOES IT HAVE AIR-CONDITIONING   STOP   IF NOT CAN QUOTE REASONABLEST TERMS   STOP   I RUMPLE YOUR HAIR   STOP   MELISSA

At breakfast-time next morning Selmar boarded the Bucharest plane at Croydon.

Enter the Baron de Bahl

THE streets of Bucharest were hot and dusty in the sunny October afternoon. The Baron de Bahl had doffed his wide-awake hat disclosing a shock of snow-white hair and was sponging his face and neck with his handkerchief as he turned in out of the glare and clatter of the Calei Victorei under the cool porch of the Hotel Metropolis. It was the hour between tea and dinner and the big hall was rather full. The sensuous strains of a Viennese valse softly played came through the palms where a gypsy orchestra in national dress made a patch of white. Faint perfumes and the languid murmur of voices overlaid the air. People came and went. Rumanian officers in gay uniforms, with lack-lustre eyes and powdered cheeks, established at small tables, ogled the women over their grenadine.

The newcomer bowed amiably to an elegant brunette nursing a griffon who smiled at him, and saluted with a condescending wave of the hand a grizzled Rumanian colonel who read the evening paper at one of the tables. He did not stop but, with the relentlessness of a tank, made straight for the telephone desk. He was a big man in a loose, rather over-plump way, but it was less his bulk than the air of authority he dispensed that made people get out of his path. A young fellow well tailored in a dark suit had risen in the rear of the hall on de Bahl's appearance and now with cat-like gait came towards him. His skin was olive and he had dank black hair.

At the telephone desk the Baron coughed diffidently. 'Anything for me, Fräulein Ileana?' he asked in German.

The pretty Austrain telephone attendant was most deferential. 'Your friend, Monsieur Volkoff, called from Monte Carlo, Herr Baron — the Herr Baron's secretary took the communication. Trieste rang. The gentleman left no name. He wished to speak to you personally — he'll call you back. And, *warten Sie ein Bissl*, Paris was on the line ...'

'Monsieur Jaffé, was it?'

'That's right. Your secretary spoke to him. Prague announces a personal call for the Herr Baron at 7 P.M.'

The big man nodded composedly. 'Get me Monte Carlo at once, a personal call for Monsieur Volkoff. You have the hotel number? I'll take Prague at seven — I'll be up in my suite. Here!' He fished out a large leather purse, extracted a note and put it in the telephonist's hand with a friendly pat on the cheek. The girl reddened with pleasure when she saw the note. 'Oh, *danke, Herr Baron!*'

De Bahl turned to find the olive-skinned young man at his side. 'Ah, there you are, Amanescu!' he said in French. 'What did Monte Carlo want? Wait!' He drew him into the gangway between the telephone booths out of earshot of people passing in the hall.

'It was Volkoff. He seemed most anxious to speak to you — I'd quite a job to persuade him that I'm your secretary.'

The Baron had a dry cough that seemed to be chronic with him. He gave it now and asked: 'Did he leave any message?'

'Yes. He said "Tell him to sell."'

'To sell, eh? Jaffé called, too, didn't he? Did you give him my order about those shares?'

'Yes.'

'How was the Bourse?'

'Weak towards the close.' De Bahl seemed pleased. 'A man named Rapp was asking for you at lunch-time,' Amanescu went on.

'Ah!' The Baron's tone was eager. 'What brought him round?'

'He says they've heard from Selmar.'

'The American, yes?'

'He's in London. He's flying over today — he should be here tonight.'

De Bahl's nostrils twitched. His nose was clear-cut and aquiline: with his white hair and regular features it gave him a distinguished air. 'Where's he going to stay — did Rapp tell you?' he questioned sharply.

Amanescu's finger pointed downward. 'Here.' Mechanically the other repeated the gesture. Then he clapped the young man on the back. 'Thanks, my boy. I shan't need you any more tonight. Run away and amuse yourself with the pretty Rumanian ladies. Wait!' Once more the leather purse appeared. The secretary's rather sullen eyes came to life as he perceived the extended note. 'Thanks, Baron!' Then de Bahl sought the lift.

As he entered the sitting-room of his suite, the telephone was pealing. He went to the desk. 'Monte Carlo, Herr Baron,' the operator announced. 'Monsieur Volkoff is on the wire.'

'Vladimir?' spoke the Baron softly into the instrument.

'Is it you, Alexis?' a cautious voice came back in French.

'Speaking.'

'You had my message?'

'Yes. Your Vienna man examined him, then?'

'Yes. He gives him a month.'

De Bahl's dark eyes glistened. 'Good. But it means we shall have to work fast. Are you sure you can keep it dark?'

'Cannot an old gentleman of seventy-five keep his room while the mistral lasts? Listen, Grenander's up to something. He and Wahlczek have been visiting works all over the place for the past fortnight.'

'I know all about Grenander. They won't touch him with a barge pole.'

'Don't be too sure. I hear they're due at Trieste at the end of the month for a conference with certain parties. Apostolou is there already. I think they're cooking something up.'

'You're right, they are. But don't worry, their broth won't be ready by dinner-time.'

'Meaning that yours will?'

'I shouldn't be surprised. Meanwhile, if Grenander turns up at Monte Carlo, as he surely will, keep him at arm's length until I arrive, you understand?'

'You may rely on me.'

With an enigmatic air de Bahl hung up. A furrow between his dark, hot eyes, he stared down at his hands, planted palms down on the blotter. His hands were large and white, but beautifully formed with long, delicate-looking fingers.

He had reached for the telephone again when a sound behind him brought him quickly about. It was the scratch of a match that had caught his ear. A jaunty individual with a restless eye, his hat on his head, stood with his back to the fireplace, nonchalantly lighting a cigarette. 'How many times have I told you, Miklas, that I won't have you sneaking in here without knocking?' said de Bahl.

He spoke in French. His voice was soft and husky, the furred voice of the chain cigarette smoker — one had the impression that he rarely raised it. He did not raise it now: his tone was one of mild reproach. The other blew out his match and dropped it in the fireplace behind him. 'Was I to know you were talking secrets? Besides, the door was ajar.'

The Baron puckered his brow. 'I feel sure I closed it behind me.'

'It was ajar, I tell you.'

De Bahl had helped himself to a cigarette from a tin box on the desk. They were enormous cigarettes, almost as long as a fountain pen. He lit one now, coughed a spiral of smoke and said throatily: 'Rapp was round from Grigorescu's. Selmar will be here tonight.'

Surprise appeared in his companion's face. He was a smartly groomed fellow in his black jacket and striped trousers and wore a large pearl in his tie. His eyes, jet-black and liquid, were round as a cat's, and the teeth below his small, dark moustache were magnificent. Against this he was almost bald, and bags under his eyes gave him a worn and dissipated air. 'So he bit, eh?' he remarked admiringly.

'As I told you he would.'

'But what does an American millionaire want with an old ruin like this? And in Bessarabia, of all Godforsaken places!'

'Castle Orghina is not a ruin. With a little intelligent restoration . . .'

Miklas guffawed. 'And you really think you can persuade him to let us restore it for him?'

'He knows me for a reputable antique dealer and interior decorator. When he was at my place at Geneva this summer ——'

'Bah, a millionaire and his dollars aren't so soon parted. If he has any sense, he'll hand Orghina over to the State.'

The Baron laughed contemptuously. 'For a Greek, my dear Guido, you're a singularly poor psychologist.'

'My mother was Spanish,' was the sulky retort.

'Your mother was out of a Tangier dance hall, and you can put "dance hall" in quotation marks, as well you know, and the less said about her the better. In certain enterprises in which we have been associated together in the past you've proved your worth as architect and draughtsman and as an exponent of direct action — a quick knife thrust, a shot in the nape of the neck or a bomb in the self-starter — I gladly concede that you have few equals.' As he spoke the blood ebbed out of Miklas's face and his eyes glittered venomously. But the Baron proceeded serenely. 'Psychology, however, is not your forte, so kindly leave the psychology to me. Stephen Selmar has all the money he wants, but like most self-made men, he lacks background. If I know anything of the American mentality the Countess Boreanu's bequest has made the strongest appeal to his imagination. Castle Orghina establishes his pedigree, so to speak. It's also a gift, and I've yet to learn that the possession of wealth ever predisposed anybody against getting something for nothing. The fact that Selmar's on his way here proves I'm right.'

'It doesn't prove that he's willing to saddle himself with the place.'

De Bahl veiled his eyes. 'I propose to organise his trip to the Castle and I think I can promise you that he'll accept the legacy.' He blew a cloud of smoke. 'Grenander and Company are having a meeting at Trieste at the end of the month ——'

'With the Ukrainians, it is?'

He nodded. 'Apostolou will keep me posted. But I don't trust him, so I'm sending you down there. But, if all goes as I plan, I shall want you to come down to Castle Orghina with Selmar and me first.'

Miklas laughed. 'You seem very sure of him.'

'I *am* very sure of him. I saw a lot of him at Geneva this summer. I believe I may say without boasting that he eats out of my hand.'

'He must have a better digestion than most American millionaires,' said the other sneeringly. A shadow fell across his face. 'I wanted a word with you about that secretary of yours.'

'What about him?'

'Have you run into an Englishman called Armitage, Geoffrey Armitage, out here, an engineer from London?'

'No. Who is he?'

'He's supposed to be connected with the oil industry. He and Amanescu are as thick as thieves. They meet almost every day.'

'Well, and supposing they do? What about it?'

'Only that Armitage is a British secret service man.'

The Baron's fat cigarette, halfway to his lips, stopped. His eyes glinted between half-closed lids. 'You're sure of this?'

'I know him as well as I know you. He was at Addis Ababa during the Abyssinian business and at Beirut the other day. I ran into him only this morning, coming out of a café with this secretary of yours. I thought I'd make some inquiries. They play billiards every evening at this place.'

De Bahl nodded. 'Did Armitage spot you?'

Miklas laughed. 'He wouldn't know me if he did, I'm too old a hand for that. The British Intelligence, smart as they are, have never been wise to me. I know Armitage, but he doesn't know me.'

He broke off sharply, for the Baron, with a finger to his lips, was pointing with his other hand at the door communicating with the bedroom. In two noiseless bounds Miklas reached the door and softly opened it. From somewhere out of sight came the sound of a door gently closing. Miklas disappeared and re-entered from the corridor. 'There was someone in the bedroom,' he announced, 'but he's gone. Now we know how that door came to be ajar.'

The Baron nodded placidly. 'You'd better keep an eye on our British friend, Guido.'

'And what about Amanescu?'

The other smiled. 'When they're going to hang a man in England, Guido, the hangman visits the jail the day before the execution and peeps at his victim through a spy-hole in the door to calculate the length of drop he'll give him. Not a word to our smart young friend for the moment. I'll watch him and see how much rope he'll take.' He chuckled. 'They don't call me "The Fox" for nothing. You leave the young man to me.

He laughed with great good humour. 'Go now — I have some more telephoning to do,' he said. Miklas went out, leaving him at the desk, his loose frame shaking with laughter interspersed with coughing.

A Wanderer Comes Home

IT WAS only mid-October, but the first fog of the year had dropped down over London. The day had broken dim and windless and the risen sun showed itself to Londoners going to work as a pink disk glowing through an orange pall. By noon the lights were on and along Oxford Street and Regent Street the shop-fronts blazed. In Piccadilly the electric signs were flashing above the silvery furrows cut by the head-lamps of the slowly groping traffic.

With the falling of dusk the fog thickened. In London's vast acreage of suburbs, away from the glare of the shopping streets, it was night. As Boulton's taxi chugged into the quiet square, the trees stood like dim wraiths behind the battered railings of the central garden, and the street lamps, ringed with brown radiance, had the dull gleam of sequins sewn on the curtain of fog. The air was raw and smelt of soot; the young man shivered in his thick scarf and heavy Melton overcoat. 'What a day to come home!' he murmured.

The taxi stopped at one of the tall houses in the square, a 'gentleman's residence,' mid-Victorian and smug, the sort of place where you would expect a judge or a prosperous chartered accountant to live. Boulton jumped out, thrust his hand in his pocket. 'Hell!' he remarked to the dim figure on the box, 'Egyptian money is no good to you, is it? Just a minute!'

All the lights were on in the hall when Petty Officer Potts, one hundred and eighty pounds of solid muscle turning into fat, opened to his ring. 'Potts, my old salt!' was the young man's greeting.

The doorman's forefinger jerked to his grizzled cowlick. 'Arternoon, Mr. Boulton, sir! We ain't seen you in a row o' Sundays! Blow me down, it must be all o' three months! My word, you 'ave bin out in the sun, 'aven't you? As nice a coat o' tan as ever I see!'

The young man shuddered. 'Does the sun ever shine in this cursed town, I wonder?' he remarked feelingly. With a flick of the hand he sent his rather grubby felt flying in the direction of the hat-stand. It landed adroitly on one of the hooks. 'Bull's-eye!' he murmured with gratification. The doorman helped him out of his overcoat. 'Ouch! Mind my shoulder!' the visitor warned.

'Still 'ave trouble with it, do you, sir?' said the other, folding the garment and laying it on the chair.

Boulton nodded. 'It's this cursed damp weather. Ah, my Potts, never sell your farm and go up in the air!'

The doorman grinned. 'No fear, Mr. Boulton, sir! I copped mine at Jutland. I'm ashore for keeps!'

'A Jutland veteran, a hero full of honours, with a snug berth and a pension — you're on velvet, Potts. Look at me! A choked feed pipe crashes me and because it's in peace time and I'm not on duty, I'm just a blinking civilian with a busted shoulder and darn glad to have landed a job. The trouble is, Potts, my hearty, I was born too late!'

The doorman chuckled. 'There was times in the war when some of us allowed as we was born too early!'

'And to think,' the young man continued, unwinding his

scarf, 'that I might have flown one of these marvellous new 'buses they're dishing out to the troops at present instead of the sudden-death contraptions which were all we had when I was in the Force. Oh, hell!' He dropped his scarf on top of his overcoat. 'Don't shut that door for a moment: I have to pay off my cab. Hey, Hanky!'

A plain girl of indeterminate age, very neat as to dress and hair, was crossing the hall. At his hail she advanced composedly under the rays of the hall lamp, peering through horn-rimmed glasses. 'So you've arrived at last!' she observed without enthusiasm.

He struck an attitude and in a voice that shook the hall, chanted:

> At home at last, all danger past,
> I hail my native vill—age!

dwelling tenderly on the last note, which ran up an octave. He held out his hand. 'Half a crown for the taxi, please. I've no English money. Why on earth do you have to live in the suburbs?'

'Stop that noise at once! The Chief's in conference.' She was hunting through her purse. 'Mind you pay me back! No charging it against the petty cash. Your expense allowance ceases when you leave your post, you know.'

'But not when my post leaves me. Thanks, loveliness!' He took the half-crown she gave him and handed it to the doorman. 'Discharge the charioteer, my ancient sea-lion!'

The girl said severely: 'The Chief expected you for lunch. Why are you so late?'

'The fog, angel, the fog. Ceiling zero and visibility even less. They put us down at Lympne.' He had slipped his arm in hers. 'Tell me, dear heart, are you still in love with me'?

Firmly she detached his arm. 'Couldn't you have telephoned or something? The Chief has asked for you at least half a dozen times.'

'And how is my aged employer?'

'Worried. The Foreign Office has been playing up again. Sir Herbert's with him now. You'd better wait in my room.'

She led the way towards a door at the end of the hall. Boulton said, 'How do I stand with him?'

'You'll find out fast enough!'

'He realises they were on to me, that I had to skip. I mean, when he recalled me like that ...'

'You can't teach him anything about the Service!'

She showed him into a plain office lined with white cupboards. There was a typewriter and a very neat desk on which stood a bunch of asters in a vase. She sat down at the typewriter and began to type. Boulton picked up a photograph from one of the desk trays. 'Who's the pretty girl, Hanky?'

'It's Melissa Selmar, Stephen Selmar's daughter.'

'The millionaire, the American motor-car fellow, do you mean?'

She nodded, typing on.

He pursed his lips appraisingly. 'Rather fetching. What's her picture doing here?'

'It's the Chief's. And don't go poking about in my trays! I don't like it.' She took the photograph away from him and thrust it in a drawer. Boulton's eyes followed the picture to its resting place. 'Old man stepping out, is he?' he observed whimsically. 'My, my, what a time you must have, Hanky dear! When you're not receiving lovely American heiresses for our beloved Chief, you're entertaining a never-ending succession of romantic and, if I may say so without vanity, un-usually good-looking Intelligence officers.'

The secretary turned up her line to rub out a word. 'Those must be the ones I haven't met,' she observed witheringly, plying her eraser.

Her companion placed his hand on her shoulder. 'No, no, dear Hanky, you must not speak like that. Verily 'tis piteous when a refined young female allows the iron to enter her soul. Child, if you have not discerned the qualities of your fellow labourers in the vineyard, is it not because your glance has failed to penetrate through the dross to the — er, solid ore beneath? Beauty, dear maid, is but skin deep. What if the faithful Armitage is but five feet high with hair a peculiarly loathsome shade of red, if our brother Elkington has a wall eye and the somewhat dreary Dyson's teeth fit badly so that it is like a whistling solo when he talks — what are these trifling blemishes by comparison with the sterling merit that gleams like minted gold beneath the surface? And there are others, notably one, whom modesty forbids me to name, who com-bines the — ah, external husk of a Prince Charming with the soul of a Sir Galahad, oh, my Hanky.'

She shook his hand off. 'Stop pawing me about and let me get on with my work. These letters have to catch the continen-tal mail.'

He sighed. 'When I joined the Service three years ago, I followed the lure of romance. Did I find romance? Yes, I did not. I live the life of a travelling bagman and when I come home with my honours thick upon me, I have to traipse out to the darkest suburbs only to have the aged Potts blow his beery breath all over me and to be kept kicking my heels in the antechamber.'

'You'll be kicking them in the hall if you don't stop talking,' Miss Hancock promised grimly.

The Chief's room was spacious and lofty. The elaborately moulded ceiling, the crystal chandelier and the marble fire-place suggested that it had been the drawing-room formerly: a very large map of Europe almost filling one wall, a wireless set, a row of steel filing cabinets and a large safe built into the wall oddly contrasted with these embellishments.

High Foreign Office officials are not frequent visitors at Secret Service headquarters. But a quarter of a century before in the Great War Sir Herbert Ashcroft, then a Third Secretary in the Diplomatic Service, and the grizzled man who now sat opposite him across the desk had undergone sundry unrecorded but none the less exciting adventures together at various neutral centres, and the link endured. At that time Ashcroft had been a young man about town with a Guardsman's silhouette and a neat Guards moustache. He was still sleek and well-groomed and retained the moustache; but he was losing his hair, and if his back was still straight his Guardsman's figure was nearer that of a Guards sergeant-major than a subaltern's.

With a plaintive air he was saying: 'You know what he is, old boy. He wants Armitage. He was greatly impressed by that report of his from Beirut. Why can't he have Armitage if he wants him?'

'I've told you already, Bertie — Armitage isn't available.'

'How do you mean "not available"?'

'He's away on a job. In Rumania, to be precise.'

'You can bring him home, can't you?'

'Not off this job, Bertie.' He paused. 'This is for you and

nobody else, not even your old man. Armitage is keeping an eye on an old friend of ours.'

'Not "The Fox"?'

'"The Fox," no less!'

First Blood

ASHCROFT whistled. 'You haven't heard of him so lately, have you?'

His friend shrugged his shoulders. 'We're always coming across his traces. Wherever John Bull's in trouble his agents are never very far away. "The Fox" has cost me the lives of three of my men during the past eighteen months.'

He stood up and went to the window. The curtains had not been drawn: outside the fog clung to the panes. There were even wisps of it in the room, a faint haze lurking in the shadows above the chandelier. 'Back in the war when I first went into this job,' he went on, staring sombrely into the outer greyness, 'there were at least certain rules, a sort of unwritten code that both sides honoured. But with international morality at its present low level how can you expect anyone to play the game? International spy-masters like de Bahl, who buy and sell information as if it were tea, least of all. It's a grim prospect, Bertie! When I look at the world today, it seems to me I can see no farther ahead than if I were out in the fog there. And of course with everybody arming all round, big operators like "The Fox" with plenty of brains and plenty of capital are on velvet.'

'He has brains all right or he'd have been laid by the heels before this.'

'He's diabolically clever: he never leaves us with a shred of proof against him. To the world at large he's the wealthy art dealer who's obliged to be constantly travelling in the interests of his affairs.'

'Does he still run that antique business of his at Geneva?'

'Very much so. It would be hard to devise a better cover for an espionage bureau.'

'What's his nationality? Swiss, is he?'

'A man like that probably has a different passport for every day of the week. As he steers clear of England we've had no opportunity of checking up on this point. But I'm told he was born in Tunis, father unknown, mother Tunisian. He's a pretty elusive person and not many people have seen him, but he's said to be a fascinating personality remarkably handsome, with a shock of white hair that contrasts with his black eyebrows and olive skin. That's just façade, however — beneath it he's a rapacious, cold-hearted rascal with the outlook and methods of the Barbary pirates from whom he's sprung.'

Miss Hancock glided in with a letter tray. 'Your letters, sir.'

'I'll sign 'em presently, Hanky.'

'Mr. Boulton is outside.'

The Chief frowned. 'Send him in when I ring.'

The secretary glided out. Ashcroft said, 'Boulton? Isn't that the fellow you had out on the Italian-Sudanese frontier, used to be in the Air Force?' The other nodded briefly. 'He came to see me once, about that business at Malta, remember?' his visitor pursued. 'A crazy bloke, but that's the way you like 'em, isn't it? Wait a minute, surely he's the chap the Italianos made all the fuss about the other day? What was the trouble exactly?'

'Strictly against orders the young gentleman crossed into Italian territory and proceeded to get himself involved in a spot of bother. I don't remember the details, but some askaris, a dancing girl and a bottle of chianti were mixed up in it. No doubt I shall hear the story from the young man himself. It wound up by his having to ride for his life on a racing camel. It seemed more prudent to recall him.'

'And now he's waiting outside to catch hell?'

'I shouldn't wonder.' The smile was rather grim. 'He's a good lad and a fine linguist. He'd done all kinds of things after a crash put him out of the R.A.F. before he joined us — rubber planting and the Lord knows what else.'

The visitor drew down his mouth primly. 'I regard a fellow like that as a public menace. Why, he might have provoked an international incident if the Duce had not behaved most reasonably about it. What's "The Fox" up to in Rumania?'

His friend shrugged his shoulders. 'That's what Armitage has gone to find out. He was traced through a certain Guido Miklas, who's been his righthand man for years.'

'I never heard of him.'

'By profession he's an architect — he's supposed to help de Bahl in the business. Actually, he's been mixed up in all sorts of dirty jobs for "The Fox." This office has a long score chalked up against Mr. Miklas.'

The telephone on the desk rang. Ashcroft stood up. 'I've wasted enough of your time, old boy. I understand about Armitage. But my master won't like it.'

'Tell him to try the War Office!' Okewood pressed a button on the desk and lifted the telephone as his friend went out.

It was Miss Hancock. 'Mrs. Armitage on the wire, sir.'

'I'll speak to her, Hanky. Send Boulton in when I've finished.'

The lady was voluble. Her rather shrill voice welled out into the quiet room. The Chief listened impassively. Then he spoke with careful deference. 'I shouldn't let that worry you, Mrs. Armitage,' he said. 'No, I'm afraid I can't tell you where he is. But he's all right — I heard from him quite recently. So far as I know, very fit. Of course, as soon as we hear.'

He hung up. There was a tap at the door. 'Come!' he called. Boulton appeared, an ingratiating smile on his face. His Chief aroused himself from a brown study. 'Don't get married as long as you're in this job,' he observed bleakly. 'No fellow in this game ought to marry. The wives never understand.'

'No, sir!' said the young man jauntily.

His tone seemed to jar on his superior, for the other bent a cold blue eye on him. 'You're late!'

'The fog grounded us at Lympne. I caught the first plane out of Khartum on receiving your message. I wrote my report on the way home — I have it here.' He laid a thick envelope on the desk. 'I feel I should explain, with regard to that unfortunate incident, sir ——'

'I've no use for officers that disobey orders,' his Chief broke in sternly. 'Your damned insubordination has almost wrecked the most delicate negotiations which the Foreign Office is at present conducting. If the Treasury didn't keep me so infernally shorthanded, I'd lay you off for three months, just to teach you that an order's an order. As it happens, I've a job for you at this moment, but I tell you frankly I'd never put you on it if you didn't happen to be the only man available. I do it with the utmost reluctance because I don't trust you, because you've let me down.'

'I assure you, sir ——'

'I don't want any excuses. There's one tradition in this service, and that is that officers don't let the office down. You're to consider yourself severely reprimanded. Now sit down!'

Much of the young man's self-assurance had evaporated. With rather a dazed air, he drew up a chair. The Chief's hand dipped into the silver cigarette box on the desk. Then he pushed the box at the visitor. With a questioning glance at the other's face, the young man helped himself, stooped to the proffered match. Their eyes met. Boulton cheered up: he discerned a glint of humour in his superior's glance that gave him confidence. Unexpectedly the Chief chuckled. 'That must have been a good camel you had!' he said.

The young man grinned. 'I had to pinch it. Off the major commanding the Italian meharists, as a matter of fact. I thought I might as well bag a good one while I was about it. Gosh, I bet he was raving!'

The other flung himself back in his chair and laughed silently. 'Lord,' he observed with a sigh, 'you make me wish I was your age again.' He began to brandish his big ivory letter-opener. 'Now pay attention to me, young Boulton. When you leave here this afternoon you'll go to an address Hanky will take you to and await the visit of a certain Amanescu who's arriving from Bucharest. He speaks only Rumanian and French — that's why I'm sending you. He'll bring a letter from Geoffrey Armitage addressed to "Captain Dunlop." You're "Captain Dunlop." Is that clear?'

Boulton nodded. 'Does Armitage say anything about the fellow, sir?'

'He's been acting as private secretary to a certain party in Bucharest who's a very old acquaintance of this office. Did you ever hear of one Alexis de Bahl, better known as "The Fox"?'

The young man's eyes widened with excitement. 'I should say I did. Why, the Mediterranean was ringing with his name during the Abyssinian crisis! Do you mean to say you've got a line on him at last? And in Bucharest, of all places!'

'It looks like it.' The Chief's tone was measured. 'Armitage, who's handling the situation for us, has got hold of this bird, Amanescu. Amanescu has a story to sell, but he's opening his mouth wide and won't deal except with a principal. You'll have to comb him out and see what his information is worth. You'll refer to me before closing with him, but I can tell you we'll go to a pretty high figure for the pleasure of putting Alexis de Bahl where he belongs, and that's behind the bars. Is that clear?'

'Yes, sir.'

'Have you ever met a fellow called Miklas, Guido Miklas, one of de Bahl's men?'

Boulton shook his head. 'No, but I know about him. He's supposed to be "The Fox's" trigger man. What's he up to?'

'He's been in Bucharest with "The Fox" in tow. I can't tell you what they're up to, but there's the situation as far as I know it. Something appears to be stirring in the Ukraine — at any rate, Trieste reports the arrival there of a party of Ukrainian Nationalists who are in constant touch with a certain Apostolou, a well-known international agent and a notorious doublecross. Armitage says that de Bahl has been in almost daily communication by telephone with Trieste and has now gone off to Bessarabia, which, I need not remind you, is conveniently close to the Ukraine. With him are Miklas and an American millionaire called Selmar who makes motor-

cars. I've had Selmar vetted and he appears to be a respect-
able citizen: all I can say is that his reputation is better than
the company he keeps. Maybe this fellow Amanescu will be
able to throw some light on what all this portends; but at present Armitage seems to be as much in the dark as we are. Three
days ago, however, he wired me that he was leaving for Bessarabia on "The Fox's" trail, so we should be hearing something from him soon. What is it, Hanky?'

The secretary stood there with a telegram. 'From Bucharest,
sir.'

The Chief's eyes snapped. His face hardened as he read the
telegram. 'All right, Hanky,' he dismissed the secretary. 'It's
from Vermuiven, our resident man at Bucharest,' he told
Boulton. 'Apparently Armitage instructed him before leaving
for Bessarabia to keep track of de Bahl's movements. At any
rate, he wires that de Bahl and Selmar returned to Bucharest
last night and left again by car this morning in the direction
of Budapest.' He frowned. 'So "The Fox" has thrown us off
the scent again. I wonder what the devil Armitage is up to —
we should have heard by this. Well, there's Amanescu to go
on with and if he fails us, we'll have to start afresh from the
Trieste end.'

He broke off, staring in front of him. Then he picked up his
letter-opener again. 'About Amanescu,' he said, drumming
with the paper-knife. 'He was due at seven, but fortunately
his train's nearly two hours late owing to the fog, so you've
plenty of time. Hanky will go along with you to Pierce Street
to lend things an air of respectability, and here' — his hand
dived into a drawer and brought out a folder — 'you'd better
be glancing through Armitage's reports while I polish off these
letters.'

He drew the pile of letters towards him. The secretary was back again. 'All right, Hanky, I'm just signing 'em.'

'You ought to see this.' She thrust a copy of the *Evening Standard* at him, pointing with a finger that was not very steady at an item on the front page.

'See what? What is it?' he said testily, taking the newspaper from her.

The long silence that followed caught Boulton's attention. He looked up to see the Chief staring fixedly at the newspaper spread out before him on the desk. 'Poor old Geoffrey,' he murmured. 'He always liked to have two strings to his bow and now there's only one.' Silently he handed the newspaper to Boulton, his finger indicating a Reuter telegram from Bucharest, printed at the foot of the first column. Boulton read:

> Bucharest. Tuesday.
> A telegram to the *Romania* from Orghina, a village in Bessarabia, announces that the body of an English engineer named Armitage, who was visiting Rumania on business, has been recovered from the Dniester. The local police have opened an enquiry.

The Chief took off his glasses and passed his hand wearily over his eyes. 'Well,' he said, 'with poor old Geoffrey gone, Amanescu's our only source.' His glance rested sternly on Boulton. 'It's up to you, young man.'

Rendezvous in Pierce Street

SOHO is an elastic term. The precise boundaries of this Continental quarter of the London West End are as vague as the origin of the name. From Oxford Street it merges into the London theatre district somewhere in the triangle of which Shaftesbury Avenue is one leg, Leicester Square and Piccadilly Circus the others. Not all of Soho is given over to cheap eating-houses, delicatessen shops, waiters' clubs and the film trade. One corner harbours the wool industry, and the accents of Bradford and Leeds are strong in certain modern office blocks which stand up incongruously between the Hogarthian houses in and about Golden Square.

To one such block, bleakly utilitarian product of neo-Georgian London with its six floors of concrete already discoloured by the London grime, Miss Hancock conducted Boulton. On account of the fog they went by tube, alighting at Hyde Park Corner, as Boulton insisted on calling for letters at his club in Piccadilly. The fog was thicker than ever. It came billowing in from the Park. Piccadilly was a chaos of groping headlights and sounding klaxons. Boulton proposed dining at his club, but his escort protested there was no time. It was already past eight: they must not be late at the rendezvous. They fumbled their way to the club. Miss Hancock was kept waiting a good ten minutes on the ladies' side. She was fuming when her companion appeared. 'Do you realise that it's twenty-five minutes to nine?' she demanded irately. 'It's no good taking a taxi in this fog — we'll have to walk. If his train shouldn't be as late as they say...'

'He'll wait,' said Boulton. 'He has something to sell, hasn't he? Don't worry. If the train's in, we'll find him on the mat.'

'You talk like a fool,' was the sharp rejoinder. 'We've a job to do and I'm here to see we do it. For heaven's sake, stop loafing about and come on!'

He saw she was on edge and glanced at her wonderingly. He had never seen Hanky indulging in the luxury of nerves before.

The lights of Soho swam in the fog. Here on all sides were names, faces, too, that evoked the Mediterranean sunshine — there was something preposterous about the brown clamminess of Berwick Street and its roaring street market, with its cheerful costers chaffering under the naphtha flares and the moisture beading on the bright windows of the provision and radio shops. At the street corners the public-houses were oases of light and noise; but in the sparsely lit back streets the fog seeped over all. One such street was Pierce Street, a narrow lane running between the shabby Georgian houses with the gaunt silhouette of a new office building breaking the line of the roofs. 'It's here,' said Miss Hancock, plunging into the gloom of the lane.

A distant clock struck nine as they turned in under the entrance to Beltran House. There was no porter visible, but the outer door was open: it remained open until midnight for the convenience of the wool firms in the building with country mails to catch, Miss Hancock explained. They had a glimpse of a bare lobby, a panel with the tenants' names, a lift. Behind them the street was quiet and deserted, a funnel of fog.

The fog was in the lobby. It clung to the electric lights. The lift was automatic. Miss Hancock pressed the button, not once, but again and again. The lift did not descend: someone was using it. 'D'you think he'll ever find his way here in this fog?' Boulton asked her as they waited. She did not reply but pushed the button again.

The elevator came down and they mounted into the stillness, past floor upon floor of silent offices. They got out at the third floor. Two men were waiting there, nondescripts in felt hats and heavy tweed overcoats, who, entering the lift, descended out of sight.

The whirr of the dynamo as they went down seemed to be the last sound of life in the whole building. Only the corridor was lit — room after room, all exactly alike, was dark as Miss Hancock led the way along. At last she stopped, fumbled with a key and a light went on showing an anteroom with an office beyond. 'The Higgs Company, Importers' was painted on the door.

It was a banal office, banally furnished — light oak desk and chairs, waste-paper basket, telephone, and a typewriter in the outer room. 'We'd better find out about his train,' said the secretary and, without removing her hat, went to the telephone, while Boulton was hanging up his hat and coat. He heard her speaking to Victoria. She was replacing the receiver when he joined her. 'The train came in five minutes ago,' she announced.

He glanced at his watch. 'Nine-five! If he's here before half-past I'll eat my hat.' Producing a small parcel, he went on, 'Since you spurned my invitation to dinner, my Hanky, I made so bold as to ask the club to put up a few sandwiches.' He began to undo the string.

She was at the glass, taking off her hat. 'Thanks, I don't want anything!'

'You've had no dinner!'

'All the same.'

'Look!' He held up a half bottle of champagne. 'I got them to put in a pint of pop. We'll have a little celebration.'

She whirled round to face him. 'Because a man's been killed, is that it?'

She spoke with such feeling that he stared at her blankly, the bottle in one hand, one of the two tumblers he had unpacked with it in the other. 'Why, Hanky!'

'Geoffrey Armitage was a friend of yours, as he was the friend of us all at the office,' she cried. 'I dare say you knew him better than I did, a quiet, kindly creature, a gentleman in the real sense. Now he's dead, foully murdered, for all we know, and it means so little to you that you speak of celebrating. Celebrate what, in God's name? Celebrate the fact that you may be the next to go?'

He smiled at her whimsically. 'You know, Hanky, it isn't a bad toast.' He lifted the bottle to her. '*Moriturus te salutat!*'

But she swept on. 'Last year it was Hereford, and before him young Lumley. You don't talk about it because it's supposed to be bad form to mention such things, but you know you took your life in your hands on this last trip of yours to the Sudan. God, when I think of the mess men make of things! Boys like you are brought into the world to marry and have families, to be happy and do great things, not to be slaughtered like sheep!'

He shrugged his shoulders. 'I'm nearly thirty, if you call that being a boy, and I'm very conscious of the fact that if I'd been born ten or fifteen years sooner, I'd probably now be pushing up daisies like most of the war generation. I don't want to marry and settle down, Hanky: I want to enjoy life in my own way. And that means getting a thrill out of it. That's why I joined the Air Force — it was the bitterest blow of my life when that crash grounded me for good: that's why I knocked about the world for a couple of years before the Chief took me on. There are lots of fellows who feel the way I do; there always have been and there always will be. That's how the British Empire was founded.'

He unwound the wire round the champagne bottle and let the cork go with a pop. 'We'll drink a toast,' he said, 'but it'll be to you.' He filled the two glasses and handed one to her. He raised his glass. 'To Hanky! And may she always be waiting for us at the end of the journey!'

She smiled at him then through her gig-lamps and, having blown her nose, declared contritely: 'Sorry for flying off the handle, Don! But this Armitage business upset me.' She took the glass. 'Champagne's quite a treat for me. Well, here's how and thanks for your nice toast...'

At that moment they heard the scream.

It came from the distance, welling up suddenly out of the silence and fog that enveloped them and as suddenly dying, a high, gurgling cry, shrill with some mortal anguish, that seemed to climb the octave but was cut off before reaching the top. The secretary dropped her glass, and its clatter on the hair carpet was swallowed up in the crash of the outer door rebounding against the wall as Boulton tore it open and dashed out into the corridor. No sound greeted him as he sped along, no murmur of voices, no opening of doors, to match the clatter of his feet along the passage, and he told himself that, but for them, the entire building must be empty.

The landing, its floor shining in the electric light, was deserted. The young man did not wait for the lift but raced down the stairs. The vestibule with its glass doors framing the curtain of fog was as they had left it. He ran to the street door and peered outside. There was nothing there but the fog and the dim vista of the street. He turned back into the lobby and came face to face with Miss Hancock as she emerged from the stairs.

Then only did he perceive what lay almost at his feet.

It was the body of a young man that sprawled, half in, half out of the lift, in a lake of blood. He was wearing a heavy overcoat, from the back of which something shining protruded, the white metal handle of a dagger that winked and glittered in the electric light. His hat had fallen off, disclosing a head of raven-black hair. What could be made out of the face below was sallow.

Boulton made a long arm and picked up the hat. With a glance at the interior he put it on the ground. 'Vienna' was his muttered comment.

The girl spoke in a frightened voice. 'Look!' She pointed past him at the interior of the elevator.

Apparently in falling the dead man's hat had covered the white envelope that lay on the lift floor, just clear of the spreading scarlet pool. Boulton picked up the envelope, glanced at the address and his face hardened. The envelope was unsealed and he shook out of it the letter it contained. He unfolded the sheet, ran his eye over it and returned it to its envelope.

'Armitage's letter to Dunlop,' he said briefly and added, with a sort of rage in his voice, '"The Fox" has beaten us to it again!'

Stephen Blurts Out a Secret

THE *Rex* had come to rest in the harbour of Villefranche. Between the towering heights, chocolate brown thatched with the dark foliage of pine or the sicklier verdure of olive, the great liner lay far off shore, a motionless white mass on a deep green sea, foam-flecked, under a sky of brilliant cobalt, washed clean by a night of November rain. A tender, a flock of motor launches, some rowing boats, snuggled against her soaring flanks, bobbing in the swell, with the gulls swooping and hovering and crying harshly all about: from the smokestacks high above, supremely disdainful of the rattle of a winch and the seabirds' calls, little plumes of vapour mounted steadily into the glittering air, as though the giant were taking a breather after the long run from New York.

It was at Stephen's wish that at the beginning of November Melissa Selmar had left America in the *Rex*. Melissa had been faintly worried about her father. He had always been more prone to communicate with her by cable than by letter; but for a long time past his letters ceased altogether and his telegrams were little more than a chronicle of his movements from place to place. Following his wanderings by car through Switzerland and Italy, a strange restlessness seemed to have overtaken him. Scarcely back in Paris and London, he was off again. Now he was at Bucharest, now somewhere in the wilds of Rumania, inspecting this castle some lunatic had left him (how like Steve to go and see the place and say no more about it!), now in Paris, now Geneva. His final word to her had come from Monte Carlo. She was to 'hop on' the *Rex* and get off at Villefranche, where he would meet her. There was a certain firmness of tone about this last cable that suggested he desired to be obeyed: as it coincided with a vague suspicion on Melissa's part that her father was getting into mischief, she caught the *Rex*.

Having come off in the tender, he found her in her stateroom, a rather forlorn figure in the midst of a chaos of discarded dress- and hat-boxes, mountains of tissue paper and a bewildering assortment of hand luggage, some still open, others already packed. At the sight of the familiar form, in tussore and panama, in the doorway, she flew into her father's arms with a little cry.

'Steve!'

'Melissa, honey!'

She clung to him ecstatically. 'Darling, darling, darling, it's so lovely to see you again!'

He kissed the top of her head. 'You've changed your perfume. M-m, it smells nice. What is it?'

'Some frightfully expensive stuff Andy Barnes sent me to the boat.'

He smiled. 'Rather like taking coals to Newcastle, isn't it? I mean, giving perfume to a young woman who's on her way to France.'

'Andy means well, but he's really an awful sap!'

Selmar smiled at her affectionately. The thought was in his mind that their meetings, after long separation, were always like this. It was probably his fault that they spoke of indifferent matters: he could not get used to the notion that he was the father of this beautiful, vital person, and it made him tongue-tied. A little while — until they had grown accustomed to one another's company again — and the old intimacy would come back. But at first there was always this faint feeling of embarrassment between them.

She made him sit down on the bed beside her. 'My,' she exclaimed, settling his tie, 'how smart we look in our Palm Beach suit! And you're thinner, Steve — it becomes you!'

He picked up her hand. 'You look like a million dollars, Melissa. And I like the way you do your hair. Had a good trip?'

'Uh-huh!'

'Any new beaux?'

'Only an Italian who wants me to marry him and go and live in Abyssinia. The most thrilling-looking person, Steve — he sent shivers down my back. But Abyssinia, I ask you!'

Her father looked faintly uncomfortable. 'How's refrigeration these days?'

She made a little face. 'I'm stone cold on refrigeration. Andy's a nice boy, but he doesn't wear. Not at a summer camp, at any rate. He's too darn serious, Steve — six weeks was all I could stand of him. So Mr. Selmar's little girl is going places again.' She jumped up. 'Help me to shut these darn cases, will you, and we'll go ashore. Did you bring the car?'

'You bet you. It's on the dock. Honey, she's a whiz!'

'Hooray. I'll drive you back to Monte!'

At the foot of the gangway leading to the shore a grey-haired, gangling individual, clean-shaven, with the mournful eyes and button nose of a French comic actor and a twist of war ribbons knotted in the buttonhole of his sober broadcloth, touched his hat gravely to Selmar and advanced to relieve Melissa of her coat and motion-picture camera. When she instinctively clung to her property, her father laughed. 'It's all right, sweetheart, it's Charles!' And to the man he added, in his somewhat fragmentary French, '*Charles, c'est ma fille.*'

'Charles?' repeated the girl.

'He's my valet,' said Stephen. 'The hotel people found him for me. He doesn't know much English but we manage all right. Now you've come, you can interpret for me if I get stuck. *Mademoiselle parle très bien français,*' he confided to the valet.

Charles made Melissa a low bow. 'I trust that mademoiselle has had a pleasant crossing,' he said gravely in French. Mademoiselle would not have to occupy herself with the baggage: if she would give him her keys, he would see everything through the customs.

It was not until she was at the wheel of the car and they were bowling along the Lower Corniche that Melissa broke a somewhat ominous silence. 'So now we have a valet?' she remarked with a touch of grimness. More than once, after her mother's death three years before, she had tried to persuade Stephen to engage a manservant to look after his clothes and attend to his packing. But Stephen had stoutly refused, protesting that he was not yet so decrepit that he couldn't put the studs in his shirt and pack a bag for himself — like most American men, he was independent in such matters.

He laughed rather guiltily. 'As a matter of fact, he's more of a butler than a valet.'

'And what do you want with a butler at a hotel? You're still at the hotel, aren't you?'

'Sure, sure. I just thought he might be useful if we took a place for the winter.'

'A villa, do you mean?'

Her father cleared his throat. 'A villa or, maybe, a château.'

'A château?' The car swerved dangerously as she took her eyes off the road to stare at him. 'You're not talking about this Rumanian castle of ours, by any chance?'

With a muscular hand Selmar caught the steering wheel, brought the car into the straight again. 'I thought maybe we might spend the winter there, just to try it out,' he remarked with elaborate casualness.

Melissa drew up at the side of the road, stopped the car and squarely faced him. 'My poor lamb —— ' she began.

'Listen, Melissa,' her father broke in, 'I've been down there and it's a marvellous old place, a real, old, honest-to-goodness castle straight out of the picture books, standing up there on the banks of the Dniester. Generations of our family have lived there, and after them Turks, and Tatars, and Russians, and the Lord knows who else, as they came raiding across the river. The Turks were there for ages and would you believe it? they built a mosque, the cutest little mosque, and it's still there, right in the courtyard.'

His daughter shook her head. 'I had a sort of feeling I shouldn't have let you go to Europe alone. It's the devil the mischief you get into when I'm not with you. There was that deer forest on top of some God-forsaken Highland mountain you'd have bought if I hadn't stopped you, and that tumble-down castle in Wales that that phony Lord What's-his-name tried to stick you with. The trouble about you, Steve Selmar, is that you've never grown up. You've a fairy-tale complex or something.'

He laughed rather shamefacedly. 'Well, maybe I have. But this is different. When I stood on the very battlements where the great Stephen cel Mare himself must have stood — you know, you can look out across the river straight into the Ukraine and see the Soviet sentries pacing the farther bank ——'

'But that's Russia!' she cried, aghast. 'And you propose to spend the winter there? My dear man, we shall freeze to death!'

His enthusiasm was undiminished. 'There'll be snow, of course, and the Dniester's ice-bound pretty early. But by the time I've made the place over a little, we'll be as snug as two bugs in a rug.'

'Are you trying to tell me that you actually think of restoring this old ruin?'

He coloured up. 'Not restore exactly, honey, just fixing up one of the towers so's we can live there, and putting in a bath-room or two and some central heating. And the roof of the great hall wants patching. But don't worry, I've a first-class man attending to everything...'

A little spot of red appeared in her cheeks. 'You must be out of your mind if you think I've the slightest intention of spending the winter with you in this old dump! I'm only sorry you went ahead and started wasting money on the place without consulting me...'

He patted her hand. 'Now don't get mad at the old man, sweetheart. It's not as though I were going to spend a lot of money on the place, just enough so's we'll be able to stay there from time to time and maybe entertain a few friends for the shooting — you know, I can afford it. Besides, it's going to give me something to do — gosh, if you knew how bored I get, now that I'm out of the business. After all, this is our ancestral château, the — er — cradle of our race ——'

'A cradle,' she broke in crisply, 'is what, to judge by the way they behave, some people require!'

But he ignored the sally. 'Baron de Bahl, who's taken charge of the work, has entered right into the spirit of the thing. He's a grand person, one of the most interesting fellows I've ever met. He's at Monte Carlo now. You'll like him, honey. We've been running round, buying furniture and stuff together. He's a marvellous judge of furniture. He has a big antique business at Geneva — I met him there on my tour this summer.'

She shook her head firmly and slipped into gear. 'I guess it's your money, Steve, and you're entitled to spend it as you like — the Lord knows, you worked hard enough for it,' she said as they moved forward again. 'But I think your plan's plumb crazy. I won't say it mightn't be fun to spend a few weeks at this place in summer. But in winter! Why, you admit yourself the country's snow-bound! Don't you realise you've let this furniture-dealing Baron of yours talk you into this goofy scheme? Go ahead and make the castle livable in if you want to: but let you and me live like civilised beings at Monte or Cannes or somewhere for the winter, and maybe the castle will be ready for us to take a trip down there in the spring.'

'De Bahl didn't talk me into anything. If we're going down there this winter, it's for a reason.'

'What reason?'

His manner had grown faintly mysterious. 'Well, he made me swear not to breathe a word to anyone, not even you. You see, he said it's essential the Government shouldn't hear about it. He says that nobody dreams of going to this remote corner of Bessarabia in winter — there'll be very little likelihood of our being disturbed. It seems there are all kinds of stringent laws about treasure trove, and if the local authorities should get a sniff of it ——' He broke off, dismayed. 'Oh, my gosh, now I've let it out.'

She said witheringly, 'Are you trying to tell me we're going to look for treasure in this castle of yours?'

'Honey, it's serious!'

'Serious, my foot! It's like a comic strip. Steve, you're nothing but a kid. It's pathetic!'

He shook his head stubbornly. 'I haven't spent my life in one of the most competitive rackets in America to fall for the old gold brick swindle — you ought to know me better than that, Melissa. I have the actual documents.'

'What documents?'

'An old parchment in Turkish left by the Pasha who buried the treasure somewhere in the little mosque at the castle I told you about and a letter referring to the same story written by the castle bailiff to Prince Balthasar Celmar, one of our ancestors who owned Castle Orghina in the eighteenth century ....' Stephen was getting into his stride. 'You know, the history of Bessarabia, where this castle of ours is located, is pretty complicated. If I have it right, for centuries the country was divided up between the Moldavians, the rightful owners, and the Russians and the Turks, who were always fighting about it. There was a Turkish garrison at Castle Orghina for years; but in 1788 — I think that's the date — when Russia and Austria were at war with Turkey, the garrison was driven out and the Pasha in charge, lighting out in a hurry, had to dump his money and jewels. But being a careful guy he had his orderly-room clerk or someone make a note of the fact on this sheepskin — I suppose to put him right with the Sultan — though he omitted to mention the exact hiding-place. Then Orghina returned to the possession of the Celmars for a bit, and it was during this time that the bailiff, a Jew called Moses Aaron — it seems that most of the big landowners had Jews to collect their rents for them — wrote this letter, telling the Prince about finding the sheepskin with the story of the treasure, and asking permission to dig for it. Apparently, before they did anything about it, the Russians overran the country again, the castle was once more lost to the Celmars, and, well, the story about the treasure seems to have been forgotten. It was de Bahl, digging into the history of the old place, who came across these two documents among the family papers of old Countess Boreanu, who left me the castle.'

'It was your friend the furniture Baron who produced the documents, then? My poor Steve, don't you realise ——'

'I know what you're going to say. But you're wrong. As a matter of fact, de Bahl makes light of the whole thing. I ran across him quite by chance in Bucharest when I was there to look the castle over and he agreed to go down to Orghina with me — I thought it was darn decent of him. He had a friend of his along, fellow called Guido Miklas, who's a very clever architect — as a matter of fact, it's Miklas who's drawing the plans. He's down at Orghina now supervising the work.'

She shrugged a disdainful shoulder. 'Oh, Steve,' she cried in exasperation, 'don't you see, all they wanted was to get you to commission them to restore the place?'

'Honey, you're wrong. It was I who started it. Just for a rag I asked them what it'd cost to fix the place up so's a fellow could live in it and, well, you know the way one thing leads to another — we got talking about Stephen cel Mare and all the

rest of it and when we were back in Bucharest, de Bahl started
to dig into the history of the Castle and discovered these
documents.'

'Of course,' she broke in with delicate sarcasm, 'I was for-
getting that you read Turkish fluently. Not to mention Yid-
dish, or whatever language this Jewish bailiff of yours wrote
his letter in.'

He chuckled. 'Aaron's letter's in Rumanian. I'm not such
a sap as you think me, sweetness. I insisted on getting my own
translators to work on the documents. Of course, this restoration job means business for our friend, the Baron; but he's not
much impressed with this treasure story, really, and at first
he was dead against my going down there this winter, and
especially against my taking you. I got him to admit, however, that, if we're seriously going after the Pasha's hoard, the
winter's the best time, when there's no one much about. His
suggestion was that he and Miklas should start restoring the
place and at the same time fossick round in the mosque and if
they found anything, send for us. But once I heard about the
treasure, there was no holding me — if there was going to be
a treasure hunt I was going to be in it from the start. And I
knew you'd feel the same about it. Why, darling, we'll have
rafts of fun — it's like an adventure story!'

They were rolling up the long slope leading to the Square in
front of the Casino. Melissa turned her head to smile at her
father. 'Dear old Steve,' she said. 'I love your enthusiasm.
It's so American. It all sounds perfectly crazy to me; but it
might be fun.'

He clamped his hand down on hers as she grasped the
wheel. 'Then you're on?'

She laughed and shook her head. 'Wait till I've had a peek
at this Baron of yours!'

Melissa Meets the Baron

MELISSA could not help admitting to herself that Stephen had been right about the Baron. He interested her profoundly. Ever since she was twelve, after her mother's death, she had usually accompanied Stephen on his business trips to Europe. Englishmen, and Frenchmen, and Germans she knew; but the Baron de Bahl was a new kind of European in her experience.

Even at a cosmopolitan centre such as Monte Carlo he struck a bizarre note, with his topknot of snow-white hair combed back in a high pompadour contrasting with his jutting, jet-black eyebrows. There was something vaguely Oriental about the faint brownness of his skin, the high-ridged nose and rather prominent cheek bones, the dark lustre of his eyes. The eyes were remarkable, almond-shaped and mostly half-veiled by lashes as long as a girl's. The pupils were curiously dilated: it lent his gaze a certain compelling power which, Melissa felt, had something of the hypnotic about it. She fancied he must have been very good-looking as a young man, though in a lush, Oriental way. In his fifties now his muscles had sagged and his nondescript suits, usually of black or grey, hung loosely on a form that, once well knit, had become bloated and flabby. It was quite evident that the Baron cared as little about his dress as about his figure, and Melissa discovered, rather to her surprise, that she scarcely noticed his clothes.

That was because the personal charm he exuded had the effect of banning all other considerations. It was not hard to see how he had captivated Stephen, whose simple, rather volatile nature always responded to a frank approach. He had an irresistible manner. He was an autocrat — you could tell that by the way he ordered the hotel servants around — but behind his somewhat lordly air was not condescension but rather the blank assumption that all men were his friends and eager to serve him. His air was indolent, sleepy, even, and his husky voice was never raised above a level, velvety tone; but these externals only stressed the more strongly the unflagging vitality of his mind, a reserve of strength, physical as well as mental, so much in excess of the ordinary that he seemed able to impose his will upon everybody with whom he came in contact.

He was highly cultured. There was a faintly foreign tang about his English, which was otherwise flawless and marked by an exquisite choice of words. French was his native tongue inasmuch as he had been born in Tunis; but he appeared to have no difficulty in passing from French or English to Italian or German or even Arabic, which he spoke with his servant, a chocolate-hued Tunisian called Ali, gorgeously arrayed in a gold-braided monkey jacket and sky-blue, flowing trousers. He was installed in a flat down by the Summer Casino, but made the big lounge of the Selmars' hotel his headquarters. All day long he was to be seen there, at a buhl table facing the reception desk, his big body oozing over the arms of his high-backed chair, one of the giant cigarettes he favoured between his fingers and a mounting pile of stubs in the ash-tray at his elbow, drinking innumerable cup of coffee prepared by Ali while he pored over blue prints, and drawings, and photo-

graphs that littered the table. Stephen had daily discussions
with him over the plans for the restoration of Castle Orghina;
but he had to go to him in the hotel lobby. 'He'd be much
more comfortable upstairs in the suite,' Selmar confided to his
daughter. 'But he insists on sitting in all that racket in the
hall. He says he likes the sensation of movement about him —
it gives him inspiration.'

At the Castle workmen were already busy carrying out the
essential outdoor repairs before the first snows came down —
he hoped that the Green Turret, where, it seemed, they were to
be lodged, would be ready to receive them early in December,
the Baron told Stephen. Meanwhile, plumbing had been
ordered from England, girders, cement and tools from Czechoslovakia, furniture from Paris, Geneva and Bucharest. It
seemed to Melissa that Stephen must be spending a great deal
of money, and she wondered whether he seriously counted on
recouping himself out of the more or less problematical Pasha's
treasure. Stephen, however, in daily conference with de Bahl
over ways and means, was radiant. Melissa had an indulgent
smile for his enthusiasm. Whether it was a business or the
fallen walls of a medieval stronghold, Steve loved to be building
something.

The winter season was not yet under way and Monte Carlo
was quiet. Stephen was rather apologetic to Melissa about it.
'Dave Harness and Leila from Detroit and the Marchmont
Buchanans from New York are at Cannes, I believe,' he informed his daughter, 'but I've been so darn busy with de Bahl
I haven't found time yet to go over and look them up. Actually, I don't know a human being here at Monte except de
Bahl and the bank manager, unless it's old Ardza, you know,
the chap they call the "armaments king."'

'The man who's supposed to have a finger in all the wars, is it? The one they made all the fuss about in the Senate Committee?'

'That's the guy. I showed him round our works once and we met once or twice later in New York. A quaint old buzzard and as rich as they come.'

'Out of slaughtering millions of people! I must say, Steve, you have some darn odd friends!'

He laughed. 'Well, it takes all sorts to make a world. We're not likely to be troubled with old Ardza, even though he lives right here in this hotel. It appears he's over seventy and very rarely goes out any more. At least, so his secreaty told me. He's a Russian called Volkoff who was out in the States with him — I met him in the elevator one day. De Bahl knows him.'

'Well, don't go introducing *me* to the old vulture,' said his daughter.

For the first week of Melissa's stay it was wet. She found much entertainment in the Baron's company. He rarely quitted his post in the lounge until dinner-time, when he hauled his ungainly body to its feet and departed homeward, clutching his large portfolio. He ate no lunch and protested that he never dined out, although he relaxed his rule to the extent of sharing an occasional meal with them and of dining once or twice with his friend, Volkoff, in the great Ardza's suite.

Most days Melissa and her father took their coffee with him after lunch at his table in the lobby. Sometimes, when it was too wet to go out, she would spend the whole afternoon there while Stephen was away, hunting up antique furniture or tapestries at Nice or Grasse, and de Bahl would hold forth to her while he worked — however occupied he seemed to be, he always had time for a chat. He suffered from a smoker's cough, a little rasping hack from the back of the throat: he had a trick, when pausing for a word in his fluent and graphic English, of giving this little cough, flashing his dark eyes at her. She came to identify him with his cough: when she came down in the elevator in the morning and heard it, she knew he had arrived and was in his accustomed place.

The man was a fascinating talker. His mind was stocked with knowledge and ranged far beyond the prosperous antique business he conducted at Geneva. He told her wild, strange stories of blood, and lust, and slaughter, about the old Beys of Tunis and the Barbary pirates, the Turkish sultans and the fantastic life of the seraglios.

In his husky voice, punctuated by his little, hesitating cough, he described to her the remote corner of Europe for which they were bound — Bessarabia, cradle of modern Rumania, ancient and war-scarred, torn away from its original Moldavian possessors by Hungarians, Poles, Turks, Tatars, and finally Russians, in turn, before coming back to the arms of Mother Rumania after the collapse of Russia in the war, its soft Latin tongue and Christian faith still intact.

He showed her photographs of Bessarabian scenes, but the most glowing pictures of the country were those which fell from his eager lips. He made her see the deep, swift Dniester rushing between high banks, from which hoary strong-holds like Castle Orghina looked down, the wide steppe and gaunt wooden windmills, the bright, clean villages, few and far between, buried in cherry orchards, with the bulbous domes of the little Orthodox churches stabbing with their spires the sky above the endless plain; he brought to her nostrils the tang of dung fires, the scent of the rich, dark earth turned over by the

patient water buffalo trudging before the plough. He conjured
up a vision of the Castle, rearing its lofty mass from the river
brink, lone outpost of Christendom against the barbarian
across the stream, the desolate splendour of its ruined great
hall, the exotic charm of its little mosque.

'This country,' he told her one afternoon of rain when
Stephen was upstairs writing letters and they sat alone together, 'is like one of those old parchments to be found in
monasteries, with one set of writing effacing that below —
what we antiquarians call a palimpsest. A succession of civilisa-
tions have left their mark upon it. Thus, for years your illustrious ancestor held back the infidel flood. But when he died
at the end of the fifteenth century — you must visit his tomb
at Suczava, the old Moldavian capital — the Turks came
swarming in. For centuries these old Sultans in their palaces
on the Bosphorus were lords of Bessarabia, though the Tatars
from across the river made many raids against their garrisons.
After that the country was the battlefield of countless wars
right up to Napoleonic times, when the Russians drove out the
Turks and seized Bessarabia for themselves. The rule of the
Muscovites was worse than that of the Turks. The soldiers
stripped the peasants of everything and when the people com-
plained to the General he made the historic reply, "You still
have your eyes to weep with."'

'The horrible brute!' Melissa exclaimed.

The Baron hoisted his vast shoulders. 'I think he spoke no
more than the truth. Your General Sherman said to his soldiers
as I have read, "War is nothing but hell, boys!" and he knew.
'This General Kutusoff must have been a good soldier — I
should like to have met him.'

'I'd run a mile from a monster like that,' declared the girl
indignantly. 'Those poor people! What a savage!'

De Bahl paused to jot down a figure from a paper he was scrutinising. 'A man of the Kutusoff type was probably no new experience for the Bessarabians,' he observed philosophically. 'All through history we find them being knouted and tortured and hanged and plundered by one set of invaders after the other. Even today the land has a strange, sad air, especially in such far-away parts as Orghina, where your castle is situated. When you stand on the battlements and look across the river at Russia, opposite, you forget that Bucharest, so noisy and modern, is only a night away by train from Kishineff, the capital. Since Bessarabia was reunited to Rumania Kishineff — Chisinau, as they now call it — is a fine, growing place; but it is three hours by carriage from Orghina, so bad are the roads they still have in this part of Bessarabia. We. find it more convenient to use the station on the branch railway, thirty kilometres from Orghina — an hour and a half by carriage: quicker by sleigh.'

'It sounds pretty remote,' the girl observed rather dubiously.

'It *is* remote. But, good gracious, as your father says, nowadays, when every year the world grows smaller, isolation, privacy, is a luxury which only the truly wealthy can afford. When he first told me he would like to restore the Castle, I thought he was crazy. But in reality what he says is good sense. Today you may buy an estate in England, a château in France, and yet find no peace, with the road at your gates full of automobiles and noise and tourists. But at Orghina there are no automobiles, no tourists, hardly any roads, even. Civilisation has stood still: a little effort of the imagination and you are back in the days of your famous ancestor defending the country in his fortress against Russian and Turk. It will be a new experience for you, I promise. You will not have your

American luxury, but you will not be too uncomfortable. You are young, Miss Melissa, you are American, that is to say, you have a great capacity for enthusiasm. Take with you to Castle Orghina your American spirit of adventure and maybe' — he screwed up his eyes and coughed — 'you shall not be disappointed — I cannot say more for the present.'

She knew what he meant, of course. Stephen had shown her the documents referring to the Pasha's treasure, which he kept in a steel box — the original record on its yellowing parchment, a few lines of closely written Turkish script, and the bailiff's letter, a long effusion in Rumanian couched in a spidery hand. Beyond the fact that the Turkish document spoke of the treasure being interred in the mosque, neither manuscript threw any nearer light on the hiding-place of the treasure, her father assured her. By the way de Bahl looked at her, she knew he guessed that Stephen had told her about the treasure. On the instant she made up her mind to have it out with him. 'I think I should tell you,' she said, 'that my father and I have no secrets from one another.'

For a moment his eyes searched her face uncomfortably. Then he nodded understandingly. 'Am I right in thinking that your worthy parent might be a trifle indiscreet at times? I shall rely on you to restrain him.' He rasped his little cough. 'You must remember that the Rumanian Government is jealous of its rights and that the old Turkish tradition of baksheesh is still strong, down where we go. The slightest whisper of hidden gold and we shall have a horde of petty officials descending upon us, ravenous for pickings. In principle, the Bessarabian frontier is strongly held. But the region about the Castle is so remote and so sparsely populated that a handful of frontier guards can do all the policing that's required, especially

is there's absolutely no communication between the two sides
of the Dniester — for one thing because, what with rocks and
rapids the river is unnavigable and for another, the Russian
guards open fire on anybody trying to cross. When I was at
the Castle with your father I made a point of becoming ac-
quainted with the head of the local gendarmerie, a comfortable
old gentleman who asks nothing better than to be left in peace,
especially as his headquarters are five or six miles, over a fearful
road, from the Castle. He believes your father to be an eccen-
tric archaeologist who does not wish to be disturbed, and I en-
couraged him and his men to act in accordance with this belief
by leaving with him a contribution to local charities, which I
have an idea may be applied on the principle that charity
begins at home.' He chuckled and his eyes twinkled. 'As long
as we keep our mouths shut, therefore,' he concluded, 'we are
not likely to be interfered with. So, Miss Melissa, discretion,
I beg.'

She nodded. 'I can answer for my father, I guess. But what
about the workmen? Won't they go spreading the news
around?'

'It is a difficulty we have to consider. Already we have
trouble to find the necessary skilled labour to work on the
Castle. We shall have Rumanians, Ukrainians, Ruthenians —
a veritable *macédoine* of different languages, different nationalities — my architect, Mr. Miklas, who is in charge in my absence, is at his wits' end to obtain trustworthy assistants
speaking these languages to help him out. As to the other
matter, we shall include in our working force a certain number
of picked men who will do the digging when the time arrives,
men on whom we can depend not to talk. When the restoration
work is finished, the other men can go; but these we will keep.'

'Then you really think there's something in this treasure story?'

He laughed and cocked his head. 'To hear your father talk, you'd think that all the gold of the Orient was buried in the mosque, waiting to be turned up by our spades. Remember, my dear, that there was a Russian garrison at Orghina for more than a hundred years — who knows but that the treasure wasn't found years ago?' He patted her hand. 'Let's treat it as a little gamble, hein? Then no one will be disappointed and we shall all pass a pleasant winter together.'

She laughed happily. She liked his point of view. Clearly, in his eyes, the whole thing was no more than a novel and amusing experience. Her misgivings evaporated. The Castle loomed up as a large and exciting question mark on the horizon, and for the first time she found herself looking forward to their stay at Orghina.

A King Is Dead

AFTER a solid week of rain, cold winds and grey skies, the sun had come back to Monte Carlo. Melissa awoke to just such another morning as that on which she had landed from America. The sun's rays were warm on her face as she stood on the balcony in her dressing-gown, breathing in the balmy air and delighting in the peerless blue of sea and sky laid behind the wedding-cake whiteness of the Casino. Stephen was in Paris, seeing about some panelling he had heard of that he thought they might use at the castle. He was flying back that morning and would be in the hotel by lunch-time. Seeing that the weather was so fine, Melissa telephoned down to the porter and ordered her father's car, the cherished Selmar Eight, to be brought round. She realised she would require some sports clothes for the Bessarabian trip; she thought she would have time to run over to Nice and back before lunch and see what she could find there.

It was about ten o'clock when she went downstairs. As she passed through the hall she was vaguely aware that the hall was unusually crowded. She looked for the Baron, but he was not in his accustomed place. Outside the hotel Stephen's convertible, a-glitter with chromium and black cellulose, was at the kerb, parked in a long line of cars. She was backing out when an enormous roadster shooting up behind her caught her rear wing a glancing blow. She stopped, jumped out and ran back to find the right rear mudguard badly scraped.

The car that had struck her was a powerful-looking Isotta, splashed screen-high with white mud, which was just drawing up at the steps of the hotel. A man in a heavy ulster came scrambling out, followed by three others, each bearing a large portfolio. With a resolute air Melissa stepped in front of them. 'Are you the owner of this car?' she asked the man in the ulster. 'Spik to my chauffeur, yess?' he replied and, unceremoniously elbowing her aside, dodged into the hotel, his three companions at his heels. Melissa was about to dash after them in pursuit when a voice, an English voice, drawled in her ear, 'Sorry. But why not try looking round the next time you start to back?'

She swung about in a fury. A young man in a close-fitting black béret, a bright green scarf wound about his neck partially concealing his grey pullover, was craning round the screen of the Isotta. He looked like a tramp, his face spattered with mud and darkened with several days' growth of beard. She glared at him. 'I did look round,' she said icily. 'How was I to know that you'd come swooping up behind me like a maniac? Hasn't that car of yours a horn?'

He grinned at her imperturbably through his grime. 'Sure, it has a horn. But it went flat on me coming through Venice, and my singularly objectionable employer was in such a hurry he wouldn't let me stop to have it fixed.' He peered backward to where her car stood, projecting from the line. 'I scraped you a bit, I see. I expect it was as much my fault as yours.'

'Pardon me, I was not in the least to blame.'

He yawned. 'I daresay you're right. Excuse me! I'm not fit to drive another yard really; I'm all in. We've come all the

way from Trieste in one jump in every sort of weather. What's
the date?'

'November the eighteenth.'

'Thursday, is it?'

'It's Friday.'

He counted on his fingers. 'That's right.' He glanced at her
car again. 'Well, it might have been worse. A lick of paint'll
put that wing right again. It's a Selmar, isn't it?'

'It is. And it's brand new.'

He wiped a piece of mud out of his eye. 'Nice line. Is it any
good?'

She stiffened. 'The Selmar has always been the best medium-
price car on the market. This particular model is not out yet.'

He nodded. 'Demonstrating, are you? I know — I once sold
cars myself. Do Selmars still have that lousy clutch?'

She coloured angrily. 'The Selmar never had a bad clutch
at any time.'

He laughed. 'All right, all right. You can't sell me one;
you don't have to give me that salesman stuff.'

'It's not salesman stuff. And if you want to know, I'm not
demonstrating, either. My father happens to be chairman of
the Selmar Corporation. What he's going to say when he discovers that some lunatic's been and chipped all the paint off his
rear wing, you can figure out for yourself!'

With an anguished air the young man closed his eyes. 'Oh,
dear!' he sighed. 'Both trotters in the mash-tub!' He gave her
a contrite look. 'I'm sorry — I should have known.'

She passed over this rather enigmatic remark. 'And
now if you'll be good enough to give me your employer's
name and address.'

'It's Grenander,' he answered soberly. 'I believe we're going to stop at a villa, but where I don't know yet. He'll tell us when he comes out.' His eyes, very grey and limpid behind his patina of mud, implored her. 'Do you think you could raise me a cup of very hot, very black coffee? I'm falling asleep in my tracks and goodness knows when I shall see my little bed again.'

With a weary air he flung himself back in the driving seat and proceeded to wipe his face with an exceedingly grubby handkerchief. 'This bloke of mine's a regular slave-driver,' he remarked philosophically. 'He keeps me sitting around with the bus for hours, but if I'm not ready to shoot off the instant he appears there's the devil to pay. You could send a waiter out here, couldn't you? I hate asking you, but honest, it's as much as my place is worth to leave the car. I picked up this Grenander person at Trieste and he hired me to chauffeur him and his friends. I don't mind telling you the job was a godsend to me at that particular time — it still is, as a matter of fact — and I don't want to lose it. Since he took me on three weeks ago I've driven him and his pals half across Europe — Jugoslavia, Hungary, Czechoslovakia, goodness knows where we haven't been. He's a jumpy packet of fun, is our friend Grenander, and if he hadn't been in too much of a hurry to notice I bumped you, he'd have sacked me as sure as eggs is eggs. But if I don't get something to keep me awake I'll crash into something else as sure as God made little apples, and next time it mayn't be so harmless. You know, I don't like the look in the eye of the gendarmes in this town. Oh, my hat, here's one of 'em now!'

A Monte Carlo policeman in a sky-blue uniform festooned with aiguillettes, enormous moustaches sprouting from under his white helmet, bore down upon them. '*Défense de s'arrêter!*' he screamed. '*Mettez-vous en ligne, nom d'un chien! Allons!*'

The young man gave the girl a comic look. 'It's war,' he murmured. 'They've mobilized the army on us. *C'est bien, c'est bien, sergot,*' he observed in accentless French to the gendarme. '*On y va!*' He parked the Isotta beside the kerb under the fiercely rolling eye of the law, touched his hat to the policeman in a flowery salute and stiffly hauled himself out of the driving seat. Seeing that the gendarme remained there, glaring at him, and that the girl had disappeared, he jumped into her car and ranged it behind his, on which the *agent*, with a parting comminatory glance, went on his way.

The young man doffed his béret, disclosing a tangle of fair hair, and was lounging against the railings when the girl came back, bearing a cup covered by a plate on which reposed a couple of sandwiches. 'Well, well, well,' he said, taking the cup from her, 'if that isn't real friendly! You're an absolute brick!'

Melissa scrutinised him discreetly as he ate and drank. He was rather an ugly young man, tall and broad-shouldered, with a snub nose barred by freckles and a wide mouth, by his accent obviously British. In his rumpled grey flannels and a blue shirt that was far from clean, with his unshaven face deeply burnt under its grime, he made a singularly unprepossessing impression. But for all that he looked and spoke like an educated person. And he had nice eyes, grey in the shadow, blue when the light was on them, steady, unconcerned eyes, lit by the merriest twinkle. They twinkled at her now as he lifted his cup to her and said: 'To my life-saver! And may I do as much for you some other time!'

In order not to embarrass him while he ate his sandwiches and drank his coffee, she turned away to her car, found a packet of cigarettes in the recess under the instrument board, lit one, and handed him the packet. Putting the cup and plate down on the stone ledge of the hotel railing, 'You know,' he remarked casually, as he pulled out a cigarette, 'if I had such a lovely name as Melissa I wouldn't stifle it with a mere initial — I'd wear it in full all over my chest!'

Her eyes followed his downward to the front of her jumper with its small 'M' embroidered over the heart. She laughed. 'How did you know the "M" stands for Melissa?' she asked.

He flushed a little. 'I saw a picture of you once...'

'Where?'

'I don't remember. In a newspaper or somewhere. My name's Boulton. My Christian name's so utterly leprous that I try and forget it, but my friends call me "Don"!'

She smiled at his anguished expression. 'Let's hear this first name of yours!'

He gave her a look of comic resignation. 'It's Alfred — isn't it too ghastly? The full name goes "Alfred Donnington Montgomery Clinton Boulton." Can you imagine any parents being so revoltingly inhuman as to weigh down a poor defenceless babe with a load of names like that at the font? It's a wonder I wasn't sunk without trace.'

At that she laughed outright: she found the young man amusing. He said: 'I've never met anybody called "Melissa" before. It's a lovely, liquid name, like — like milk and honey. Would you mind terribly if I called you "Melissa" just once, to see what it sounds like?'

She laughed again. She had china blue eyes that danced when she laughed. 'Please yourself,' she said. 'It's a free country.'

He took her hand solemnly. 'Then here goes!' He declaimed:

> 'O, woman in our hour of ease.
> Uncertain, coy and hard to please,

When pain and anguish wring the brow
You bring us food and drink. And how!

'In other words,' he wound up, 'thanks for the coffee and the kind words, Melissa!'

As he betrayed no willingness to release her hand, she withdrew it firmly. She was suddenly aware of the intimacy that had sprung up, as it were unbidden, between her and this surprising, shabby young man. She liked his easy air, the pleasing timbre of his voice, his firm hand-clasp, his unexpected mind, and realised that she was parting from him with regret. 'Now, of course, he's going to spoil everything,' she reflected. 'He's going to ask me when he can see me again, and serve me damned well right for letting him pick me up.'

'I must be going now, if I'm to get over to Nice and back before lunch,' she told him, and cursed herself inwardly for feeling self-conscious.

He walked with her to her car. 'I'm sorry about that wing,' he told her. 'If I were you I'd get your garage to fix it and have them send the bill in to one Baron de Bahl at the hotel here. He's a friend of my respected employer: he'll be bound to know where the old devil is.'

She nodded. 'We know the Baron, too. But don't worry. We'll stick my father with that wing, and say nothing to your boss about it. I should hate to think of your losing your job.'

He smiled at her out of his grubby face. 'Thanks. Thanks for the coffee, too. In fact, thanks for everything. Don't go running into any more cars!' he added mischievously, as the self-starter whirred.

She smiled and fluttered her hand. As she drove away, she was conscious of a faint feeling of chagrin at the thought that he had made no attempt to contrive another meeting.

On leaving the Isotta, Grenander, obese, short-necked, gold-spectacled, led his three companions at a rapid amble through the rotating door into the bustle of the hotel vestibule and straight up to the reception desk, where he buttonholed a clerk. 'Monsieur Ardza?' he said in throaty French.

The clerk looked startled. 'Monsieur Ardza, monsieur?'

'That's right!' Grenander thrust a card at him. 'The name's Grenander — Axel Grenander. You can announce me and my friends. Monsieur Ardza is expecting us.'

In a helpless fashion the clerk gazed about him. Then, lowering his voice, he said: 'I'm sorry, monsieur. Monsieur Ardza is dead!'

'Dead?'

Aghast, Grenander stared at him, then whipped round to the two men who accompanied him. 'The gentleman died last night,' the clerk explained.

'Then announce us to Monsieur Volkoff,' Grenander ordered in a stifled voice.

The clerk spread his hands. 'I regret, monsieur, the suite has been vacated. The body was taken out before dawn this morning. It has been despatched to Bellaggio, to Monsieur Ardza's Italian property, where the funeral is to take place. Monsieur Volkoff accompanied it.'

With an air of consternation, Grenander turned to his friends. But they had stepped back, and he found himself confronted by a large man, loosely dressed with a shock of white hair. He recoiled, his pudgy face livid, his small eyes fearful. 'You?' he gasped in English.

The other clutched his arm — he had fingers of steel. Smiling gently, 'You don't seem pleased to see me, Axel,' he remarked in a fluty voice.

Grenander stood his ground. 'Ve came to Ardza — by abbointment,' he said in guttural English, his small eyes hostile.

De Bahl wheezed his little cough. 'Quite! I was expecting you. For nearly three weeks already I have awaited your arrival.' He flashed a glittering eye round the group. 'But Ardza is no more. The arms king is dead.' He smiled and dropped his voice to a purring whisper. 'Gentlemen, *le roi est mort. Vive le roi!*'

The fat man scowled. 'Meaning what?'

'You came to submit a certain proposal to Ardza, and are remaining to submit it to me. Do I make myself clear?'

Grenander turned and consulted his companions with a glance. He grunted, but did not speak. His air was very sullen. De Bahl said: 'You and your friends will give me the pleasure of your company at breakfast? The restaurant will be deserted at this hour, and we shall not be disturbed. Come!'

Breakfast over, the host passed his big cigarettes around, lit one himself and, inhaling deeply, said in his velvety tones: 'I shall waste no words, Axel. Two months already you discuss this scheme without making headway. The idea is excellent — it's the execution that's faulty. I say nothing against your friends, Rypnik and Vassenko...'

The blood mounted in Grenander's florid cheeks.

'Vun day, mebbe, you poke your nose vunce too often in other people's affairs, Alexis,' he growled.

De Bahl smiled composedly. 'Maybe. But for the time being, my friend, I am aware of your discussions at Trieste. I likewise know that you've been all round Europe, trying to get support for this project of yours. You've tried governments, you've tried industry, and neither will look at it. In the last resort you come to Ardza, as I felt sure you would. Am I right?'

Grenander glowered at him. 'Ardza is dead. So what? I do without him. The plan is mine — if you t'ink you steal it, I say, No!' And he brought his fist down with a crash on the table.

The Baron was unmoved. 'Partnership is not stealing, Axel. I have elaborated a perfectly simple scheme for the successful execution of your idea, and I'm prepared to take you and your friends in. Indeed, I'm relying on your help if, as I have reason to believe, you've taken certain preliminary steps with a view to securing the — ah' — he cleared his throat — 'the necessary rank and file.'

The other rolled a bloodshot eye round the table. 'By yimini now,' he growled, 'I vunder who's been leaking to you!'

De Bahl laughed. 'I like to keep my ear to the ground — it's an old habit of mine.' He shot a rapid glance round the circle of attentive faces. 'Gentlemen, I need have no secrets from you. This is my plan ...'

Lowering his voice to a purring whisper, he began to speak.

The Baron Presents His Friends

It was past two by the time Melissa got back from Nice. The hall porter said her father had returned and had asked for her. Upstairs, outside their suite, there was a coming and going of waiters with service trolleys, the loud murmur of voices from the salon. She made a little face. There was company for luncheon, men, by the sound of it. She slipped into her bedroom next door to wash off the dust of the Corniche road and put on some powder.

She was at her dressing-table, making up her lips, when in the mirror she saw Stephen, napkin in hand, at the door communicating with the sitting-room. 'Hullo, big boy,' she said. 'Had a good trip? How's Paris?' Through the half-open door behind him the noise of voices, the clatter of knives and forks, were loud.

He came over to where she sat and kissed the top of her head. 'All right,' he replied. 'But that panelling was a washout. You're late. Hurry up and come in. De Bahl brought some men to lunch — they're going to help us out down at the Castle.' She stood up, and they went into the salon together. 'Gentlemen, my daughter!' said Selmar. 'Baron, will you present your friends?'

All the men at the table had sprung to their feet with alacrity. There were four of them, besides de Bahl, and in one she recognised the rather porcine contours of the fat man in the Isotta, Don Boulton's employer. The four guests left their places and crowded about her, bowing and kissing her hand in the foreign fashion as the Baron introduced each in turn. A nondescript lot, was her thought, all except a tall, rather elegant individual with a monocle and a lean, aristocratic face marred by a long scar running from eye to chin. He made room for her at the vacant place at the table between him and a little dark man rather elaborately dressed, with a big black pearl in his tie and a white carnation in his buttonhole.

'I have a name not easy for English tongues, Miss Selmar,' said the man with the scar in very good English. 'It's von Wahlczek. But as nobody could pronounce it when I was up at Oxford, they called me Wally, as I hope you will also, since we shall be spending the winter together.'

Melissa laughed as she started on her grapefruit. 'It certainly sounds easier. It's a German name, is it?'

'It's Czech. But I'm a Hungarian subject, actually. First, under the Habsburgs, I was Austrian; then when Czechoslovakia was formed, I was Czech. But since I didn't approve of the way the Czechs treated their minority subjects, I became Hungarian. In other words, I'm a sort of chameleon!'

'A thoroughbred mongrel,' observed the dark man on Melissa's other side airily.

'Our friend, von Wahlczek,' said de Bahl from the end of the table, 'speaks both Russian and Ukrainian. He'll be very useful with the Russian and Ukrainian workmen at Orghina. Mr. Apostolou on Miss Selmar's other side speaks Rumanian.'

'You're Rumanian, are you?' Melissa asked, turning to her neighbour.

The latter shook his head. 'I spend many years in the

country, but actually I am Maltese. I'm a British subject,' he added, rather defiantly. His accent was rather foreign. He had a slightly furtive air.

'For reasons which, with your permission, Mr. Selmar, I have explained to our friends,' said the Baron, rolling his eyes meaningly round the attentive faces at the table, 'it is important that the Rumanian authorities do not suspect we do anything except restoration work at Orghina. This is why, as I was about to tell you when Miss Melissa came in, I have entrusted the transport of the building materials we shall require to our good friend, Frangipani, here.' On this a broad-shouldered, rather swarthy individual in the business garb of black jacket and striped trousers, who sat beside him, bowed and smiled with a flash of white teeth. 'Aldo Frangipani,' de Bahl went on, 'who was in the Italian motor transport in the War, and now runs a trucking business at Trieste, will be indispensable in organising the transport of our materials from the railway over the bad roads when the winter sets in: moreover, he will let us have half a dozen of his own Italian lorry-drivers, picked men, whose discretion we may rely on. It was Grenander' — his glance drifted to the fat man — 'who suggested this plan, and I think it is a good one.'

Grenander grunted. 'Sure, I t'ink it's good,' he growled, 'so long as he gif us drifers who keep their heads shut.'

Frangipani outlined a polite shrug. 'How shall it be otherwise, per Bacco, when they do not speak Rumanian?' he observed urbanely.

This evoked a general laugh. Under cover of it Melissa said to von Wahlczek, 'What exactly is Mr. Grenander going to do at the Castle?'

'Grenander? He'll be in charge of the steel construction work,' her neighbour answered. 'He's an engineer.'

'A German, is he?'

'Not on your life. He's a Swede. Or it might be a Finn — I don't quite know.'

Melissa laughed gaily. 'Well, I declare, it looks as though we should have a regular Tower of Babel down here at Orghina. Let's see! There's my father and I, Americans, and de Bahl, a Swiss or something, to start with; then there's you, a Czech ——'

'Pardon, a Hungarian. Or, if you will, a chameleon. But not a Czech!'

She could not help laughing at him; he was so serious about it, staring at her gravely with his glass in his eye. 'A Hungarian, if you like,' she told him. 'Then there's Grenander, and this Maltese, and the Italian who's going to manage the trucks. Not to mention my father's French valet and the Baron's Tunisian servant.'

Von Wahlczek was polishing his eyeglass on his napkin. 'Well, it's a mixed bag, I agree. But it's a land of many nationalities, and some of these languages are not so easy to come by.' He dropped his voice. 'But don't worry: you'll not come much in contact with your friends. I believe de Bahl was good enough to suggest to your father that Grenander and I should take our meals with you; but the others will mess apart — they will be mostly with the men. Grenander's a pretty rough diamond; but I shall be there to keep him in order. Do you think you can put up with me as a table companion all through the winter?'

His eye sought hers ingratiatingly. She found his scrutiny embarrassing: to change the subject she said: 'There's one nationality in our Tower of Babel we've left out. The Englishman!'

'The Englishman?'

'Grenander's chauffeur.'

'So you know our young friend, Don?' He broke off. '*Ach!* ... It wasn't your car we hit this morning?'

She nodded. 'I'm surprised the poor young man was able to drive you at all. He was half dead with sleep. I got him some coffee.'

He tittered. '*Ei, ei*, the good Samaritan! Was your car much damaged?'

'Nothing to speak of. And there's no need to say anything about it to Mr. Grenander or the young man might lose his job.'

He shook his head. 'No fear. He has to drive us down to Rumania.'

'You're taking him to the Castle, then?'

'As far as Bucharest, anyway.'

At the end of the table Grenander was holding forth. 'A foreman, a boss of the gangs, ve must haf,' he declared ponderously. 'But he must be vun of us, foreign. I know these people, all of dem at each other's t'roats. Ve put a Ukrainian, a Rumanian, in charge of the gangs — plenty trobble.'

'It seems to me it will have to be Herr von Wahlczek or Mr. Apostolou,' Baron de Bahl suggested in his quiet way.

Grenander snorted derisively. 'Put a Czech over a bunch of Ruthenians — you're crazy. And Apostolou, they'll count him as a Rumanian.' He grinned. 'Better, I t'ink, I find you someone.'

'No time,' de Bahl objected, shaking his white head. 'The winter's coming on, and Miklas is already recruiting the labour. You speak of going down there tonight; well, I want you all to get busy on the job as soon as you arrive. You'll have to look around for a foreman when you reach Orghina.'

Melissa spoke up. 'How would an Englishman do?'

'An Englishman?' repeated Stephen. 'What Englishman?'

Von Wahlczek struck in. 'Mademoiselle is speaking of Don, Grenander — the chauffeur who brought us here from Trieste,' he explained to Selmar.

'I was talking to him this morning,' said Melissa. 'He struck me as being a very wide-awake young man.'

Grenander seemed impressed. 'Vell, von qualification he has. He's bossed gangs before.'

'You don't say?' Selmar exclaimed.

'*Ja.* In the rubber plantations in Malay and Brazil, on engineering vorks in the Sudan. What you call a rolling stone, this yong man. I find him as the English say on his beam ends at Trieste, when my French chauffeur got dronk and I sacked him. Vorked his vay across from Alexandria as a fireman, he told me.'

The Baron interposed suavely but firmly. 'Just a minute. This is a responsible position. Your young man sounds little better than a tramp, a beachcomber.'

'He's educated,' Melissa struck in. 'He's what you'd call a gentleman — at least, that's the way he impressed me. And is he sure of himself! He doesn't care a hoot for anybody.'

'That's right,' von Wahlczek agreed. 'He's a little crazy like all the English, but his nerve is first-class — you should have seen him bringing that big Isotta of ours round some of the mountain curves. As for being a tramp, good gracious! the world today is full of Englishmen of good family who can't get a job at home. If all these mixed nationalities we're going to employ can't have one of their own sort over them for

obvious reasons, I believe they'll work better under an Englishman than anyone else. And take it from me, they won't put
anything over on Boulton. The young man is tough.'

De Bahl drew on his cigarette, rasped in his throat and
carefully flaked his ash into the saucer of his coffee cup.
'And the language question?' he enquired gently. 'Have you
thought of that?'

'He speaks Russian,' said Apostolou. 'He told me so
himself. Ukrainian will not come so hard to him, I think.'

Grenander guffawed. 'Rossyan, Oukrainian, what does it
matter? All the foreign languages a gang boss vants, he has
in the toe of his boot.'

The Baron dropped his eyes. Selmar was radiant. 'A first-
class suggestion of yours, Melissa,' he told his daughter.
'I'll see the young man after lunch,' he informed de Bahl,
'and if he measures up to specification, he gets the job!'
Melissa was watching de Bahl and it seemed to her that a
shadow crossed his face. With a laugh Stephen went on:
'With all these different lingoes flying about down there, it'll
be a comfort to have at least one guy around who speaks the
same language as we do, won't it, Melissa? You know,' he
added to de Bahl, 'he might come in useful helping me with
my letters and so on, as I don't propose to take a secretary
with me — Melissa says he's apparently well-educated. He'll
be a sort of contact man for me. Gosh, it's the ideal solution,
I'd say, and if the young man's willing to take the job on, I
guess we can regard the matter as settled.'

Steve with a new idea always reminded Melissa of that
moment at a rodeo when the gate opens and the cowboy sails
into the ring mounted on a squealing, bucking bronco: he
would cling to it as tenaciously, as regardless of consequences,

as the rodeo rider to his steed. She saw the Baron's face
harden — it was evident he did not approve her suggestion;
but she knew her father better than de Bahl did, and had no
doubt in her mind but that he would have his way.

The Baron said no more, but only lit another cigarette
while Selmar, always practical, began to question Grenander
as to what wages the young man would expect. She was dimly
aware that de Bahl appeared less suave than usual in the
marked foreign setting of the luncheon party, not towards
her father, but towards Grenander and the others — it struck
her that he barely troubled to conceal his contempt for the
four of them, singly and collectively.

It occurred to her that the fascinating Baron might be a
bad man to cross.

'The Voice of Fate'

LUNCHEON over, Melissa left the party to their *fines maisons* and cigars over the contents of the Baron's big portfolio spread out over the tablecloth, and strolled up, hatless as she was, through the gardens to the garage to see about having the car repaired. She was conscious of a gratifying sense of accomplishment at having secured young Boulton in his job, of no less pleasurable excitement, too, at the thought that a reasonably presentable young man was going to share their winter exile. The strongly continental atmosphere of the luncheon party had rather depressed her — the different brands of spoken English, all, except von Wahlczek's, definitely exotic, the unfamiliar types among the guests, were a little bewildering: she had suddenly realised, with a sort of dread, the prospect of having Stephen as her sole companion 'speaking the same language,' as he had put it, during the long months that stood before. Of course, the Boulton person wasn't an American. But he was the next best thing. And he wouldn't bore them: he had a quality of mind that she found definitely refreshing.

At the garage, under the wide, cool roof, she gave the necessary orders about having the wing of the Selmar tapped out and repainted. She was turning to go when she saw, across the driveway, the grey Isotta streaming with water and Boulton in gum boots spraying it from a hose. She strolled over there. He was in shirt open at the neck and trousers, face and hands streaked with lubricant: there was even a smear on a yellow hank of hair that dropped down over his forehead. 'Why is it,' he demanded gravely as he looked up and recognised her, 'that you always see me at my filthiest?' — he did not desist from his hosing.

She laughed and, sitting down on the running-board of an adjacent car, fished out a cigarette from the packet in the pocket of her jumper. 'I'm an American,' she said. 'In America we never mind seeing a man doing an honest job of work.'

The water hissed. 'Our idle rich don't mind it, either!' he answered drily.

She flushed. 'That's not what I meant. I meant...'

He turned round to her with a grin. 'Don't be so literal! Can't you see I was pulling your leg?'

'I don't find it amusing to be called one of the idle rich. Especially when I was only paying you a compliment. I know lots of men who, when they strike a bad patch, are quite content to sponge on their friends instead of getting themselves a job.'

At that he made chortling noises. She said, 'What's funny about that?'

'Nothing. It was just something I thought of.' He stood back and dashed the hair out of his eyes. 'Don't you think I'm a great car-washer?'

'I don't think I should leave all that dust between the spokes if I were you!'

'*Touché!* My withers are unwrung!' He directed the stream of water at the wheel. 'Was your father a friend of Ardza's?' he said.

'Of Ardza?'

'The armaments king, the old guy who died at your hotel last night.'

'Then that's what all the excitement in the lobby was about this morning! I didn't even know he was dead. Of course, he was pretty old, wasn't he? Yes, my father knew him. They met in America.'

'Did your father see much of him here?'

'He didn't see him at all.'

He turned and looked her in the eye. 'You're sure of this?'

'Of course I'm sure. My father has no use for a man who makes his money stirring up wars, and I haven't either. As far as I know the old man was shut up in his suite all the time we were here and nobody saw him except Baron de Bahl.'

He plied his hose once more. 'Ah! So de Bahl was a friend of his!' he said evenly.

'He's a friend of Volkoff, Ardza's secretary. He used to dine up in Ardza's suite sometimes. Whether he was a friend of the old buzzard's, I can't tell you.'

He smiled. 'Buzzard — a bird of prey. "Buzzard" is good. I like that.' He went on with his spraying.

She said, 'What would you say to a new job?'

The water gurgled. 'Who's giving me a new job?'

'My father.'

With the detached air with which he seemed to do everything, he laid the spurting hose on the ground and, going to a tap in the wall, shut off the water. Seating himself beside her on the running-board, he said: 'You seem to spend your time doing me good turns, don't you? It's terribly nice of you, but I can't leave old Grenander, however objectionable as an employer, in the lurch.'

'You don't have to. He and his friends are going to spend
the winter with us in Bessarabia — that's part of Rumania,
you know. We've inherited an old castle down there and
Baron de Bahl is restoring it for us.'

'And your father seriously contemplates staying there all
the winter?'

She reminded herself that she must not breathe a word
about the treasure. 'Part of the winter, at any rate,' she
answered. 'It depends on how we like it.'

He gazed at her bleakly. 'He must be out of his mind.
What on earth put it into his head to think of such a thing?'

'Castle Orghina was originally built by one of our ancestors.
My father's thrilled to the bone at the prospect of living there.
After all, he's a rich man — he can afford to indulge his
whims.'

He nodded. 'Quite. As your friend the Baron no doubt
appreciates. Of course he talked him into this. He's a furniture dealer, isn't he?' He turned and glanced at her sharply.

'As a matter of fact, it's my father's own idea, entirely.
It was he who first suggested restoring the place.'

He grunted, sucking on an empty pipe. 'And Grenander
and his friends, you say, are going down there with you?'

'That's right. Mr. Grenander's an engineer, as you probably know — he's going to look after the steel work.'

'And von Wahlczek and the other two — are they engineers
as well?'

'No. They're going to help out with the languages.' She
explained about the different languages in Bessarabia. 'They
want someone to act as foreman, someone to keep all these
mixed nationalities among the men in order. So I suggested
you. Steve — my father — thinks it the whale of a good idea,

especially as you've bossed gangs before, Grenander says. They'll probably send for you this afternoon and offer you the job, so I thought I might as well put you wise.'

He was silent for a long moment, staring in front of him, his hands hanging down between his knees — he had well-shaped hands, she noticed. Suddenly he sprang up, took a turn up and down the floor in his clumsy boots, stopped in front of her. 'And you're going down with the party, too?'

She nodded serenely. 'I am.' She flicked the ash from her cigarette. 'You don't have to take this job, you know.'

He ignored her remark. 'Why should they drag you off down there? Couldn't you get out of it?'

'Why should I? It's a fascinating country, Baron de Bahl says, and the Castle's a marvel.'

He scowled. 'Bessarabia in winter's no place for anyone like you. It's the end of the world as far as civilisation is concerned. This castle's probably a draughty old barrack and you'll freeze to death. If your father's set on going, let him go. But you, take my advice, stick here on the Riviera and enjoy yourself in the sunshine or go back to America, if you want — do anything you like, but give the Castle a miss.'

Her laugh was rather scornful. 'I'm not afraid of roughing it, and, if I were, I really don't see it has anything to do with you.'

He nodded resignedly. 'Well,' he observed with a whimsical air, 'it looks as though we were going to spend the winter together.'

'Am I to infer, then,' she asked cuttingly, 'that you'll take the job if my father offers it?'

'I'll take it all right.' He paused, his eye on her. 'I'd have taken it anyway, but knowing that you're determined to be along makes a difference.'

She sighed impatiently. 'When you know me better, you'll realise I hate compliments. Especially cheap compliments.'

'I'm not paying you a compliment,' he replied very simply. 'I don't have to tell you that you're a most attractive person, because you know it already. But you're impulsive, and eager, and, with it all, terribly unsophisticated under that New York veneer of yours, and you're badly in need of someone to look after you.'

She laughed. 'Thanks, but I'm quite capable of looking after myself.'

He shook his head dubiously. 'In New York, London, Monte, perhaps. But Bessarabia's a different pair of shoes. You may be glad to have Mrs. Boulton's little boy around before the winter's out.'

He spoke jestingly, but there was no laughter in the level glance he gave her. She thought of de Bahl and his rather frightening air, of Grenander, loud-voiced and vulgar, and of their ill-matched companions, and it seemed to her that her spirits slipped a notch. Then a man came over from the garage office. He bowed to Melissa. 'Pardon, mademoiselle!' To Boulton he said in French: 'Your *patron* telephoned. You're to be at the hotel without the car at four o'clock.'

The Englishman grinned at Melissa. 'The voice of Fate!' he murmured. Then he went to the tap and turned on the water again. 'If I'm to be cleaned up by four ready to see your father, you must let me finish washing this blinking bus,' he told her, picking up the hose again.

Castle Orghina

MINK-WRAPPED against the biting cold, Melissa stood on the little platform on which her turret chamber opened and gazed out across the frost-bound Dniester. Below her the castle wall, red brick brownly toned by age, with great stone blocks let in, dropped sheer to the icy hummocks of the riverbed. To either side, beyond the line of crenellated battlements high above her head, the flat whiteness of the snow-covered steppe stretched to the low horizon, with hoary wooden windmills, sails stripped and arms still, looming through the smother of fine snow.

Across the river the cluster of pinnacles and gilded domes was Soviet Russia. In this remote frontier region it was a forbidden land, for Soviet Russia (the Baron was her inform-ant) was still rancorous at the thought that, on the collapse of the old Tsarist Empire, Bessarabia had escaped the Red em-brace and returned to the bosom of Mother Rumania. Here there was no communication between the opposing shores: the Dniester was the barrier. In the frosty air of the early afternoon the sky had a greenish glow — against it the distant spires and cupolas of the little town across the stream were laid as though cut out of cardboard.

The setting, she told herself, was sheer Russian ballet — a design by Bakst. Her mind was still a little blurred by the swiftness of the change from the glitter and luxury of Monte

Carlo and Paris to the stark picturesqueness of this forgotten corner of Europe. Here the blue skies and bluer seas, the chattering cocktail bars and gleaming limousines, of the South of France, the warm, perfumed air of the Paris dress salons, the moving chain of lights up and down the Champs Élysées at night — she had stipulated for a week's shopping in Paris before she and Steve caught the Orient Express — were as of another world. Bucharest, where they had taken the evening train for Chisinau, the Bessarabian capital, was a fleeting news reel in her mind of clanging trams, languorous mondaines and aggressively modern concrete contrasting with peasants in sheepskins; Chisinau, where they had transferred to a little local train, a glimpse of broad streets flanked by mostly low and shabby shops, a great white cathedral. They had travelled straight through at the Baron's suggestion — 'for an American millionaire, even in Rumania, is news, Miss Melissa, and the less attention we draw to ourselves just at present the better' — looking backward from the balcony over the confused incidents of their journey half across Europe it seemed to her that she had stepped straight out of the twentieth century as it seethes along the rue de la Paix into the illustrations of some old Russian fairy-tale book, replete with boyars in be-furred robes, enchanted castles and shaggy serfs.

Behind her as she leaned on the coping stone of the balcony overhanging the beetling wall above the river the Castle rang to the clink of hammer and trowel. The snow had stopped work out of doors: the Baron and his men were concentrating on the restoration of the Great Hall, the selfsame high-roofed chamber where Stephen cel Mare and his boyars had feasted. This, on the first floor, ran the whole length of one side of the inner courtyard: below it, on the ground level, were the Selmars' living-rooms — a sitting-room, dining-room and a nondescript apartment which Steve used as an office. These had been the Commandant's quarters when the Castle was a Russian fortress — furnished and redecorated, they were waiting for the Selmars on their arrival.

The Baron had travelled down ahead of them, while they were in Paris. Their first impressions must be favourable, he insisted: he would not have them arrive until he had personally assured himself as to their comfort. Boulton she had not seen again, for the motoring party had set out forthwith: she gathered from Stephen, however, that he was not unfavourably impressed with the young man and had agreed to give him a trial.

She had fallen in love with the Castle at her first glimpse of it from the sleigh, with three horses abreast troika fashion, in which the Baron had met them at the little local railway station. After a long, cold drive they saw it from afar across the gently undulating plain, four-square and grim in the early winter dusk, the blankness of its mighty walls rarely broken by arrow-slit or loophole, a vast pile of reddish masonry crowning a low eminence above the river, with a tower projecting from each corner. They had their first view of it on emerging from the village of Orghina, where the jangle of their sleigh bells brought peasants in gaily embroidered shirts running to the doors of their large thatched houses, each with its little verandah of carved beams in vivid colours and farmyard and orchard enclosed in wicker fences. Thereafter, there were no houses or farms, but only the stark fortress with its towers and battlements, between them and the mystery land of the Soviets beyond the river. Melissa found herself thinking of it as their legendary ancestor had built it, last bulwark of Chris-

tianity against the pagan horde across the Dniester: her heart
leaped within her as, with a final spurt from the steaming
horses, the sleigh swept up a steep ramp to the main gate
straddled by an enormously solid tower.

Within, everything was on the heroic scale — the vast outer
court with the old Russian barracks along one side, where the
workmen were now housed, and across the way, accommodation for the Baron and his staff in what had formerly been
the officers' quarters: the smaller inner yard, divided from the
outer court by a massive iron gate and flanked on the far side
by towers which, jutting from either angle of the main exterior
wall, commanded the river up and down. In the right-hand
tower (as you entered from the outer yard) — called, from its
oxidised copper roof, 'The Green Turret' — Melissa and
Stephen had their bedrooms, tower chambers, high of ceiling
and spacious, communicating by means of a corkscrew stair
leading from the vestibule below.

Melissa loved her bedroom. Cheerful blue and white hangings on the walls and blue and white Rumanian rugs on the
floor hid the naked stonework of the octagonal chamber, and
brightly painted peasant furniture lightened the rather sombre
effect of the two deep window embrasures — one had a door
leading out upon the little balcony. A huge white porcelain
stove of the German type kept the apartment warm and dry.
True, she and her father had to forego their private bath-
rooms — they shared what had been the Russian officers'
steam bath on the ground floor, adapted to their use, with its
vast wood-burning furnace to heat the water. But there was
electric light furnished by the plant supplying the whole Castle
— the patient chugging of the Diesel engine was one of the
accompanying sounds of life at Orghina: what with the taste

and comfort of their sleeping quarters, as well as of the rest of the accommodation prepared for them, Melissa and her father considered that the Baron had surpassed himself.

The tower forming the corresponding angle of the wall on the other corner of the inner court was known as the Boyar Tower. A gateway under it gave access to the rough, precipitate track by which the lorries with building materials reached the Castle — their loads were temporarily stored on the ground floor of the tower or in the cellars beneath. The trucks, with caterpillar treads that made light of the snow-covered roads, came at all hours — in the middle of the night Melissa would wake to hear them clanking up the steep incline to the Boyar Tower.

But it was the little mosque, guardian of the Pasha's secret, that thrilled her most. It stood facing you as you passed through the gates between the outer and inner yards, a shabby, forlorn little building once alternately squared in red and white stone courses but now faded and dilapidated, built against the Castle wall between the Green Turret and the Boyar Tower, with a slender minaret quite dwarfed by the soaring battlements above. The low door tucked away under its tiny porch was locked; coming upon Melissa trying it, the Baron told her that the place was filthy and filled with rubbish inside. It would have to be cleaned up before it would be fit for her to visit.

A week had elapsed since she and her father had arrived at the Castle, a week so fully filled with unpacking and exploring their new home that they were content to postpone visiting the mosque or even undertaking excursions beyond the Castle walls, had the weather made such trips possible. Huge packing-cases, with furniture and rugs and pictures, mainly destined for the great hall, were waiting to be opened, and others continued to arrive, mixed up with the crates of tools, the girders and bags of cement dumped by the lorries under the Boyar Tower.

Meanwhile, she found the definitely masculine atmosphere of the Castle somewhat overwhelming. On the night of their arrival they had driven into the outer courtyard to discover that the whole working force had turned out to greet them. In the gathering darkness torches flared and smoked, and in their flickering light she was aware of a sea of peasant faces hairy and unkempt, with staring eyes — shaggy men in blouses, some bare-headed, some in flat Russian caps. Von Wahlczek was there and the sallow Maltese, and Frangipani, in a cluster of figures in leather jackets smiling a welcome out of cheerful brown faces — the Italian truck-drivers, she surmised. It was a moment or two before she recognised Don Boulton, looking oddly Russian in a high-peaked fur cap, suède jacket and plus-fours thrust into high boots; but the sleigh flashed by before he appeared to see her.

The workmen had their barrack-rooms like soldiers, she discovered next day when she went on a tour of inspection with Stephen, lines of truckle beds with blankets neatly folded and a steel wardrobe beside each for the man's belongings. As their quarters were in the outer court, and she and Stephen were lodged in the inner yard, she came little in contact with the workmen. But the Castle was alive with their presence from early morning when gongs improvised from steel bars summoned them from sleep, to nightfall, when the same gongs sounded the 'Lights Out' — all day long the ancient walls reverberated to the shrill of the foremen's whistles, shouted orders, the tramp of feet.

It rather amused her to find herself the only woman in this quasi-military setting. She could have brought a maid with her from France, as Stephen had urged. But, feeling that a

Frenchwoman was likely to prove more of a liability than an
asset in the wilds of Bessarabia, she had preferred to rely on
the Baron's undertaking to find her a maid, when they were
settled in, probably a German woman from one of the old-estab-
ished German farm colonies in the region. Meanwhile, she
made her own bed, while Charles and Ali, the Baron's Tunisian,
did the rest of the housework, prepared the meals with the
assistance of one of the Rumanian workmen as kitchen boy,
and waited at table.

Charles would be serving tea, she reflected as she quitted the
balcony and, passing through her turret bedroom, made her
way downstairs. As she crossed the lobby below she saw
through the window Don Boulton coming through the gateway from the outer court. He strode purposefully into the
yard and up to the entrance of the Green Turret, then stopped,
irresolute, and looked behind him.

Melissa opened the window. 'Hello, there,' she said. 'Were
you looking for my father?'

As he raised his eyes and saw her there, his face lit up. It
seemed to her that he had a faintly excited air. 'Because if
you are,' she continued, 'he's with the Baron at the office.'

He nodded. 'I know. It seemed a good chance to catch you
alone.' He glanced back over his shoulder again. 'Do you
think I might come in for a minute? I've something to tell
you — something pretty important.'

He spoke hurriedly with a sort of desperation in his voice
that gave her a sudden sense of misgiving. 'Come in, of course,'
she told him. 'I'm just going to have tea. That ought to
appeal to you as a good Britisher.'

But his face showed no appreciation of her jesting tone.
With the same hunted air, he cast another stealthy glance
backward and hastily entered the turret.

The First Warning

HE FOUND her waiting for him in the doorway of the living-room, framed in a pool of light that spilled out into the gaunt stone vestibule, groined of ceiling and dank with the chill drifting in from the yard, an ultra-modern silhouette in her smartly tailored fur coat. A very faint fragrance came to him as she stood back to let him pass and he brushed by her into the warm radiance of the room beyond. His rough working clothes were powdered with snow and smeared with clay: there was snow on his fur cap and snow on his eyebrows, and his gloveless hands were blue with cold. 'My gracious,' she declared aghast, 'you look half frozen. Come to the fire and warm yourself.'

The room was high of ceiling and tapestry-hung, with a fire of tremendous logs blazing in a great stone fireplace. Though the furniture, apart from the red leather settee before the fire and a couple of club chairs to match, was period, a line of open bookshelves, a table of American magazines, gave the apartment a cheerful, modern look. The leaping flames gleamed on silver and porcelain where the tea was set out on a low table before the hearth. Boulton appeared to notice none of these things. Disregarding the girl's invitation, he said brusquely, 'What's going on here?'

She bristled a little at the bluntness of his tone. 'Has anything happened?' she asked.

'Shut the door!' he bade her, and when she had complied, 'What's the game?' he demanded with the same uncompromising air.

She was thinking to herself, 'He's heard about the treasure and wants to pump me.' Going forward to the fire, she sat down on the couch and, removing the cosy from the teapot, said composedly, 'Wouldn't you be more comfortable if you parked your hat and found a chair?'

Glancing demurely backward, she saw him whip off his fur bonnet. 'Sorry,' he muttered. Then he stamped over to the fireplace and confronted her. 'Have you taken a look at the last lot of workmen?' he demanded.

She knew what he was alluding to. On the previous evening a fresh party of workmen had arrived, hard-bitten, sturdy types. These were the picked men provided by Grenander to dig for the treasure, her father had confided to her. She shrugged her shoulders as she poured out the tea. 'Not particularly.' She laughed. 'You know, all these peasants, Rumanian or whatever they are, look much the same to me. I mean, they're all pretty shaggy, aren't they? Cream and sugar?'

He gazed at her stonily. 'These are not Rumanian-speaking Moldavians — they're Ukrainians to a man. Grenander paid off every Moldavian in the place this morning and sent them packing. There are twenty-eight in the new bunch and they're supposed to be skilled labour — at least, that's what Grenander told me. Would it interest you to know that, out of the whole boiling, there aren't ten who can use a plane or plaster a wall? And there isn't a skilled workman in the lot. And I'll tell you something else. There were a number of perfectly good carpenters and masons among the Moldavians, yet Grenander lets them go. Why?'

She handed him his tea. 'Well,' she observed delicately, 'I wouldn't want to be quoted, but I don't believe the Baron has much use for the native article.'

'So he replaces them by a bunch of scallywags who can't tell one end of a saw from the other!' He broke off impatiently. 'Listen. With this fresh batch there are about fifty men on the works here. If your father thinks de Bahl can get anything done with this outfit, he's nuts! To complete the work on the Great Hall alone, what with the repanelling and the reflooring, calls for expert woodworkers. Well, you can take it from me that there are not half a dozen men left in the Castle who know the first thing about it. If you don't believe me, go up to the Great Hall tomorrow morning and see them falling over each other, just killing time. From now on the restoration work's a farce and de Bahl knows it. And so I ask you again — what's the game?' With an angry air he drank his tea.

She was conscious of a little thrill at the thought that the preparations for the treasure hunt were seriously afoot, at the same time remembering that she must be discreet. She offered him a plate of biscuits. 'I wish you wouldn't stand there barking questions at me,' she said. 'Why don't you sit down?'

He took a seat on the cushioned fire-rail. 'You haven't answered my question,' he reminded her.

She shrugged her shoulders. 'I think you're being rather dramatic about something that probably has a perfectly simple explanation. The Baron told me at Monte Carlo that he intended to get rid of the local labour as soon as possible.'

'Why?'

She felt the colour rise in her cheeks. 'Maybe because he prefers to employ his own people.'

'An unwashed rabble who'd rather sit round talking politics than do an honest day's work — are these his people?'

'You call them a rabble. But I don't suppose it was so easy to find men who'd be willing to come and work in the wilds of Bessarabia. Naturally, they'd be of the adventurer type.'

He laughed on a hard note. '"Adventurer type" is right. Well, it may satisfy you, but it don't satisfy me.'

She was sorely tempted to ask him what business it was of his. But he looked so forlorn standing there, there was such a hurt, suspicious look in the grey eyes, that she refrained. 'Oh, well,' she remarked, helping herself to a cigarette, 'I'll tell my father what you say. We'll see what he thinks.'

His manner changed instantly. From being arrogant he became urgently imploring. 'No, no, no, please,' he entreated. 'Not a word to your father!'

'Really,' she said coldly. 'Don't you think I'm the best judge of that?'

He shook his head. 'No. Definitely not. Your father and de Bahl are in this together.'

'Are you suggesting that my father and the Baron are mixed up in some crooked deal?'

'I don't know,' he said very simply. 'Your father impresses me as being a very honest sort of man ——'

'Thanks!' she broke in sarcastically.

'But he believes in de Bahl ——'

'And why shouldn't he? Baron de Bahl's a grand person and devoted to my father.'

'All right. But don't you see, if you take this story to your father and he repeats it to de Bahl, the first thing that happens I'm out on my ear. And that's what we have to avoid at all costs.'

She shrugged indifferently. 'Then if you want to keep your job, surely it's unwise to go around spreading tales against your employers?'

On that he flushed. 'Naturally, you'd think that.' He gazed
at her steadily. 'I told you at Monte Carlo the time might
come when you'd be glad to have me around. Well, it's coming
all right, and coming with giant strides: if you've any regard
for your own and your father's safety, I do beg of you not to
give them the slightest chance to get rid of me ——'

He broke off and put his finger to his lips — there were
voices outside. 'Not a word to your father or anyone,' he whispered imploringly as the door opened and Stephen appeared.
Grenander was with him. At the sight of Boulton Grenander
scowled. 'Don't you know the staff ain't allowed to come beyond the outer yard without permission?' he growled to
Boulton.

The Englishman moved his shoulders unwillingly. 'Miss
Selmar was kind enough to ask me in to tea,' he answered
stolidly.

Grenander's hard eye sought out the girl. 'The yong man
belongs in the barracks vith the rest,' he rasped. 'It's a rough
crowd ve got here and vithout ve use a iron discipline, ve can't
handle them. Then please, no favourites, ja?' He swung
fiercely to the Englishman. 'Now get back to your quarters
and, in future, keep the rules or, mebbe, you find yourself
vithout a yob again!'

'All right, all right,' Selmar, who had gone to the tea table
and was eating a piece of cake, broke in testily. 'That wasn't
a very bright idea of yours,' he observed to his daughter in an
undertone.

Melissa had crimsoned. She found herself disliking Grenander exceedingly. She was about to come to Boulton's defence when she caught sight of the Baron wiggling a warning
finger at her from the doorway. She had rather hoped that

Boulton would have stood up to Grenander, but he only shrugged his shoulders and saying, 'Thanks all the same, Miss Selmar!' went out.

De Bahl drew Melissa aside. 'Don't pay any attention to Grenander,' he whispered. 'His bark is worse than his bite.' He gave her an understanding smile and patted her shoulder.

She felt, as she had felt before, that one could always depend on the Baron to do the tactful thing.

Blood in the Snow

ON COMING down to dinner that evening Melissa was relieved to hear from Charles that Grenander had sent word he would not be able to join them. It was pay night for the workmen, and he would be busy until late — he would dine with Apostolou and Frangipani, who, with Miklas the architect, had their own mess in the buildings of the outer yard. She felt she could get on very easily, not only then but always, without Grenander, who, with the Baron and von Wahlczek, took his meals with them — especially after the encounter of the afternoon. By contrast with the elegant von Wahlczek, the big engineer had the grace of a farm hand, surly and taciturn, with a rough way with the servants, and really deplorable table manners.

They did not dress for dinner at Orghina, but Melissa usually changed her frock, while Stephen liked to slip on an old smoking jacket to which he was attached. The living-room was empty when she appeared in the black taffeta dinner dress she had bought in Paris with a silver fox across her shoulders. Charles had put the cocktail service out and she busied herself, while waiting for the others, in shaking up a dry martini. It was still snowing outside: the snow clinging to the windows made the room with its roaring fire seem very cosy. She was pouring out the cocktails when her father, very distinguished with his grizzled hair and black velvet coat, came in. 'None of them here yet?' he said.

'Grenander won't be dining — he's paying the men,' she told him.

He frowned. 'He's a tough egg, that one. I didn't like the way he spoke to you this afternoon. I must have a word with de Bahl about him.'

'You know that he paid off all the local workmen today?'

Selmar's frown deepened. 'Who says so?'

'Boulton just told me.'

He grunted. 'It's the first I've heard of it. Of course, now that that new batch has arrived — they're a husky-looking lot, I must say. Still, he should have told me.'

'Are we going to start looking for the treasure right away?'

'I tackled de Bahl about it this morning. But he said there was no hurry — as they've begun work on the Great Hall, he thinks we should finish with that first.'

The opening of the door interrupted him. Von Wahlczek was there, very dapper in dark grey — however grubby he might appear in the daytime, as Melissa had seen him, shouting orders in the Great Hall, he invariably turned out well groomed at night. He came up to her with alacrity, bowed over her hand, then straightened himself up with an audible sniff. 'Delicious!' he cried, beaming at her through his eyeglass. 'Your perfume, like your frock, mademoiselle, proclaims the rue de la Paix!' And, turning to Stephen, 'How grateful we should be to your charming daughter, Mr. Selmar, whose always so ravishing appearance brings a touch of civilisation, as delicious as the airs of spring, into this company of savage men!'

Her father made growling noises in his throat — he had an inherent distrust of compliments — while Melissa gave the newcomer his cocktail. Selmar said abruptly, 'So Grenander has been sacking some of the hands, eh?'

Von Wahlczek shrugged his shoulders and laughed. '*Ach was*, merely the surplus labour, my dear sir. A lot of loutish peasants only fit to till the ground. To your good health, mademoiselle!' He raised his cocktail to her. 'You'll appreciate that our friend Grenander is continually concerned with keeping down the expenses — what you call in America the overhead,' he remarked to Selmar, and sipped elegantly.

Stephen thawed — here was an argument he could understand. 'I've nothing against that, certainly. But I think I should have been consulted about it. Now that the diggers are here, I want the work on the Great Hall finished as soon as possible so that we can start operations in the mosque.'

Von Wahlczek stared at him through his monocle. 'The mosque? Yes, yes, of course. But, with the men we have in ten days, a fortnight, the work on the Hall is finished, *terminé!*'

His answer produced an unpleasant impression on Melissa. He's too glib, she thought, he's lying. It was on the tip of her tongue to ask him how many of the remaining working force were really competent to carry on with the work still to be done on the Hall; but she hesitated, loth to give young Boulton away. While she was debating the matter in her mind, the Baron came whirling in upon them, casting off his fur cap and heavy fur-lined overcoat all speckled with snow and wheezing apologies for being late; and they went in to dinner.

The dining-room, guard-room of the Castle under the Tsars, was under the Great Hall, with a groined ceiling and a row of high, narrow windows along one side, overlooking the inner yard. Some trophies of arms, survivals of the Russian occupation — bucklers bristling with old-fashioned bayonets, brass-handled swords, rifles of ancient pattern — made geometric designs on the naked stone walls between the windows. An immense mahogany buffet elaborately carved from the Baron's Geneva stock — he told them it came from a Lisbon palace — imposingly filled one end of the hall, a huge fireplace with a blazing fire the other, while a great Dutch dresser laden with pewter faced the windows; but even their massive lines were dwarfed by the lofty proportions of the chamber.

They dined at one end of the long refectory table, of solid oak from an English country-house, just the four of them in the rather ghostly radiance of the beeswax candles, fat and yellow, set in heavy brass candlesticks. Outside the wind whistled and tore at the windows, with flurries of snow that whirled against the panes — the wildness of the night, however, seemed far removed from the pleasant warmth and studied quiet surrounding the little party, with Charles, grave as an image, and the dark-faced Ali, moving noiselessly in the shadows beyond the candlelight.

That night von Wahlczek did most of the talking, as, indeed, he usually did. He was an excellent raconteur, with a fund of curious stories about Court life in the Vienna of the Emperor Francis Joseph and his period of active service as a cavalry subaltern in the campaign against the Russians in the war. On this evening, before even they had started on their caviar, he embarked upon a description of the Jewish Rabbi's family at Lodz on which he had been billeted during the operations in Poland, and soon had them chuckling with him over the 'Rav,' his large progeny and their countless relations, and imitations of their contorted Yiddish-German.

It seemed to Melissa that her father listened to their guest with some unwillingness at first — she could guess that Steve was impatient to tackle the Baron about Grenander's action in dismissing the Rumanians, as well as about Grenander's behaviour in general. But von Wahlczek was a finished actor. He knew how to win and hold an audience, and it was not long before he had Stephen listening to him as intently as the others and laughing as heartily at his mimicry.

It was a good story, but a long one, and it was still unfinished when, halfway through dinner, Ali brought the Baron a note. Von Wahlczek broke off while de Bahl found his glasses and, with a muttered 'Pardon!' broke the seal. With a perfectly stolid face he read the message, then, flinging down his napkin, stood up. 'If Miss Selmar will excuse me,' he said to Selmar, and without further explanation went rapidly out through the door at the far end of the dining-hall, leading to the corridor where the staff quarters were situated.

Von Wahlczek resumed his tale. Ali removed the fish plates and Charles served the sweetbreads. Melissa let her attention wander. She was thinking of Boulton out there in the snow, wondering what sort of life he had, a lone Englishman marooned among so many different nationalities. She remembered Steve's idea that Boulton might act as liaison officer between him and the working staff and decided it was time something was done about it. She saw no reason why the young man should not take his meals with them. He would be a useful counterpoise to Grenander; besides, it would annoy Grenander — she had a score to pay off against her *bête noire*.

It appeared to her, as dinner proceeded, that some kind of disturbance was going on outside. Her ear caught a growing murmur of voices, and turning towards the windows, she was aware of flickering lights in the snow without. Stephen seemed to hear something too, for, brusquely interrupting von Wahl-czek, he said sharply: 'Listen! What's that noise?'

In the silence that fell sounds of tumult welled in to them out of the night. Von Wahlczek laughed. 'It is nothing. The men have received their first wages this evening and maybe one or two of them have drunk a little too much schnaps — so it was always in the army, too, on pay nights.' But Selmar said, 'Please!' quite crossly and twisted his head round to Charles, who was behind his chair, serving the wine. 'What is it? What's happening?' he demanded irritably.

The valet went to the window. 'It is the workmen, who come into the inner yard, monsieur,' he informed Selmar with his usual impassive air. The voices were now much louder. Confused shouts and cries rang in the inner yard and a sudden fitful glare danced from outside. Selmar rushed to the window, flung it open. The court was thronged with defiant, gesticulating men, some carrying torches. Von Wahlczek jumped to his feet and hurried to the door through which the Baron had disappeared. Selmar would have followed, but von Wahlczek stopped him. 'Please, you stay here and take care of Miss Selmar,' he entreated earnestly. 'I find out what is the matter and let you know.' He stormed out.

Peering over her father's shoulder as he gazed from the window, Melissa saw by the light of the torches that the crowd in the yard was gathered about a solitary figure, a man who, with collar torn and face bleeding, was plunging in the grip of two shaggy-looking workers. It was Apostolou. The crowd swayed about him as he tried to free himself, while angry cries, in which one word was constantly repeated, echoed from their ranks.

Then without warning it happened. There was a red flash somewhere out there against the snow and a report that shook the windows and seemed to awaken every echo of the castle; Apostolou spun round so violently that he jerked himself out of the grasp of the men who held him, pitched forward on his face, twitched and lay still. The crowd fell away like magic, swirled about and closed in again, while a stentorian voice reverberated through the yard, excitedly shouting orders.

Selmar had sprung back from the window. Melissa had a glimpse of him vanishing into the adjacent living-room and followed after. She caught up with him under the turret entrance. With a line of tossing torches the crowd was trailing away to the outer yard, leaving the inner court empty and dark, save for the lightening effect of the snow. The body on the ground had disappeared. As Melissa and her father stood there they saw two figures move into the path of light flung by the vestibule lamp. It was the Baron and Grenander, arguing in angry tones. Selmar cried, 'What's going on here?'

De Bahl turned swiftly. At the sight of the two Americans, his manner changed on the instant. 'A little trouble with the men, Mr. Selmar. But it's settled now,' he said reassuringly.

'But, good God, man, Apostolou's been shot,' Selmar exclaimed. 'Look!' He pointed downward. There was blood on the trodden snow. 'What happened?'

It was Grenander who replied. 'Best you keep out of this, I t'ink, Mr. Selmar!' he said thickly.

'Keep out of it?' Selmar's tone was apoplectic. 'Don't you realise that a man's been killed, shot under our very eyes? Who shot this man and what did they have against him? I insist on knowing.'

The engineer grunted. 'You leave this to us, *ja?* Meanwhile, you take Miss Selmar and go back inside the house!' 'Just a minute...' Stephen broke in, but Grenander was loudly apostrophising the Baron. 'What for ve stand here, vasting time?' he roared. Seizing de Bahl by the arm, he hurried the other across the yard at a shambling run and disappeared into the court beyond.

'By the Lord Harry, I won't stand for this,' Stephen trumpeted. 'Hey, you, Grenander!' he cried, setting off in pursuit of the two men. The Baron had disappeared when they reached the gateway, but Grenander's squat outline bulked black against the lantern under the arch. Selmar began to bluster. 'Look here, Grenander ——'

The other cut him off. 'You heard my order ——'

'Order? Who's giving me orders?'

'I am. You go back to the house and stop there, ja? And from now on see that you and the girl don't pass this gate without my permission.'

Stephen's anger flamed. He sprang forward. 'Now you listen to me, you dumb Swede...' But the darkness under the gateway had swallowed Grenander up. In his place a stalwart figure, fur-capped and armed with a rifle, barred the way.

'This is my house — you can't stop me!' the American shouted. But the sentry, muttering some unintelligible phrase, menaced him with his rifle.

Melissa had followed her father to the gate. While he was engaged in his altercation with the guard, a firm hand seized her by the arm and drew her into the shadow beside one of the buttresses of the Great Hall. It was Boulton. 'Listen,' his fierce whisper rustled, 'you must get your father back to the house and keep him quiet, or they'll kill him, the same as they killed Apostolou.'

She stared at him aghast, unable to speak. He went on:

'They accused Apostolou of dickering with the Russians across the river. I don't know who shot him, but it was deliberate murder. I'm telling you this, not to scare you but so that you'll restrain your father from raising trouble. For the present, let him think it was a drunken brawl, anything, as long as it isn't the truth, because if I know anything of him, once he hears the truth he'll fly straight off the handle and then we're all in the soup.'

'But why should they want to harm my father?' she asked earnestly.

He was glancing rapidly about him. 'I've no time for explanations now. I've to get through that gate and back to my quarters before I'm missed. But make up your mind to this — you and your father are prisoners here for the present.'

In the dim light under the arch they saw that the iron gate had been shut. Stephen was visible plodding across the snow-covered ground. They heard him call: 'Melissa! Melissa! Where are you?'

Boulton gave her hand a little squeeze. 'That sentry mustn't see me talking to you. Remember what I told you — try and keep your father quiet!

She stepped out of the shadow to meet Stephen, while Boulton slipped away into the darkness.

Boulton Blots His Copybook

In the excitement of their dash from the dinner-table, Melissa had not noticed that the snow had stopped. Clouds hid the moon, but the night was dry and clear. The cold was pitiless — in the silence that had dropped down upon the dark void of the inner yard she could hear the dull reports of the ice in the river. All about her the Castle walls stretched upward to the stars — the oblong of sky above the court was gemmed with them blazing brightly in the frosty air.

Earlier in the day the workmen had made a path through the snow from the Green Turret to the dividing gate. Melissa ran along it now to meet her father, who came hurrying towards her, spluttering with wrath. 'It's unbelievable!' he stormed. 'There's a dumb sentry on the gate who refused to let me pass, and when I tried to brush past him, darn nearly shoved my ribs in with his rifle. This is Grenander's doing, and I'm not standing for it; no, by heck! Where's de Bahl? I'll have somebody's blood for this. By Gad, it's worse than a sit-down strike back home!'

Melissa took his arm. She felt pierced through with the cold: she had only a fur thrown across her shoulders and she was shivering. Now she discovered that her father was bareheaded and without even a muffler. 'What you're going to do,' she said, 'is to march straight back to your dinner. We shall both catch our death of cold if we stay out here.'

'I'll show them who's boss of this outfit,' Selmar raged. 'They shoot a man and when I demand an investigation, all they give me is a rifle in the ribs. But I'll get to the bottom of this business, if it means canning the whole bunch, de Bahl included, gosh darn it!' But he allowed his daughter to shepherd him indoors.

Charles, lantern-jawed and unmoved, was at the turret entrance looking for them. 'I put the sweetbreads back on the fire, monsieur, but I fear they're spoiled,' he said gravely. 'Shall I go on serving the dinner or will monsieur wait for the other gentlemen?'

'Serve the dinner, Charles,' Melissa bade him. 'We won't wait for the others.'

'I'll wait for nobody,' her father barked. 'Get on with the dinner, damn it, and listen! — you can mix me a highball, and make it strong!'

The dining-room, with napkins flung aside and chairs pushed back as they had quitted it, welcomed them with its warmth and quiet. But Melissa found herself thinking of that scarlet stain in the snow; it was hard to realise that a man's life had been sheared away in the few minutes during which they had been absent from the table. There was where von Wahlczek had sat and made them laugh with his story; there beside her plate the handkerchief with its Paris perfume he had praised; a few ticks of the clock and the peace of that dinner-hour — indeed it might be of the whole long winter before them — had been rudely shattered. She shuddered a little. Boulton's warning cast a black shadow over her mind. He had told her that Apostolou had been killed because he was believed to be a Russian spy. Did it have something to do with the Pasha's treasure? She felt bewildered and much disturbed in mind. She wished the Baron might come. He was always a tower of strength; he would make everything clear.

Charles brought Stephen his whisky and soda and Stephen drained it at a gulp. Melissa watched him wiping his moustache with a determined expression on his pink and healthy face; she saw no longer the retired business man on holiday, but the hard-bitten American industrialist used to having his own way. From now on — she read it in his eye — he meant to make his authority felt; it might not be easy, she reflected, to carry out Boulton's injunctions to keep him in check.

When Charles reappeared with the sweetbreads, Selmar said, 'Tell Ali to find Baron de Bahl and say I wish to see him here at once.'

'Ali is not here, monsieur.'

'Then go yourself, damn it!'

Melissa signed privately to the valet to disregard the order. 'Now, Steve,' she said, 'you're going to calm down and finish your dinner. You can give everybody hell afterwards.'

Her father shook himself unwillingly, but resumed his place at the head of the table. 'Do you know what I think?' he growled. 'There's been some monkey business about the treasure. It's always the same story — where there's hidden gold, there's trouble. Well, de Bahl can't say that I gave anything away. It's one of these fellows of his, I guess — you can't expect a secret to be kept that's shared between half a dozen people.'

At that moment Ali came in and pulled out his master's chair. And here was the Baron himself, sliding into his seat with his little cough. 'My dear friend,' he declared, picking up his napkin, 'I cannot say how sorry I am for our friend Grenander's unpardonable rudeness to you tonight. But, *mon*

Dieu, you know him, how he is, a rough diamond, and he was much upset by this unfortunate accident. I hope you will not bear ill-feeling towards him.'

'*Accident?*' Selmar snapped back. 'Accident, my foot! The man was shot, and shot deliberately, wasn't he? He's dead, isn't he?'

'I fear — yes.'

'Who shot him?'

The Baron helped himself to bread. 'We don't know yet. Grenander is inquiring into the matter now.'

'Are you aware that one of your dumb workmen prevented me by force from leaving the inner court tonight? He had a rifle. Who gave him a rifle?'

De Bahl sighed. 'I shall ask you to be very patient — patient and understanding. I have not mentioned it before in order not to alarm you, but the Soviet people have been giving us a little trouble. We have a few rifles — this is a fairly unsettled region, remember — and it seemed wise to distribute them tonight — you know, to keep the men in check.'

Stephen laid down his knife and fork. 'The Soviet people? What in Hades have they to do with it? This isn't Soviet Russia.'

'No. But Soviet Russia is only just across the river, as you know. For more than a hundred years this was a Russian province. The Soviet Secret Service is very active on this side of the Dniester.'

'But ...'

De Bahl cast an appealing glance at Melissa. She said, 'Steve, you might let him explain.'

'The gentlemen across the river,' said the Baron composedly, starting in upon his sweetbread, 'are apparently incapable of believing that you are restoring the Castle as a private residence. Our activities here appear to have aroused their strongest suspicions.'

'You mean, they've got wind of the treasure?'

'If it were only that.' The Baron's tone was gently condescending. 'No, dear friend, they appear to have taken into their heads the idea that Castle Orghina is being put back on a military footing in connivance with the Rumanian General Staff and — well, in short, we have reason to believe that they have planted spies among the workmen. The best way to do this was to take advantage of the unskilled labour recruited more or less as it could be found in the immediate neighbourhood. That is why our good friend Grenander has taken the first opportunity to get rid of the bulk of the unskilled labour today — all the Rumanians and such Russians and Ruthenians as we had: the Ukrainians, who are bitterly opposed to the Bolsheviki, we can trust. But it seems he was too late.' He swallowed a little wine thoughtfully. 'To speak ill of a dead man I do not like, especially of one for whose engagement you are certainly entitled to hold me responsible, but I'm afraid that Apostolou — with whom, I may tell you now, I was never very favourably impressed — was in touch with the Soviet Secret Service.'

Stephen glanced at him sternly from under his bushy eyebrows. 'That's a pretty serious charge, Baron. Apostolou struck me as being a harmless enough sort of guy. What proof have you?'

'A Soviet questionnaire, a favourite device of all secret services for obtaining information, was found on him, as well as a considerable sum of Russian money.'

Selmar grunted. 'I can't for the life of me see what the Soviet people could discover here.'

'Agreed, but who knows what stories this Apostolou has not told them? He might have dropped a hint about the treasure, for example — the Russians, having occupied Castle Orghina for so many years, might certainly think they had a claim to it.' His eyes rested tentatively on Selmar's face.

Melissa spoke up. 'How did you get on to the fact that Apostolou was spying for the Bolsheviks?' she asked him.

'He was seen drinking in the village with a notorious Russian agent,' was the impressive answer. 'When he returned to the Castle some of the men accused him of being in the Soviet employ. They were paid tonight and some of them were a little drunk, there was a row and — well, somebody shot him.'

Stephen pushed his plate away. 'Well, spy or not, the murderer has to be found and handed over to the Rumanian authorities for punishment. Is that clear?'

'But, of course, Mr. Selmar, of course.' His voice became silky. 'In the meantime, feeling is high among the workmen and I think it is wise, especially as we have a young lady with us' — he bared his teeth in an expansive smile at Melissa — 'that you do not leave your quarters for the present.'

Selmar was in the act of selecting a cigar from his case. He looked up sharply. 'Did Grenander send you to me with that message?'

The Baron spread his hands. 'Let me remind you that I had nothing to do with the hiring of the labour. That was Grenander's job, and if he reports that political passions among the workmen are so inflamed that it's unsafe to...'

The door communicating with the living-room was rapped, then opened. Young Boulton was there. He advanced to Stephen at the head of the table. Hand to his cap, he saluted.

'Mr. Grenander's compliments, Mr. Selmar, and you and Miss Selmar will please not leave this wing of the Castle until further orders. I was to add that armed guards have been posted at the doors to see that these instructions are complied with.'

Stephen crimsoned. Making a visible effort to control himself, he threw himself back in his chair.

'Is that so? Well, young man, you can trot right back to Grenander and tell him that this is my house and no one's going to give me orders as to what I can do and can't do.'

The messenger hoisted his shoulders. 'You can please yourself about that: I'm merely carrying out my instructions. But if you take my tip, you'll stay indoors until this unpleasant-ness has blown over. The men are devilish worked up about that dirty rat Apostolou and his Communist pals across the river, and they suspect everybody of being in league with him.'

Selmar laughed shortly. 'Me, too, perhaps?'

'Certainly. They say that modern America is run by Communists....'

Melissa cast an agonised glance at Boulton. Communism was to Steve as a red rag to a bull: Fascism was an almost equally sore point with him. She could not think what possessed the young man to get into such an argument with her father. 'They'd suspect me if they didn't know I was heart and soul a Fascist,' Boulton added calmly.

Selmar stuck out his chin. 'Well, I'm not, so you'll oblige me by taking your Fascism and getting the hell out of here.'

The young man laughed. 'Right-oh. But I shouldn't try and leave this wing until Grenander gives you the word, or you might get shot.' He turned to de Bahl. 'Grenander would like to see you in the office. He said it was urgent.'

The Baron rose. 'I'll have a word with Grenander,' he promised Selmar confidentially. 'In the meantime, if you'll take my advice, you'll go to bed.'

Boulton stood back to let him pass. De Bahl went out, the young man at his heels. Melissa, who had been staring wrathfully at Boulton, was about to avert her gaze contemptuously as the Englishman passed in front of her when, as their glances crossed, she saw his right eyelid flutter at her in an unmistakable wink.

Melissa Has a Midnight Visitor

SHE and her father usually played backgammon after dinner. Back in the living-room, she brought out the board and set the pieces, her mind busy with her thoughts.

One had to face the fact — she was scared. She could not rid her memory of that vision of Apostolou crumpling up in the snow in the light of the torches. or banish from her ears the primitive hate in the angry voices crying out against him as the rabble seethed around. The Baron had told them that the murderer was unknown: she wouldn't put the deed past Grenander, she told herself, Grenander with his flaccid cheeks and piggy eyes, and brutal, hectoring air — she shivered at her recollection of him. After all, it was Grenander who was behind everything. True, the Baron was nominally in charge at the Castle, but actually it was Grenander who appeared to be running the show. It was he who had filled the place with roughnecks of his choosing, he who had cleared out the real workmen, if Don Boulton was to be believed. If the Baron could do nothing about it, it meant that he, who had brought the Swede in, was as much his dupe as she and her father were. Of course, de Bahl was a charming and delightful companion, but on looking back she began to have a vague feeling that he had not supported them very vigorously. Steve had sent for Grenander but he had not showed up, and there was no sign of the Baron, either.

Her eye rested on her father, smoking his cigar with a froward air and absently watching her as she arranged the board. Knowing him as she did, she guessed he was more concerned with Apostolou's death than any consideration of their own safety. He had always taken a high stand regarding his responsibilities towards his dependents. At the Selmar works they had idolised him and there had been no labour troubles as long as he was President — she knew he felt himself morally liable for this man's death and responsible for bringing the murderer to justice. She must not let him suspect that she was frightened, she reminded herself. Once she came into it, nothing would stop him from clashing with Grenander, and then anything might happen. She wished she could have a word in private with Boulton. That steady regard of his lent her courage. She found herself anxiously looking forward to seeing him again. She had the feeling that somehow, before very long, he would contrive another meeting between them.

They started their game, and for a time the rattle of the dice was the only sound. Presently Selmar broke a long silence to say unexpectedly, 'Do you know what I was thinking when we saw that blood on the snow out there tonight, Melissa?'

'What, darling?'

He moved his pieces forward. 'I was thinking how many men must have died by violence in this old place since it was first built. Why, the very walls are red, as though the mortar were mixed with blood.'

'But, Steve, what a horrible thought!'

They both started for the door had opened softly.

'Do I disturb monsieur?' It was Charles.

'What is it, Charles?' said Melissa.

'I thought monsieur should know, mademoiselle' — his manner was as restrained as ever — 'the doors are guarded. At the turret entrance, at the back, everywhere, there are men with rifles posted — they will not let me out.' For Selmar's benefit he spoke in his broken English.

'It's merely a precaution, Charles, on account of the trouble tonight,' Melissa replied.

The valet lingered. 'There was something else, mademoiselle.' He hesitated. 'As I heard this Englishman tell monsieur that mademoiselle and monsieur were not to leave your rooms for the present, I thought I would see about supplies. I rang up Rabinovici, the Jew who keeps the village shop at Orghina, but the telephone does not function. One would say that the wires have been cut.' He made a pregnant pause.

Stephen's face was expressionless. 'Very good, Charles. I'll speak to the Baron about it in the morning.'

'Then good night, monsieur; good night, mademoiselle!'

But when the door had closed behind the servant, Selmar put down the dice-box and stared blankly at his daughter. 'Oh, my darling,' he said, greatly moved, 'what a mess this crazy notion of mine has landed us in!'

She went round the table to where he sat opposite her and slid her arms about him. 'That's all right, Steve. It's my fault as much as yours. Because you don't suppose I'd have let you begin all this unless I'd been as keen on this treasure hunt as you were.' She kissed the top of his head. 'But I want you to be sensible, darling. Don't go blowing off steam all over the place until we know what this man Grenander is up to!'

He drew away from her. 'What do you mean? What should he be up to?' he demanded suspiciously.

'I don't know,' she answered hastily. 'But what's certain is

that the Baron can deal with him much more efficiently than
you can. So let's stay home as he suggests and see what
happens, shall we?' She went back to her seat. 'It's your
throw, old-timer. You'd better make it a double six or you're
sunk!'

He shook his head and with a sudden gesture of the hand
swept the draughtsmen together. 'I can't concentrate tonight.
Let's take the Baron's advice and go to bed. I'll leave my
door open so that I'll hear you if you call. Here!' — his hand
dived into his hip pocket and produced a small automatic —
'You'd better have this: I have another, a bigger one, upstairs.
Are you sure you're not scared?'

The cold touch of the metal as he laid the pistol in her hand
sent a wave of fear chilling down her spine again. But she
was determined to show nothing. 'What's there to be scared
of, with guards outside to protect us?' she lied bravely.

His hand caressed her hair. 'I used to be sorry you weren't a
boy. But it's the girls who have all the pluck nowadays, it
seems to me. When I think of that white-livered rabbit
tonight, ranting about Fascism! Well, out he goes, first
thing tomorrow!'

She thought of Boulton's cheerful wink and suppressed a
smile. They moved to the door together and Stephen switched
off the light. There was a moment of quiet in which the ring
of iron-shod boots came to them from without, and from the
darkened room against the faint greyness of the snowy yard
they discerned the silhouette of a man with a rifle slowly passing the window. Selmar said nothing, but Melissa felt his
fingers tighten on her arm. Then they climbed the turret stair
together.

They were unloading stores again under the Boyar Tower. From her bedroom window Melissa had a glimpse of lights moving about the gateway under the other flanking turret facing her across the long vista of Castle wall, while the sound of voices and sundry thumps as of heavy weights being unloaded came to her over the frosty air against the steady throbbing of the lorry engines. Far below, the ice in the river made booming noises in the darkness.

This was her favourite hour at Orghina when the peace of night descended upon the Castle and, secure in the intimacy of her bedchamber with its fantastically thick walls and curiously timbered ceiling, she could surrender herself to the romantic thoughts that invaded her mind. In just such a setting, she would reflect as she sat at her mirror with its shaded lights and creamed her face for bed, millions of women in the Middle Ages had passed their lives, loved and brought forth children, laughed and cried and died. Girls like herself must have sat in that very room between those self-same grim walls, brushing out their hair as she brushed out hers and listening to the tramp of the sentries on the battlements, the cracking of the ice below.

Her preparations for the night ended, she shed her wrapper and switched off the light. Facing the foot of her bed was the long window giving on her little crow's nest of a balcony. The night was too cold to leave the balcony door open, she decided, and clambering on to the wedge-shaped seat of the other window, she hooked it back. The cold air streaming upon her in her thin nightdress almost took her breath away, but she lingered there an instant, peering out. It was still dark, but somewhere behind the fleecy white clouds that covered the sky the moon was shining, silvering here and there the snowy cloak of roofs and pinnacles. Under the Boyar Tower the unloading still went forward, with a voice shouting orders.

She recognised the voice. It was Boulton driving his gang. She found it consoling to have him within hail. The sound of his voice, punctuated by sundry grunts and answering shouts as the men responded to his objurgations, pursued her as, shivering with cold, she crept into bed.

Snuggled under the blankets, she suddenly remembered that she had not bolted the door leading to the balcony. But the icy air from the open window made her reluctant to hop out of bed again: after all, she told herself, the balcony was hung like a swallow's nest high up on the outside wall of the turret, a good ten feet below the battlements — no one could enter that way. She felt for the gun under her pillow and composed herself to sleep.

She never knew what awakened her, unless it was the freezing draught that blew her hair about her ears as she lay in bed. In terror she sat up to find the room bathed in moonlight and the balcony door open. A tall figure stood in the doorway right in the path of the moonbeams. 'Don't be scared,' said a hushed voice in English. 'But I had to see you and this was the only way.'

She clicked on the bedside lamp, and Don Boulton, in his fur cap and muffled up to the eyes against the cold, stepped into the room.

When a Nail Is Not a Nail

SHE said: 'What is it? What happened?' He had moved silently to the door leading to the staircase and was trying it. 'I locked it before I went to bed,' she explained. He nodded. 'I don't want your old man busting in here, demanding my intentions,' he remarked, eyeing her bleakly.

The bedroom was bitterly cold. The wall hangings shivered in the glacial breeze blowing in through the open window and from the balcony. Her knees up to her chin, Melissa had dragged the satin quilt about her. 'Hand me that dressing-gown,' she ordered, pointing to where her wrapper lay at the foot of the bed, 'and for the love of Mike close up some of those windows — I'm perishing.' He took the wrapper and tossed it to her — she noticed that he dawdled over shutting the window and balcony door to give her time to struggle into it. 'How on earth did you get here?' she demanded.

'Over the roof of the Great Hall and so on to the battlements.' Momentarily, his expression relaxed. 'Romeo went up the ladder; I came down it, although, to be accurate, it was a rope!'

'A rope? You're crazy. You might have broken your neck!'

He moved his shoulders. 'There was no choice — there are guards on every entrance to this part of the Castle. And I had to see you.'

'Was it so urgent that it wouldn't keep till morning?'

'There's no time like the present — I may not be able to see you tomorrow. Listen, is your father in the gun-running business?'

So saying, he sat down on the bed. With a severe air she drew her feet away. She prided herself on being modern-minded and the circumstances were unusual, to say the least of it. But she wasn't having any young man breaking into her bedroom in the middle of the night and sitting on her bed as if it were the most ordinary thing in the world. 'Do you mean to say you come dangling in here at the end of a rope in the middle of the night to ask me such a ridiculous question as that?' she demanded indignantly.

'So ridiculous that I risked my neck to get an answer. Is he or isn't he?'

'Of course he isn't. Who's he supposed to be running guns to?'

He made a little pause. 'Well,' he said slowly, 'across the river here is the Ukraine. They call it "the granary of Europe." They say that Germany would like to get her hands on it — the Ukrainian crops would solve many of her problems. The Ukrainian Nationalists have no use for the Soviets. They'd rise if they could, and a rising in the Ukraine might very easily bring about a European war. But before they can rise, they must have arms.' He gazed at her tentatively. 'The arms traffic pays thumping good dividends. And, after all, your respected parent's a good business man, presumably.'

'My father's a decent citizen. He'd rather be found dead than put a nickel into any such thing. What do you take him for?' Her voice had an angry ring. 'And who asked you to sit down on my bed?' she added with acerbity.

He stood up languidly. 'Sorry. You needn't get into such a wax. After all, he could be financing a stunt like this and you'd be none the wiser, couldn't he?'

'Certainly not. My father tells me everything: besides, he has a perfect horror of the arms trade.'

'He knew Ardza, didn't he?'

'Ardza?'

'The armaments king, the fellow who died at Monte Carlo when you were there.'

'Only in a casual sort of way. Why, he never even tried to see him at Monte Carlo, although we lived in the same hotel!' She furrowed up her smooth forehead. 'I remember now, you tried to pump me about my father and this Ardza person that first day I met you, at Monte Carlo. What's all this about gun-running, anyway?'

'This,' he answered simply. His hand dipped into the pocket of his windbreaker. 'These men were unloading trucks tonight. They contrived to drop one of the cases and a handful of these fell out. And what was even more curious, I was the only one to be surprised.'

He opened his hand. A clip of cartridges rested on his palm. 'That's rifle ammunition, Mäuser. The box was labelled "Nails." The point is that we've handled at least a hundred similar boxes during the past two weeks, and tonight the trucks brought another dozen whopping big cases, as heavy as lead, marked "Steel Ties." The whole lot went into the cellars under the Boyar Tower. I may be inquisitive, but I ask myself if "Nails" means cartridges, what does "Steel Ties" stand for?'

She gazed at him with frightened eyes. 'You mean that all these stores they've been bringing in are really arms?'

'Not all, but a good percentage, I'd say.' His manner grew faintly excited. 'Look,' he said, sitting down on the bed again, 'the cover's perfect. Here's your father, a well-known American industrialist of the highest standing, importing building materials into this remote corner of Europe. Nobody can say anything against it — if any questions are asked, he's restoring this castle he's been left. What's simpler than to slip a few cases of rifles or machine guns in with every load? It's been done before. There was hell to pay at the League of Nations a few years back when the Italians were caught running machine guns into Bavaria for the Hitler boys in cases labelled "corned beef."'

'You're squashing my feet. No, you needn't get up. Just shift over and don't fidget and tell me what's the idea!'

'I've told you already. All this stuff's headed for the Ukraine, I believe. I think they're planning a raid.' He paused. 'You know, only a small percentage of these fellows of ours are workmen. Most of them are soldiers of fortune. Some of them fought with Wrangel, others were with the French Foreign Legion, and two or three are deserters from the Foreign Legion in Spain.'

'And you seriously believe that my father's in this?'

'It's he who's putting the money up, isn't it?'

'That's to restore the Castle!'

He gave a dry laugh. 'Do you know what Grenander really does for a living?'

'Isn't he an engineer?'

'He's an arms salesman, representing some of the biggest international syndicates. And Frangipani's an aeroplane manufacturers' tout who, up to the other day, when the Great Powers started putting their foot down, was recruiting foreign pilots for the war in Spain, he didn't give a damn on which side — the more airmen available, the more planes the big boys would sell! Von Wahlczek's in the business, too! These blighters would cheerfully plunge the world in war, drench our cities with poison gas, blow our women and children to pulp, so's they'd earn their three-quarters of one per cent commission. God, you can smell death on them a mile away. And your father's backing these rats!'

'It's not true!' she cried hotly.

'How can you deny it?' he flashed back, his mouth bitter. 'Do you take me for a fool that you think I'd fall for all this elaborate camouflage of restoring an old ruin, situated at the back of beyond, in midwinter? If you ask me, the whole thing's a plant. They spotted the Castle as the ideal jumping-off point for this raid or whatever they're up to and bought it from the Countess Boreanu's heirs: all that stuff about the will was just to throw dust in your eyes!'

'That at least is not true,' she told him haughtily. 'I've seen the lawyer's letter.'

'That could be faked.'

'It wasn't faked. My father corresponded with this firm of attorneys.'

'All right. Let's suppose the will *was* genuine — does that explain why your father, a wealthy man with castles all over the world to choose from if he was so minded to buy one, should be willing to bury himself and you here for the entire winter, let alone the money it's costing him?'

On that she was silent. She must come to Steve's defence, she told herself: she would have to explain about the treasure. It was very still in the room. Outside the wind blustered about the battlements and the stealthy chug-chug of the electric light plant blended with the dull noises from the river. Boulton was prodding the quilt with his finger. 'I know you're loyal to your father,' he said more gently. 'But we have to face facts, haven't we? And this business has cost more than one man's life already.'

'More than one man?' she said in surprise. His glance fell away. 'One life, anyhow.'

She hesitated. Then, 'You don't know the whole story,' she said. Thereon, to the accompaniment of the wind battering the castle, she told him about the Pasha's treasure.

He listened impassively until she had reached the end. Then he uttered a mocking laugh. 'It's good psychology,' he commented, 'but it don't explain those Mäuser rounds.'

'How do you mean "good psychology"?' she demanded.

'De Bahl. Psychology's his long suit. He's deep: he studies his man.'

'I don't know what you mean. Are you implying that the treasure story's a fake?'

He made a weary gesture. 'Oh, let it go!'

'Do you suggest that the Baron's in this with Grenander and the others?' she persisted.

'He brought Grenander and Company into it, didn't he?'

'Is Baron de Bahl an armaments salesman, too, or what are you driving at?'

•He shook his head. 'The worthy Baron's a very different cup of tea, believe me!' he told her firmly.

She shook her head. 'You're wrong about the Baron. He's a dupe like the rest of us. He's in Grenander's hands.' She recounted the conversation at dinner. 'I think we should consult him,' she said stoutly.

Aghast, Boulton broke in upon her. 'For Heaven's sake!

For the present you must treat what I've told you tonight in the strictest confidence. If your father's as innocent as you say, we'll have to open his eyes. But it must be in my own good time. And that won't be until I know more of what they're up to.'

'Whatever it is, they're out to keep it from my father — that's why the doors are guarded.'

'That's in his favour, certainly. But I wish he weren't so thick with the Baron.'

She sighed impatiently. 'First it's my father, then the Baron. Don't you trust anybody?'

He looked down at her hand as it lay on the coverlet. 'I'd trust you.'

'Why me?'

He glanced at his watch. 'A quarter to four. They change the sentries at four. If you can put up with me for another ten minutes or so I mean to try and slip back while the relief is on.'

'Why do you trust me?' she repeated.

He moved his shoulders in an imperceptible shrug. 'Instinct. Do you remember that morning at Monte when I crashed into your car? I didn't really want a cup of coffee so badly as all that, but I thought I'd test you. I like testing people.'

'And was the test satisfactory?' Her tone was gently sarcastic.

He let her question pass. 'I said to myself: "Here's a millionaire's daughter. Let's see whether she's as nice as she looks."' He gave her one of his rare smiles. 'And you were!'

She laughed. 'I suppose if I'd had a long red nose and pince-nez, you wouldn't have bothered?'

'"The girl who is bespectacled rarely has her neck tickled,"' he quoted with a grin. 'You're certainly nice to look at —

"easy on the eyes," as you say in America — especially in bed. I mean, now that you've taken the paint off and let nature have a chance. You'd be surprised how few women nowadays can stand that test.'

'Yes,' she answered demurely. 'All my men friends tell me that.' He looked so startled that she broke into a laugh. 'Because, you know,' she added, 'it's a regular thing among us half-civilised Americans for the unmarried girls, especially millionaires' daughters, to receive strange young men in their bedrooms in the middle of the night.'

'Now you're pulling my leg!'

'Instinct again, is it?'

With a reflective air he smoothed out the coverlet with his hand. 'As a matter of fact,' he answered simply, 'when I realised that the only way I had of seeing you alone was by busting in on you like this, I said to myself, "If she comes up to specification, she'll be perfectly sensible about it." In other words, I thought it most improbable that you'd go all Victorian on me and holler blue murder.'

'You were quite sure of it, were you?'

He nodded with a little sigh. 'Yes. I knew you trusted me. I knew it from the first moment I saw you.'

She was about to make some flippant rejoinder when she caught the serious, almost wistful look in his eyes. 'It's true,' she said. 'I do trust you. I don't know why, but I do. I wish you'd tell me who you really are.'

He consulted his watch again. 'Five minutes to go,' he announced. Then he was off in his light mood again. 'As the saying goes, me father was a vicar — only in my case it happens to be true. Like most country parsons he lived in a rectory that was much too big for us, on a stipend that was much too small. I had a horrible time at a cheap public school and went from there into the Air Force. From nineteen to twenty-four I had the five most wonderful years of my life.' His eyes shone. 'You've no idea what flying does to a fellow — to soar out into the dawn over the Euphrates, for instance, as I used to do when we were in Mespot, makes you feel like a god. Then I had a crash — a morning of fog on Salisbury Plain. I'd had crashes before, of course, but this was the real stuff. My sergeant, poor devil, was burnt up. They pulled me clear, but my flying days were over. I've a silver plate in my shoulder and it's about all I can do to shift gear with my left hand. So there I was jobless with a tiny pension and the slump going full blast. I drifted from tea-planting into rubber, from rubber to being a store manager in West Africa and later, foreman on irrigation works in the Sudan, always moving on, as one job after the other folded up on me. I've knocked about all over the shop and done everything, including driving a taxi in New York and washing dishes in a bar at Tia Juana.'

'How old are you?'

He laughed rather ruefully. 'Twenty-nine, I think. Or it might be twenty-eight. It matters so little, I don't always remember.'

'And you're still drifting?'

He nodded. 'The British Empire's full of chaps like me. We're hoboes — the hoboes of Empire.'

She said, 'It's too bad. You never had the breaks.'

He laughed. 'I'm not asking for sympathy. I loathe self-pity. I've had a very amusing life in some ways — I don't complain. But don't let's talk about me — let's talk about you.' He held his wrist out to the light. 'I've still two minutes left. How old are you?'

'Twenty-two.'

'Why aren't you married?'

'Maybe I wasn't asked.'

'That's nonsense.'

She laughed. 'Well, perhaps, it's just that my father's enough trouble for one woman to manage. Are you married?'

'God forbid!' He added more gently, 'I've never met a girl I wanted to marry, I expect.' His eyes were on her face. She was annoyed to feel the blood rising in her cheeks and looked away.

He sighed and said irrelevantly, 'You've such a lovely name!' Then he put on his cap and wound his muffler about his throat. 'Well, you'll be hearing from me. In the meantime, stay home and mum's the word. I think you'd better put out the light: there's a sentry in front of the Boyar Tower.'

She switched off the bedside lamp and he opened the balcony door. 'Be careful going back!' she entreated, as the cold air filled the room.

He nodded. 'Trust me!' Then the balcony door closed noiselessly, and where the tall figure had been was only the moonlight.

The Light Begins to Break

'MADEMOISELLE! Mademoiselle!'

The urgent, hurried voice came to Melissa out of a loud knocking. She stirred restlessly in her bed. 'Mademoiselle! Mademoiselle!' She opened her eyes. The turret room was grey with the mournful daylight of another snowy morning, the air raw. Through the open window the snow came whirling: it was piled deep on the window seat.

She sat up abruptly, glanced at the clock beside the bed. Seven-fifteen — Charles did not usually call her until eight-thirty. It was Charles at the door now, rattling the handle and knocking. 'What is it?' she called.

'Mademoiselle, it is monsieur. He is not well. I think you should come. I have brought your hot water.'

She was out of bed, into her dressing-gown and at the door in a second. Charles, fully dressed in his invariable black, was outside, a brass can in his hand. 'I ask your pardon, mademoiselle, but monsieur rang for me. He is in much pain and I think has a temperature. He says it is the lumbago. He asked for you.'

Melissa sighed. 'Oh, dear!' She knew Steve's lumbago of old. When he got one of his attacks, to be in the house with him was like being caged with a Bengal tiger. She took the can. 'All right,' she said. 'I'll be along in two minutes.'

Her first thought was that her father's illness momentarily disposed of the danger of a fracas with Grenander. Usually these attacks lasted several days — it should not be difficult to persuade the doctor to let nobody approach the patient. She wondered about a doctor. There must be one in the village, she supposed, although he would probably speak nothing but Rumanian. Then she remembered that the telephone was not working. Well, Charles or Ali would have to go to the village: it cheered her to think that they would be re-establishing communication with the outer world.

Her father's bedroom was the counterpart of hers, but without the balcony. It was more sombre, too, with its crimson damask tapestry and the period furniture, French and Italian, they had brought from France. There was a big four-poster bed. Steve was groaning and tossing about in it under the brocade canopy, eyes haggard, face flushed. 'Well,' he growled, 'it was about time one of you came. I was ringing for that damned Charles for hours. Ouch, my back!'

She sat down beside him and took his hand. It was hot to the touch. 'Where's the salicylate, darling?'

'Charles gave me a dose already.'

'I brought you some aspirin. You're running a temperature, you know.'

'I've had all the aspirin I mean to take. Gosh, my back's giving me hell!'

'What about a hot-water bottle?'

'Charles has given me a couple.' He closed his eyes and moaned.

'It was crazy, the way you rushed out into the snow last night without a coat. It was asking for trouble. Well, what you have to do now is to stay in bed and keep warm. Meanwhile, I'll see about getting you a doctor.'

Selmar opened angry eyes. 'The doctor'll keep. It's Grenander I want to see. Why didn't he come last night when I sent for him? I'll show that dumb squarehead where he gets off, by heck, putting guards on the doors and threatening me with rifles!'

'Now, now, darling, don't go exciting yourself!'

'Excite myself? You bet I'm exciting myself. Do you realise a man was killed last night, one of my staff, and I'm to do nothing about it? What's this fat slob done about identifying the murderer, will you tell me that? Have the police been informed? Ring for Charles, or Ali, or someone, d'you hear me? Let them get Grenander now, at once. Or if not Grenander, then de Bahl. I want some action on this business and by God, I intend to have it.' A spasm crossed his face and he clapped his hand to his back. 'Gosh, this pain is awful!'

She stood up resolutely. 'It's very bad for you to work yourself up like this. If I find Grenander for you, will you promise to see the doctor afterwards?'

'Anything you like, as long as you bring me Grenander.'

She patted up his pillows for him and crept away. She had no intention of approaching Grenander: she meant to find the Baron — this was a matter for him to settle. It was not much after half-past seven by the time she came downstairs, but she knew by the aroma of Turkish cigarettes that de Bahl was already about.

The sound of voices came from the dining-room. They grew louder as she crossed the living-room. She recognised the Baron's hoarse tones; but a new note in his voice brought her to a full stop outside the closed communicating door. He was speaking French — with a sudden chill at her heart she realised that he was chattering with rage.

'And who gave you orders to shoot, *maudit?*' he railed. 'Are you aware that but for you we'd have caught not only this rat, Apostolou, but also his accomplice? I don't give a damn what Grenander told you — I'm master here and you should know by this what happens to ignorant apes like yourself who disobey my orders!' The hoarse voice rose to a scream. 'I'll smash you, you dog, as I've smashed men worth ten of you! Get out, before I choke the life out of you! Get out! Get out!' The other voice seemed to expostulate, but the Baron's shrill trumpeting bore it down. 'Out of my sight!' it thundered. 'Out of my sight!' A door slammed. Then silence, and Melissa found herself trembling on the threshold, knowing that beyond it the door had closed on Apostolou's murderer.

In a daze she sat down on the nearest chair. Her eyes were open now. Grenander didn't count. It was de Bahl who, as he had put it himself, was 'master here!' and he knew — he had probably known all along — who had shot Apostolou. She had a sudden feeling of being trapped. She realised now how greatly they had depended on the Baron. The discovery that he was behind the dark plans of which Boulton had warned her was shattering. She had a vision of him, like the ruthless spider in an old Walt Disney cartoon that had remained in her mind, luring her and Steve like flies into his web. She wondered whether the whole story about the Pasha's treasure wasn't a plant. Boulton had seemed to think so when he spoke of it as 'good psychology.' 'He's deep,' he had told her, speaking of the Baron. 'He studies his man.'

She was appalled. For a full five minutes she sat there, staring in front of her, wondering how she would grapple with the situation, with Steve sick and Boulton inaccessible. At last, she stood up and, pausing a moment at the door to collect

herself, walked purposefully into the dining-room. The Baron
was at breakfast. At the sight of Melissa he scrambled hastily
to his feet, wiping his hands on his napkin, and kissed her hand
ceremoniously, as he always did at their first meeting of the
day. 'You're down early,' he said. 'You have breakfasted,
yes?'

'I only want a cup of coffee,' she told him. 'Please don't let
me disturb you — I can get it myself.' Remembering what
Boulton had said about him, that he 'studied his man,' she
tried to put the customary warmth into her voice. Not very
successfully, she felt, for she was aware of the Baron's eyes
following her as she went to the hot plate on the sideboard.
Placidly he prepared to resume his seat.

'I trust you passed a good night, dear Miss Melissa, notwithstanding the highly superfluous military dispositions of
our excitable friend, Grenander?' he observed.

'The hypocrite,' she said to herself, 'the hypocrite! Always
this pretence that Grenander is to blame for everything!'
Aloud she remarked: 'My father's ill. I'm afraid he caught a
chill last night by going out into the yard without an overcoat.'
To lighten her tone, so as to sound as normal as possible, she
added with a laugh: 'When Steve's ill, it's a major disaster, let
me tell you. He's in considerable pain, poor lamb, groaning
with agony and filling the air with the most horrible impreca-
tions against everything and everybody, Mr. Grenander and
his sentries in particular.'

As she spoke she perceived by the expression of the Baron's
eyes that he had already heard that her father was ill. But he
did not admit it — characteristically, as she thought. Instead,
he emitted his little cough and said: 'Dear, dear, that's bad.
I'm sorry. He should have a doctor, shouldn't he?'

'Is there a doctor in the village one could get?'

'*Hélas*, no! There's not a doctor within ten or fifteen miles of Orghina that I know. But as it most fortunately happens, there's a very clever doctor at the Castle right now, Doctor Metzger, from the Russian side of the river — he came across to see a relative of his, one of our Ukrainian foremen, and they gave him a bed for the night as the snow was so heavy.'

She looked at him dubiously. 'A Bolshevik, is he?'

'Indeed, no. His sympathies lie quite the other way. As his name indicates, he's of German descent, member of a German family settled for many years in the Ukraine, and, although I believe he's a Russian subject, he's honorary German Vice-Consul at Mirapol — you know, the little town across the river — the Metzgers have been German Vice-Consul at Mirapol for generations. If you wished, I could bring him to see your father after breakfast. I understand he speaks a little English.'

The suggestion was made so tentatively, with such an air of friendliness, that for the moment she felt her distrust weaken. It was like the Baron to come to their aid — all through their acquaintanceship he had always showed himself ready with a solution for every problem. 'That's terribly kind of you,' she said. 'But there's someone Steve insists on seeing before he'll let any doctor come near him, and that's Grenander.'

De Bahl grunted. 'It is about this wretched Apostolou, I suppose.' He shrugged his strapping shoulders. 'What does he want Grenander to do?'

'He expects him to unearth the murderer and hand him over to the police.'

'Tchah!' The big shoulders went up again. 'The thing is not so simple. These Ukrainians, they hold together like that'

— he crossed his slim fingers: 'so easy it will not be to bring the guilty one to justice. As a matter of fact, Grenander will be going over this morning to the county seat to report this unfortunate affair to the authorities. Meanwhile, he has given the men the day off, to cool down.' His tone grew persuasive. 'By tomorrow, you see, the guards will be removed, *hein?* In any case I will have a word with your father when I take the doctor to him.'

She had not noticed until then the unusual air of peace resting over the Castle. At that hour the workmen should already be making the place ring with their clatter, but this morning all was silence. The snow fell softly outside — through the window she could see the muffled figure of a sentry huddled under the eaves for shelter from the whirling flakes.

The door was rapped. A sallow face looked in. Black eyes swept interrogatively from de Bahl to his companion. It was Guido Miklas, the Baron's architect. He was the only one of de Bahl's associates Melissa had not met before arriving at Orghina — the Baron had presented him when, the day after their arrival, she and Stephen had made the tour of the Castle. She had scarcely exchanged a word with Miklas; but he had a clammy handshake that repelled her and she did not like the way his lack-lustre eye dwelt upon her whenever they met. With an effusive bow and a smile that flashed the whitest of teeth, he addressed her first, saying in English, 'Pardon, Miss Selmar, if I disturb.' Then, glancing about the dining-room, 'Did I put my gloves down anywhere when I was in here just now?' he asked de Bahl.

The Baron, who was lighting a cigarette, interrupted the operation long enough to fling a contemptuous finger in the direction of the dresser. 'Ah, there they are!' cried Miklas joyfully and advancing to the dresser, he gathered up a pair of fur gloves that lay there. 'In weather like this, one can't go without gloves, eh?' he observed chattily to Melissa, lingering while his sensuous glance dwelt on her face. But de Bahl made him a gesture of dismissal, and with his rather swaggering gait he went out.

Melissa sat very still in her chair, staring down into the empty coffee cup before her. The thought of those lewd eyes made her feel rather sick. She realised now that they were the eyes of Apostolou's assassin.

A Summons from Charles

WHEN the Baron had departed in search of the doctor, Melissa mounted the turret stair again to her father's bedside. Steve had dozed off and did not wake up till around noon when de Bahl's arrival with the doctor roused him. On catching sight of the Baron, his first words were, 'Where's Grenander?'

'He's gone to the police, dear friend, to report the affair of last night,' was the soothing reply. 'I shall bring him to you as soon as he returns.'

The man in the bed repressed a groan. 'The murderer must be found; you understand that, de Bahl?'

'But, of course, my dear Selmar, of course: that's why Grenander has gone to the police. In the meantime, allow me to present our good friend Doctor Metzger. I have put our staff medicine chest at his disposal and he will give you something to relieve your pain.'

Doctor Metzger was a cadaverous individual with a sallow face deeply pockmarked and a drooping black moustache like a mandarin's. He was dressed in rusty black and carried a small handbag. On being introduced he made a stiff little bow, first to Selmar, then to Melissa, then, drawing a pair of steel spectacles from a battered case, popped them on his nose and staring hard at Melissa said: 'You go now. I mek exemination.'

Melissa returned to the living-room. The mail was wont to

arrive before lunch — a mail orderly went to the village every day to fetch it. But there was no mail today, not even the *Paris Herald-Tribune.*

She rang for Charles. The mail had not arrived, he said. The kitchen boy had told him the mail orderly had not gone to the village that morning; the whole working force was confined to the Castle. And the telephone was still out of order. Charles lingered as though he would have liked to discuss the situation with her. But she sent him away. She was not inclined to clear her mind of the increasingly alarming thoughts that oppressed it with anyone save Boulton and her father. But Boulton was not available, and she was resolved not to say anything to add to Steve's troubles as long as he was in pain.

Presently there were footsteps on the stone stairs. It was the Baron and Doctor Metzger. De Bahl stayed behind with her for a reassuring word. She was not to alarm herself about her father — a day or two's rest in bed would put him right, the doctor had said: he had left some capsules for the patient, one to be taken after every meal. Yes, Mr. Selmar was still worrying about Grenander. But Grenander would be back for lunch: he would undertake to bring him round after, the Baron declared. She thought she would lunch upstairs with her father, Melissa said, and not downstairs as usual. To which the Baron replied that the arrangement would suit him very well: he felt he should lunch at the staff mess with the others and hear Grenander's report of his interview with the police.

Charles brought her lunch to her father's bedside. Stephen was grumpy and taciturn. He took a little soup after much persuasion, then, giving Melissa his keys, bade her bring him his cheque-book from the desk. He pored over it for a long time, making notes with his pencil and groaning at intervals.

Melissa had given him his capsule and was finishing her coffee when Charles came in and said the Baron and Mr. Grenander were below. Selmar perked up at once. 'Ah!' he said, and put his cheque-book away under his pillow. 'How'd you like to do a little fade-away?' he remarked to his daughter with a touch of his old humour.

'Not on your life, big boy!'

He stuck out his chin. 'I mean it, sweetheart. I'm going to handle this alone, and I don't want you around. It'll be fighting words I'll be using to that big palooka and you'll only cramp my style. And so, honey' — he pressed his lips to her forehead as she leaned over to shake up his pillows — 'duck!'

'You've no business to see him while you're ill. You'll only upset yourself. Besides, he's a common brute — with all this trouble going on, you never know what he might do!'

Her father laughed grimly. 'I know what *I'm* going to do, and that's to beat the tar out of the big stiff. He'd gum us up here with his guards, would he, cut off our telephone, stop our mail?' There was a knock at the door. 'Come in, Baron, come in,' he called. To Melissa he said, 'Go on, sweetheart, leave us now!'

The realisation that Charles had told him of the steps taken to isolate them from the outer world made her feel that she should have taken her father into her confidence about the true nature of his friend the Baron and the plot that was afoot. But it was too late now. Here was Grenander, like a white slug, his fat face sullen and enigmatic behind the horn-rimmed glasses, and the Baron rather wheezy after the climb up the stairs, but wreathed in smiles. Stephen from the bed clinched matters. 'My daughter was just leaving,' he said. 'Sit down, gentlemen, sit down!' He waved to Melissa. 'So long, honey; I'll be seeing you!'

Head high, she went out of the door, past the bowing figures of de Bahl and his companion. A feeling of desperation gripped her. If she could only see Don Boulton again! Until she did she felt bound by the secrecy he had imposed on her. If they had shot Apostolou because he was a spy, they would show as little mercy to the Englishman once they suspected him of giving their plans away — Boulton's life might well be in her hands. Down in the living-room, seated before the fire with the door leading to the vestibule open, she found it impossible to concentrate her attention on the month-old American magazine she had picked up. Voices drifted down to her from the floor above. From time to time she recognised her father's, harsh and angry — her uneasiness deepened. Unceasingly the snow fell, blanketing the Castle with quiet: the early winter afternoon was drawing in.

At last she heard the clank of a latch, the echo of a cough, then a light footstep upon the turret stair. That patter of feet was the only sound in the hush of the ancient house: with beating heart she listened, feeling that the very air was sultry with the presage of disaster.

The lamp had not yet been lit in the lobby and the stone Hall was full of shadows. The Baron, his forehead puckered in a frown, stood at the foot of the stair waiting for Grenander, who came clattering down in the grey-green 'Loden' suit and knee boots he always wore about the works. De Bahl barked something to him to which the other muttered a reply, then, snatching up his fur coat that lay on a chair, slung it about his shoulders and strode out through the turret entrance. The snow whirled in as he opened the door and they heard the sharp challenge of the sentry without. Then the door slammed.

'Baron!' called Melissa from the living-room threshold.

De Bahl, lost in thought, started as he saw her there, then crossed to where she stood. '*Eh bien*, why so downcast?' he rasped, giving her cheek a little friendly pat. 'Everything's in order now. Tomorrow the sentries will be withdrawn, and all will be as it was before. Meanwhile, your father's asleep and if I were you, I wouldn't disturb him. I'll see you at dinner!' So saying, with another encouraging pat he turned to the door and, head down to the eddying flakes, vanished into the snow.

The look she had surprised on his face, Grenander's forbidding scowl as he had passed, belied his words. Well, Steve would tell her the truth, and this time he in his turn should hear the truth from her. Up the corskcrew stair she sped. Her father was asleep, even as the Baron had said. She tidied the coverlet, set the window open a few inches to air the room, in case he were only dozing and might hear her. But he never stirred, lying on his back, breathing rather stertorously — 'Poor darling,' she thought, 'he's worn out.' Switching on the bedside lamp she picked up the newspaper that lay there. But presently the headlines began to swim. She was conscious of feeling deathly tired; her broken night, the strain she had borne all day alone, had quite worn her out. She closed her eyes and let the peace of the dim, quiet room steal over her. The newspaper slipped from her lap. . . .

'Mademoiselle! Ps-st, mademoiselle!'

Charles stood before her, shaking her gently. She sat up, rubbing her eyes. 'I must have dropped off,' she said. He laid a finger to his lips. 'Let us not disturb monsieur,' he warned, and she saw that Stephen was sleeping on. 'Ali went with cables to the village post-office for Monsieur le Baron,' the cautious whisper went on. 'If mademoiselle will come with me, I will show her something.' She then perceived that he carried the raccoon coat she used for sleighing over his arm and had her béret and muffler in his hand. 'Follow me,' he said. 'But quickly, or we may be too late!'

Without pausing for a reply he brought her to the staircase. At the bottom he was waiting for her, holding out her coat. 'Mademoiselle will need it,' he remarked, helping her into it.

'But, Charles,' she asked, 'where are we going? And what about the guards?'

With another brusque '*Suivez-moi!*' however, he was off again, through the living-room this time, the dining-room and thence, by way of the service door, into the kitchen, where the clock on the wall marked ten minutes past six. From the kitchen a succession of small dependencies brought them to a little inside court with a glass roof darkened by its weight of snow. Here Charles switched on a flash-lamp and revealed across the court the entrance of a shed stacked with wood.

They entered the shed and Charles, once more with finger laid to lips, silently closed the door. At the far end of the shed where a space had been cleared of the billets, a trapdoor stood wide. A wooden stair led down. Her escort signing to her that they were to descend, she followed him down. At the bottom of the short flight, the beam of the torch showed the damp masonry of a low and extremely narrow passage, not much broader than a man. It brought them to another wooden stair which mounted into darkness. Then the flashlight was extinguished and Charles's whisper, light as a sigh, was in her ear, 'Not a sound now, as you value your life!'

She was aware then of a faint murmur of voices from above. Charles's hand found hers in the dark and step by step, stealthily, he drew her up the stairs behind him. They emerged into a dank, vault-like place with an opening in the far wall through which fell a faint glimmer of light. Noiseless as a shadow, Melissa's companion crept forward and the girl, setting her pace by his, went after: through an archway they came into a black, icy little room reeking of bats and birds, with a small hatch set shoulder-high in the wall and screened with intricate oriental woodwork. It was through this opening that the faint radiance they had perceived appeared. Voices were audible beyond it.

Charles motioned to her to approach. She stole across to where he stood, peering through the hatch: she realised that, with darkness all about them, they must be invisible to anyone in the room beyond. She found herself gazing into an oblong chamber lit by a single naked bulb hung on the end of a wire suspended from the high beamed roof. The striped red and white arches on slender columns, the central ablution tank, the band of Arabic inscriptions running along the top of the tiles sheathing the walls, told her that she was looking into the little mosque — she had visited mosques in Algeria and Egypt with her father.

The air was chill and filled with tobacco smoke. A group of men sat at a table set up on trestles parallel with the opposite wall. At the head of the board, dominating them all by his presence, was de Bahl.

In the Mosque

THE Baron was finishing a speech. He was speaking in his elegant French. He leaned back in his chair, his beautiful hands lightly poised on the table before him, his head turning from side to side as his glance languidly considered the faces of his hearers. Along the table Melissa perceived Grenander, stolidly puffing a large cigar, and von Wahlczek, and Miklas; the pockmarked doctor, too, and two men she could not place who sat at the end. The place smelt musty and was bitterly cold, so that the Baron's breath ballooned about him: all were well wrapped up and wore their hats. The girl looked in vain for Boulton: Frangipani, the Italian, was missing, too.

In their rich furs the two strangers made striking figures. One was a patriarchal type, his chest barred with a great spread of beard: his companion was much younger, handsome in an aquiline way, with a dark, passionate face. It was to them that the Baron appeared principally to address himself. 'My friends,' he said, 'you've heard the plan: you've also visited the stocks in the tower. Well, there'll be another hundred machine guns, another hundred thousand rounds of ammunition as well as the hand grenades you asked for added to them by the time the moon's right for us, and that should be the middle of next week. If you or your comrade have any comments, friend Rypnik, now is the time to speak.'

The great beard nodded condescendingly. 'Your plan appears to be remarkably comprehensive,' he observed in measured French. 'If to me it seems somewhat over-bold...'

His younger companion struck in hotly. 'Boldness is what we want!' he cried, eyes flashing. 'With the arms you will bring in,' he told de Bahl, 'we need fear nothing. Our organisation across the river is more than adequate to master local opposition by a swift *coup de main*, and the first shot fired on the Dniester will bring the whole Ukraine to its feet eager to shake off the cursed chains of Red oppression.'

The doctor sprang up. 'Yes, and within twenty-four hours — what do I say, within twelve, nay, six hours — the whole anti-Bolshevik *bloc* of Europe will rally to our support!' He glared at the grey-bearded man. 'You will not deny that, Rypnik?'

The old man cocked his head. 'If you rely on foreign intervention for the success of our enterprise, you are likely to be disappointed. If you wish foreign intervention to follow swiftly, then you must link a *casus belli* to our undertaking. A frontier incident, maybe.' He turned his rheumy eyes towards his young companion. 'I spoke of this to you, Vassenko.'

The doctor gave a sudden, cackling laugh. 'They shall have their frontier incident, never fear,' he declared stridently. He glanced towards de Bahl. They all glanced towards de Bahl. Vassenko said, 'I confess I am curious to know what you have in mind.'

The Baron cleared his throat. 'We will speak of this again,' he said, eyes veiled. 'The matter will be taken care of, depend on it.' He stood up. 'I think that is all for the moment...'

Charles was tugging at Melissa's sleeve. She shook him off, fearful of missing a word of what was said. Then she was dimly aware that Charles was no longer with her, and it seemed to her presently that her ear caught a muffled thud. When she peeped through the hatch again, the party was breaking up — the two strangers were leaving. On the far side of the table was a small, iron-studded door — the mosque entrance. The strangers were moving towards it now when Grenander stopped them. 'The side door is more direct: it brings you to the Boyar Tower. Here, Miklas, show them!'

Miklas minced over — to Melissa's horror he led the way straight to where she stood at the grill. On noiseless feet she fell back through the archway to the outer room where was the trapdoor by which she and Charles had entered. By this time her eyes had grown accustomed to the darkness, and she repressed a cry of dismay on discovering Charles gone and the trap closed. The flap had a ring at which she tugged, but it resisted all her efforts. The outer room had two doors. One seemed to lead into the mosque; the other was set up a few steps in the wall. But she had no time to try it, for now she heard voices close at hand on the other side of the wall, and the sound of a door opening. There was nothing for it — she would have to retreat to her post in the inner room.

She was only just in time. Flattened against the archway and peering out, she saw the door swing inward. A flash-lamp sprang into life: it showed the three men as they crossed the outer room and disappeared through the door in the wall. She was appalled: she realised that she was caught between two fires. Voices still resounded from the mosque; at any moment Miklas might return from the Boyar Tower and find her there. De Bahl's laugh rumbling through the emptiness drew her to her spy-hole again.

She saw that the party had risen from the table and was

clustered about the Baron, who was chaffing the doctor. There was a good deal of laughter, but she understood the doctor to say that they could count on him in every way: the idea was 'really ingenious.' But he added that he thought 'our Ukrainian friends' were much too optimistic. The Ukraine would not rise so easily. On that Grenander rumbled a wheezing laugh. 'What do we care?' he grunted.

The laugh ran round the circle. 'The great thing is secrecy,' the Baron struck in. 'Let these idiotic conspirators believe what they like — we don't give the signal until the moment is ripe.'

Von Wahlczek's rather snarling voice interposed. 'Why talk of secrecy when this animal of a Miklas has given the game away? What was the sense of shooting that rat right under Selmar's nose?'

'If we hadn't shot him, we'd have had the whole Soviet Secret Service on our backs by this,' was Grenander's angry retort.

'Wally is right,' said the Baron judiciously. 'Evidently there were other equally efficient ways of dealing with the traitor. But what's done is done. You may take it from me that our friend Guido will know how to restrain his trigger finger in future.'

'That may be,' von Wahlczek rejoined. 'But in the meantime, what do we tell Selmar?'

De Bahl laughed. 'Don't you think you can leave Selmar to me? After all, I brought him here!'

Grenander chortled joyfully. 'Treasure, eh?' He smote the wall beside him with a resounding slap. 'Hear the coins rattle, children! The place is full of money!'

'And jewels, Axel! Don't forget the Pasha's jewels,' the Baron put in archly.

The engineer chuckled. 'You're a double-crossing scoundrel, Alexis, but you're smart. That Turkish document was an inspiration, but the bailiff's letter was a masterpiece: I wouldn't have thought of that.'

De Bahl hoisted his shoulders. 'Psychology, my dear Axel! When you bait a mouse-trap you have to know what a mouse likes best to eat. There are not many of us who can resist the lure of buried gold.'

'Agreed. But now you've got Selmar here, how are you going to keep him quiet?' von Wahlczek demanded. 'He expects to start in on this treasure hunt right away.'

'And why not?' retorted Grenander. 'We can dig up the floor for him, can't we?'

'With the working force available, this place can be turned inside out in a couple of days,' von Wahlczek declared. 'The Yankee is no fool. Let him once smell a rat, and he'll cut off the money. What do we do then? Our fellows have to be paid, you know.'

De Bahl shook his head, narrowing his eyes until they were mere slits. 'He won't cut off the money,' he said softly. There was a sinister ring in his voice that sent a shiver along Melissa's spine as she crouched beside the hatch.

'And what about the girl?' von Wahlczek persisted.

'Maybe I shall find a use for her, too,' was the composed rejoinder.

A sudden commotion without brought them all whirling about to face the grating where Melissa stood. She ducked and at the same time heard a door bang, voices and footsteps outside. As she cowered there, a cluster of figures went storming through the gloom on the other side of the archway and burst into the mosque. It was the Italian, Frangipani: in his wake followed three of his truck-drivers in their leather jackets dragging a struggling figure in a peaked fur cap. At the sight of the cap Melissa felt her heart miss a beat — she was so sure it was Boulton.

But it was not Boulton. The prisoner was taller than Boulton, heavier too, and a stranger to her. Frangipani shouted in his broken English: 'It is the secret agent of the Ogpu, Apostolou's man. We find 'im on the stairs in the Boyar Tower.' A sudden silence fell, and out of it came de Bahl's voice, cool and collected: 'You'd better question him, Axel.'

The engineer strode forward, chin out, and growled at the captive in Russian. The prisoner was a burly fellow with a broad Slav nose and tilted eyes: his air was savagely morose. One or two sentences were exchanged and then, without warning, Grenander dealt him a blow with his fist that rang like a pistol shot under the high roof. The prisoner reeled backward with the blood running down his chin: Melissa saw that his hands were tied behind him. The engineer broke into a torrent of angry Russian, to which the man's only rejoinder was a contemptuous shrug. 'Well, well, what does he say, Axel?' the Baron demanded irritably.

'Nothing we want to hear,' replied Grenander, balefully regarding his victim, solidly held by his guards.

Melissa had her eyes on the Baron's face. She was shocked by the change that came over it. It was as though with a handkerchief the air of purposeful *bonhomie* that was its customary expression had been wiped away, leaving in its place a look of cold ferocity that filled her with panic. But when he spoke his voice was as huskily gentle as ever. 'He'll talk all right,' he said, and turned to Grenander. 'Tell him in Russian, my good Axel, that we shall know how to make him speak.'

Grenander addressed the Russian. This time the man laughed brazenly and spat on the ground. Grenander would have struck him again, but the Baron elbowed him out of the way. Then he raised his eyes aloft, to where great beams supported the roof, and dropping his gaze to the captive, said softly over his shoulder, 'Let somebody bring me a rope!'

A faint sound in the outer room distracted Melissa's attention from the scene. She turned her head and perceived beyond the archway a lanky figure in the gloom, making frantic signs to her. She glanced once more through the grill before she obeyed. The whole party was clustered about the prisoner; from under a pile of beams against the wall Frangipani and one of the truck-drivers were drawing a long rope. When they had it clear, on a gesture from de Bahl, they flung an end over one of the roof beams.

She waited to see no more. She scarcely knew how she reached the archway. In the obscurity of the room beyond Charles was a shadow that kept beckoning: she saw that the trap in the floor was open. But now she perceived that the door into the mosque stood wide: to reach the trap she would have to pass in front of it, in full view of the men in the mosque. She drew back, her heart thumping, measuring the distance with her eye.

At that moment a long, gurgling cry shattered the silence. Glancing backward through the grating she had left, she had a glimpse of a sack-like, dangling thing being jerked unsteadily upward to the roof. It was the Russian. They were hauling him up on the rope attached to his wrists tethered behind his back. He gyrated wildly, legs kicking, while scream upon scream broke from him. Melissa lost all sense of caution then. Darting across the opening she fell half fainting into Charles's arms. The trap closing noiselessly behind them shut off those terrible cries. 'Oh, Charles,' she gasped, 'did you see what they were doing to that wretched man?' But the valet said nothing: grasping her firmly by the arm, he hurried her along the passage and so up to the kitchen.

In the light and warmth of the kitchen under the solemnly ticking clock she broke from him and cried: 'We must do something. It's horrible. That fiendish creature! Why did you leave me?'

The Frenchman outlined an almost imperceptible shrug. 'Ali came back with the stores. He was calling me. If he had found us there...'

'We must stop them,' she struck in frantically. 'When I tell my father, even though he's in pain, he'll get up and stop them. Come on, Charles! I don't care if he is asleep; I'm going to wake him.'

But her companion made no move. 'Your father, mademoiselle...' he began, and paused, moistening his lips. She saw the dismay in his regard, and stared at him in consternation. 'Nothing's happened to my father, Charles?' she exclaimed faintly.

The man swallowed once, then nodded briefly. 'Mademoiselle, he has vanished! I've searched the whole wing. They must have come when we were down there, and taken him away.'

On that without a word she fled from him and sped through the dark rooms to the turret lobby and up the winding stair. Her father's door was open, the bed empty, and when she looked about her, it was to discover that his clothes, which had been piled on a chair, had likewise disappeared. Aghast, she sat down on the bed. To her ears, out of the snowy silence, mounted the ring of the sentry's feet on the flags under the eaves in the yard below.

The Man on the Balcony

THIS was disaster. Disaster black and irretrievable. She was conscious of Charles speaking to her, but she did not answer him, and presently, without quite knowing how she had got there, she found herself crouched on the settee before the fire in the living-room, alone.

How right Boulton had been to distrust de Bahl! Anger flamed within her at the thought of him. From the beginning he had been playing a game with them. One lie after the other — he moved in an atmosphere of lies. The Pasha's treasure, this bunch of armed touts he had wished on her father in the guise of assistants, even his story to her that the mosque, which they were using for their secret meetings, was filled with rubbish and could not be visited — wherever she put her mind back, she came upon lies. And now, not content with filching her father's honourable reputation to cover their gun-running and his money to pay for it, they had dared to kidnap him. At the thought of Steve, so upright and decent-minded and square, and the way they had mocked him in the mosque, she felt sick with rage and indignation.

What did they mean to do with him? De Bahl's remark to von Wahlczek in the mosque, spoken with hideous malignity, crept into her mind. '*He won't cut off the money!*' At the recollection she sprang irresolutely to her feet, the blood draining from her face. They relied on Steve for the weekly pay-cheques: without money they could not keep their unruly gangs in hand. But no one could order her father about. He was the type of man who would refuse to the last to pay ransom to a kidnapper, but would bid him go ahead and do his damned-est. What would they do to him? In terror she remembered the look in de Bahl's eyes, the glimpse she had had of that screaming figure slowly jerking aloft, and had to cram her handkerchief into her mouth to repress a scream.

To steady her nerves she lit a cigarette and sat down before the fire again. Sombre thoughts seemed to stream from the stone walls about her, every block saturated with deeds of mediaeval violence, their very hue evoking, as Steve had said, memories of the blood spilled there. The silence enveloping her broken only by the tramp of the sentries, the sense of im-pending danger — these things, she reflected, were of the very essence of the atmosphere of Stephen cel Mare's strong-hold. Thus down the centuries women must have sat in the Castle, perhaps in that very room, wrestling with their fears while their men were away at the wars, quaking at the thought that defeat would bring inexorably a cloud of arrows darkening the sun, an onrush of thousands of rancid savages, sweeping across the ice on their shaggy ponies — it was odd to think that it was the Baron who had described to her such moments in the Castle's history. An hour or two away by air was Bucharest with its gay boulevards and shops, and the Orient Express waiting to whisk one off to Paris, to Hâvre, to the snug luxury of the *Queen Mary* or the *Normandie*, with the twentieth century seething along Fifth Avenue at the end of the journey. Yet here she was, behind the ring of sullen, un-friendly guards, utterly cut off from civilisation as though, by some Wellsian time machine, she had been thrust back into the Middle Ages.

She heard the tinkle of a tray behind her. Charles was there with tea. She felt herself drawing courage from the square, ugly French face: with Don Boulton, if he ever succeeded in getting in touch with her again, Charles was now her only ally. 'Charles,' she said desperately as he set down the tray beside her, 'what are we going to do to find my father?'

His saucer eyes regarded her mournfully. 'It will not be easy with sentries at every door.' He paused. 'I think I know why they take monsieur. I was outside his bedroom this afternoon, when the Baron and this other one were with monsieur, and I heard monsieur say he would sign no more cheques.' He wagged his head shrewdly. 'I think it will be bad for monsieur, if he resists. These are desperate men, mademoiselle. They have this project, as it would seem, to bring arms into the Ukraine. It is not the habit of revolutionaries to let a single man stand in their way.'

'They're not revolutionaries, Charles, they're vulgar gun-runners. Grenander, and von Wahlczek, and Frangipani are nothing but a lot of armaments salesmen — the Baron, too, I expect. All they care about is to sell the stuff. They don't give a damn for these wretched Ukrainians — they admitted as much when they were talking among themselves in the mosque this evening.'

The Frenchman veiled his eyes. 'So,' he said, 'this I did not know. A million of my fellow-countrymen, my three brothers among them, died for France in the name of liberty; but now it seems it was only to make the world safe for those who profit by war.' His face darkened. 'No matter, the time is coming when outraged humanity will rise and exterminate these

monsters.' He broke off abruptly, abashed by the white heat
of passion underlying his words. 'For the present, we are
prisoners here, mademoiselle — we must recognise it,' he
went on more calmly. 'If we would not make things worse
for monsieur, we must not seem to oppose these *coquins.*
Let us rather see how we can outwit them.'

'But, Charles, what are we going to do?'

'The Baron and these gentlemen will be at dinner. The important thing is that they should not guess that we suspect
anything. Fortunately I locked your bedroom door when we
went to the mosque: I told Ali that you were lying down and
that I had been in the cellar chopping wood, to account for
our absence. It appears to me that the Baron must offer some
explanation of monsieur's disappearance: for the rest we will
see. But in the meantime mademoiselle must try and conceal
her real feelings.' He gave her his grave smile. 'It is not
difficult for a woman to dissemble, I have heard.'

She sighed. 'All right, Charles. But meanwhile, keep your
eyes open for any sign of Mr. Boulton ——'

'Mademoiselle means the English chauffeur?'

'Yes. Between ourselves, it was he who first warned me
about what was going on here. He's on our side, Charles: you
can trust him.'

'*Tiens!* This is something interesting.' He smiled again.
'It is then the old alliance of the war days — France, England
and the United States.'

But Melissa was destined to dine alone. The Baron sent
word by Ali, excusing himself and the others. When Charles
brought her the message she would have given Ali a note for
de Bahl, asking what had become of her father; but Ali had

not waited. She wrote a line just the same and took it to the sentry at the turret door, asking him first in French and then in her broken German to deliver it when he was relieved. But she could not make the man understand. He only growled and waved her back with his rifle so that she was forced to go indoors again. She felt more concerned than ever. The fact that de Bahl had not troubled to vouchsafe any explanation about her father's disappearance suggested that he no longer felt the need of pretence. He had thrown off the mask. She went to her lonely dinner with the sensation that the climax was at hand.

All remained tranquil in the Castle, however. The day's snow had given place to a clear, starry night, so still that the strains of an accordion, of voices raised in song, were wafted to her from the men's quarters in the outer yard as she sat by the living-room fire, trying to occupy her mind with the muffler she was knitting for her father. The voices were grave and resonant and harmoniously blended. The rather melancholy strains grated on her nerves: she felt the lowering castle walls closing in on her. If she might only get Steve back, she promised herself, she would see to it that he took her away from Orghina as quickly as possible for good and all.

With that she folded her knitting and went out into the turret vestibule to go up to bed. At the same moment Charles appeared from the kitchen. He told her he had been as far as the anteroom of the mosque, hoping to discover the exit through the Boyar Tower, but all the doors were now locked. He had thought of bribing the sentries and, as a preliminary step, had tried to make one understand that he should take a letter to the police in the village, showing a wad of money, but the man had brusquely refused. Then he had formed the plan of making a rope of sheets and letting himself down from her bedroom balcony. But even if they could fashion a rope long enough — it was a good hundred-foot drop to the ground — there were guards posted all along the riverbank after nightfall now. There was nothing to be done that night: they would re-examine the position in the morning. Meanwhile, mademoiselle need have no fear. Let her lock her door and go to bed tranquilly. He would make up a bed for himself in the turret vestibule: if she called out he would hear her. And he showed her an automatic pistol under his coat.

Up in her room the clanging gongs that sounded for 'Lights Out!' put an end to the music and singing. From her window she saw a glimmer of light under the Boyar Tower and the silhouette of a sentry at its foot. Seated at her dressing-table, staring absently at her reflection in the mirror, she tried to send a message of love and hope to Steve, wherever he was, knowing that his thoughts were likewise with her. The last thing before she got into bed she unbolted the balcony door, breathing a little prayer that Boulton would contrive to make his way across the roofs to her again. She took comfort from his memory: the image of his cheerful, freckled face and steady, rather wistful grey eyes was with her as she fell asleep.

A dazzling beam of light played upon her face. A dim figure was framed in the doorway of the balcony. She was awake on the instant. 'Don!' she cried joyfully and, stretching out an arm from under the bedclothes, switched on the bedside lamp. Then as the light went on her two hands clawed at her cheeks in sudden terror.

'Don't scream!' said Miklas, and stepped into the room.

The Dniester Squares an Account

FOR an instant he stood there, and as he gazed at her she saw the watchfulness fade from the heavily lidded eyes and give way to a gleam of gloating surprise. He was hatless and, despite the rigour of the night, the perspiration stood out in little drops among the thinning hair and glistened on the pursy, livid cheeks. He wore no overcoat and his clothes were smeared with mortar and mud as he confronted her, breathing hard. He had a pistol in one hand, a flashlight in the other. A moment while his glance ran round the room, then the lewd glitter of his eyes, searching her face, turned her blood to stone. She remembered that this man was a murderer with the blood of his victim fresh on him.

He staggered a little, catching at the back of a chair to steady himself. Then he thrust his torch into the opening of his jacket. But the automatic he kept levelled at the bed. ''Allo, missy,' he said rather thickly. 'Well, if this don't beat everything! "Don!"' — he mimicked her cry in a high falsetto and laughed ribaldly. 'Strike me frozen, but ole Don seems to know where the fresh vegetables is kept!'

His English was indescribable, half-Cockney, half-French, the English of the night guides who prowl the Paris boulevards offering to show tourists 'the sights'; his manner unspeakably familiar, a blend of bully and masher. With despair Melissa realised that he had found Boulton's route over the roof. 'I don't know what you're talking about!' she cried in a white rage. 'How dare you come into my bedroom? And don't point that gun at me! Get out of here at once!'

He chuckled while his snake-like eyes fastened themselves on a glimpse of gleaming shoulder that protruded from under the bedspread. Hastily she drew the eiderdown closer about her. ''Aughty, *hein?*' he sneered. 'So this is where our 'ead foreman spends 'is nights.' Owlishly he wagged his finger at her. 'No use your denying it, girlie. There's 'is rope an' 'is footmarks in the snow to prove it. You *must* 'ave made it worth 'is while to come over the leads in the dark. If I 'adn't of 'ad a couple I wouldn't 'ave risked it, not even to cash in at the end of the trip, kiddo!'

She realised now that he was drunk. 'You're talking a lot of nonsense, Miklas,' she said rather tremulously. 'The painters left that rope there. Now please go away and let me sleep.'

He laughed and bared his dazzling teeth. 'No painters 'ere, girlie! That's my department, an' I know. Why did you call out "Don" just now if you wasn't expecting him — answer me that!' He took a step forward. 'Let's me **an'** you be friends. We've a long winter in front of us.'

Her hand found the bell-push on its cord. 'Stay where you are, or I'll ring for Charles,' she cried sharply. 'He's close by. He's sitting up tonight. He's . . .'

'Don't make me laugh. He's snoring like a pig in the hall downstairs. And your old man won't wake up so soon, neither — he's sleeping off the doctor's visit. So ring as much as you like, girlie, ring as much as you like.'

She pressed the bell desperately as he came at her: she could hear it pealing through passages below. Then, with a sudden grab, he seized her wrist and tore the bell out of her hand: the reek of liquor swept her face. He had laid his pistol away and with his free hand was trying to pinion her other arm: she sought to throw him off by slipping out of bed sideways. But his grip on her wrist held firm: the burning eyes, the liquor on his breath, came closer and closer....

Then she was aware that a tall figure in a fur cap was on the balcony.

It was Boulton. He was no more than a shadow in the moonlight, pointing silently towards the bedside lamp. In a last convulsive effort she twisted her hand, still imprisoned in that vice-like clutch, until her fingers found the switch. The light went out and on the instant the moon flooded the room with silver. At the same moment in a noiseless, lightning spring the figure in the doorway came hurtling through the air and her aggressor was plucked away so violently that, his clutch on her wrist breaking only at the last, she was flung to the end of the bed.

She saw that Boulton had one hand clapped firmly over the other's nostrils and mouth: his other hand grasped Miklas by the arm, pulling it down over one shoulder and at the same time twisting it. Uttering inarticulate cries of pain, Miklas was swept clear of the ground, hoisted like a sack of corn on Boulton's back: then the Englishman crouched, ducked, and his victim, heaved upward and outward, shot in a wide parabola through the balcony door and over the balustrade. The quickness of it was uncanny. At one instant there was the struggling figure emitting muffled sounds: then there was only the hard moonlight tracing patterns on the floor and the stillness broken by the straining ice below.

Aghast, Melissa would have run out on the balcony, but

Boulton stepped in her path. 'They'd spot you in white,' he said, still rather breathless. 'Better let me go.' She was aware of his silhouette black against the moonlight without; then he was back at her side, closing the balcony door, drawing the curtains. 'The snow took him,' he announced, tight-lipped and grim. 'They're not likely to find him until spring. The snow's deep on the ice, the sentry apparently didn't hear a sound.'

Her teeth were chattering with the cold. 'Did you ... did you have to ...' she began huskily.

The grey eyes smouldered. 'It was him or us. If he'd got away alive, knowing I'd been up here before seeing you ...'

'You heard what he said, then?'

He nodded. 'I was close behind him on the balcony. I followed him when he left the mess — I had a hunch he was up to no good.' He frowned. 'He had it coming to him. He was a killer.'

'You know it was he who shot Apostolou, then?'

'The rumour's all over the camp.'

'It's true. De Bahl was taxing him with it at breakfast-time this morning.' And she told him of the conversation she had overheard in the dining-room.

He gave a short laugh. 'Well, the Dniester's put "paid" to a lot of old accounts tonight, Apostolou's among the rest. This is the second of our friend Guido's victims, right here at Orghina.'

'You mean he killed someone else besides Apostolou?'

His face hardened. 'An Englishman called Armitage. They found him in the river. It happened before you came, soon after your father was here the first time.'

'Steve knew nothing about it, or he'd have told me.'

'That may well be. As far as I know, Armitage was never at the Castle. He never got beyond the village.'

'But what was an Englishman doing at Orghina?'

'Officially, he was prospecting on behalf of a British oil syndicate. But it might also be that certain people in London were interested in our friend the Baron.' He broke off. 'That nightie of yours looks pretty airy to me.' He took her hand in his. 'My gracious, but you're freezing. Here, put this on and hop back into bed!'

He picked up her dressing-gown from the bed and hustled her into it. She had flushed, realising for the first time that she was clad in nothing more substantial than *crêpe de chine*. With the most matter-of-fact air in the world he pulled back the bedclothes, helped her into bed and tucked her in. She snuggled under the bedclothes. 'That brute frightened you, didn't he?' he said, gazing down at her. 'Are you sure you feel all right?'

She nodded, then put out her hand shyly and laid it on his. 'Thanks for what you did. It was jiu-jitsu, wasn't it?'

He nodded. 'A Jap on the Pacific Coast once gave me some lessons.'

'It was a tremendous decision to take. It's rather a terrible thing to kill a man.'

'Not Guido Miklas. Not a rat like that. And I'd have as little scruple in treating our friend the Baron the same way, if I had the chance.'

Her eyes rested thoughtfully on his face. 'You were right about de Bahl and I was wrong. I wish you'd tell me what you know about him.'

His laugh was grim. 'Plenty, and none of it good. For years he's been running one of the most successful espionage bureaus in Europe, if you know what that is.'

'Not very well.'

'They buy up military secrets and sell them to the highest bidder. They also undertake specific commissions as in the case of a Power that wants, let's say, the plans of a fortress or the design of a new anti-aircraft gun. It's a dirty business. They go to work very methodically to corner the person who can give them the information they want. Sometimes it's a highly placed staff officer, sometimes only a clerk, but the procedure is always the same. They discover their victim's weakness — it may be gambling, or it may be women — and use it to get him in their clutches. Then he has to come across with the information or else.... De Bahl specialises in this sort of thing. Wherever he goes, he leaves a record of ruin, suicide, behind him. And the men he employs are absolutely ruthless, like this Miklas rat' — he jerked his head backward towards the window. 'If they want to leave no traces, they kill. The Lord knows how many people de Bahl has murdered, or caused to be murdered.'

She shuddered. 'But it's too ghastly! Knowing all this, why ever didn't you warn us?'

He shook his head. 'I didn't know what your father was doing mixed up with a man of his stamp. De Bahl has always had plenty of capital. We never knew where it came from — it certainly didn't come from this antique business of his. I'm pretty sure now that Ardza supplied it.'

'Ardza? What had he to do with espionage? I thought he was in the arms industry.'

He laughed. 'And what's better for the arms trade than seeing that everybody knows just what the other fellow has got tucked away in the way of secret weapons? But de Bahl's never been in the arms business, and I must say I'm puzzled to know what he's up to here, hobnobbing with a bunch of gun-runners like Grenander and the rest of them. He's never had anything to do with gun-running to my knowledge, and Heaven knows there's been enough of it going on, these past few years.' He clutched his shoulder suddenly. 'Do you mind if I sit down for a minute?' He dropped down on the bed.

She had switched on the bedside light and in its pinkly shaded ray saw that his face, glistening with perspiration, was twisted with pain. 'Oh, you're hurt!' she cried.

He held up a restraining hand. 'I'll be all right in a minute. It's only this old shoulder of mine.'

'Let me get you some brandy. I've a flask in my dressing-bag.'

'Please. It's nothing, really. I'm not so good at all in wrestling since my crash. And that hold of mine just now wasn't as clean as I'd have liked.' He began to rotate his arm. 'I don't think the internal ironmongery has suffered. You know, I'd like a word with your father if you think he could stand the shock of finding me here. Is it too late to wake him up?'

She stared at him in consternation. 'Then you didn't hear about Steve?'

He frowned. 'No.'

'They've kidnapped him.'

He gazed at her blankly. 'That's bad!' he said and shook his head. 'That's damned bad. What happened?'

She told then of the day's events — the doctor's visit, de Bahl's and Grenander's interview with Stephen, her adventure in the mosque. When she described the torture scene she had witnessed, Boulton's face hardened. 'I saw them bring the poor devil in,' he said. 'I thought they'd give him the works.

Well, there's the real de Bahl for you — a naked savage behind all that sleek façade.'

'What became of him, do you know?'

He outlined a little shrug. 'Some of the boys took him away in a lorry. He was still alive, but by this I guess he's in a ditch somewhere, under the snow.' He took her hand. 'It won't help, thinking about it. Go on with your story.'

'I shouldn't worry too much about your father,' he said when she had finished. 'After all, he's the goose that lays the golden eggs: so long as he controls the purse strings, nothing very much can happen to him.'

She shook her head. 'You don't know Steve. He's as obstinate as a mule. He'll pay no ransom. Don, I'm so scared for him.'

'He knows you're in their power, remember — he'll do nothing to make things worse for you. But you can leave this to me. De Bahl doesn't suspect me yet — I'll find some means of discovering what they've done with your father and of getting into touch with him. For the rest, I confess I'm still puzzled. These guys haven't a hoot in Hades chance of starting a successful rising in the Ukraine, and de Bahl, who's nobody's fool, knows it as well as I do.'

'I forgot to tell you,' she said. 'In the mosque this afternoon the old fellow with the beard said they'd have to have a frontier incident in order to bring the anti-Bolshevik Powers in.'

His expression quickened. 'The only Power in question is Germany, and she's not going to risk war with Russia for the sake of a rabble of crazy Ukrainian agitators.'

'The doctor seemed to think she would. And he's German Consul at Mirapol, so he ought to know.'

'Only by courtesy, and Vice-Consul at that. It's the only thing German about him: otherwise he's Ukrainian through and through and as woolly-headed as the rest of them. But he's the German representative, all right, and he might well cook up something to embroil the two Powers.' He puckered his brow. 'A frontier incident, eh?'

He picked up her hand again. 'As for the famous treasure, I had a notion, from the moment you told me about it, that the whole thing was a ramp. Of course, de Bahl forged those documents or, more likely, hired some out-of-elbows hack at Bucharest to forge them for him.' He looked at her speculatively. 'De Bahl spoke of not starting before the middle of next week, didn't you say? That gives us a little breathing space, anyway.'

She said: 'You always give me courage. I don't know what I'd do without you. Are you sure the Baron doesn't suspect you?'

He gave her his cheerful grin. 'With that whited sepulchre you can never be sure of anything. But my little fracas with your father made quite a hit with him. De Bahl has an eye on me, no doubt, as he has on everybody, and Grenander still thinks of me as his chauffeur he picked out of the gutter; but I get on famously with von Wahlczek — I've an idea that our Wally may prove useful yet.' He glanced at his watch. 'I must be on my way. I have to lay a good, strong alibi that I was asleep between the blankets when our friend Miklas was last seen, in case they find the body.' His glance was rather wistful. 'I bet you never talked to a fellow who'd just killed a man before.'

She pressed his hand. 'You don't think I'd hold that against you, Don? When do I see you again?'

'Tomorrow night, maybe. At any rate, I'll think up some way of communicating with you.'

'Is your shoulder good for that rope? Hadn't you better return by the stairs and the turret entrance?'

He shook his head. 'The sentry might let me pass but he'd be bound to report it. I shall manage the rope somehow.' He stood up. 'Good night, Melissa!'

She put out her hand. 'Good night, Don.' She paused. 'You've told me who de Bahl is. Won't you tell me who you are?'

He smiled at her, her hand in his. '"No names, no court martials!"' he answered. Then, with gentle deliberation, he replaced her hand on the coverlet, plucked open the balcony door and was gone.

She sprang from her bed and followed him out upon the balcony. A knotted rope trailed there. Clouds veiled the moon: she saw him as a dark mass against the darker masonry above her head. He was going up steadily hand over hand but, as it seemed to her, with agonising slowness. At last he reached the top and the rope at her feet was whisked aloft. A lonely figure on the battlements, he raised an arm in greeting and she waved back. Then she was alone, looking down upon the scar in the whiteness all about that had received Guido Miklas for burial.

Stephen Hits the Nail on the Head

STEPHEN SELMAR stirred from a deep sleep. He had no idea where he was. At first he fancied himself back in his palatial hotel bedroom at the Monte Carlo, and looked instinctively for the dazzling Riviera sunshine greenly filtered through Venetian blinds. Then he remembered that he was at Castle Orghina and with eyes still dulled with slumber sought for the familiar setting of his turret bedroom — the old Moldavian chest, the Italian bureau with the ancient print of Stephen cel Mare above it, the big table with its litter of blue prints over which he liked to pore in his dressing-gown at bedtime.

He felt terrible. His head was splitting, his tongue furred — he had not had such a hangover since his days as a young engineer. What had happened to him? A violent twinge in the back as he struggled into a sitting posture brought the immediate past back to him with a rush. He called out 'Charles!' fretfully and only then perceived that he was in a strange room. And what a room! Whitewashed walls blotched with damp, an uncarpeted floor, heavily barred windows half blocked with snow, and in place of the large four-poster he was accustomed to with its linen sheets and silk-bound, fleecy blankets, he found himself lying in a hard truckle bed covered with rugs that smelled of the stable.

He was still at the Castle — through the window he could

see the angle of the Boyar Tower bathed in brilliant sunshine. 'Charles!' he bellowed in a fury, and at the same time looked around him for his watch. He found it on his wrist. The hands pointed to ten-twenty. Good God, he must have slept almost round the clock. He glanced about for a bell. But there was no bell. 'Charles!' he roared again.

A door behind him opened. He turned his head to perceive the Baron, freshly shaved, his face shining with soap, peering ingratiatingly in. At the sight of him Selmar began to collect his thoughts. The last thing he remembered, the Baron had brought Grenander to see him and there had been a furious row. The engineer had wanted him to sign a cheque for twenty-five thousand dollars, but Selmar had told him that he was gravely dissatisfied with the way things were being run, that he was the boss and meant to stay the boss, that he would have no guards restricting his liberty, and that henceforth he would take charge himself. Meanwhile, not another cent would he advance until the murder of Apostolou was cleared up. Resentfully, he recollected that the Baron had done nothing to support him, hovering aimlessly in the background while Grenander stormed that he must have the money at once to settle customs charges on stores at railhead and pay the men. At the end of a stormy scene Grenander had flung out. Selmar's last remembrance was of falling back among his pillows exhausted with rage and pain and the Baron giving him some of the medicine the doctor had left.

Observing that Selmar was awake, de Bahl hobbled briskly in, his lips pursed in a cajoling smile. The other did not give him the chance to open his mouth. 'What the devil's the meaning of this?' he barked. 'Why was I moved in here? Where's Charles? What's going on?'

The Baron drew a deep sigh. 'My dear fellow, how shall I begin to explain?'

'Answer my question!' Selmar trumpeted. 'What am I doing in this filthy room? How did I get here?'

'Please!' White hands fluttered to appease him. 'You are ill, Herr Selmar, you must not excite yourself!'

'Ill, nothing! What I want to know is ——'

'I shall explain all, if you will give me time. Both you and I are victims of this scoundrel, Grenander.'

'You mean that damned fellow had the gall ——'

'He insists that he is in charge here. He says you have not the right to cause more trouble among the men by keeping back money due for stores and wages. I have argued with him, but he is like a mule. I think, maybe, it is wiser you let him have the twenty-five thousand dollars. After all, the money is owing.'

'He's crazy. I'll sign no more cheques, as I told him yesterday. Where's my daughter?'

The Baron shrugged his shoulders. 'He is a dangerous fellow, this Grenander, Mr. Selmar — you will gain nothing by provoking him. I do not wish to upset you but I must tell you he declares you shall stay here, where he can keep his eye on you, until you sign that cheque.'

The other crimsoned with anger. 'He said that, did he? By the Lord Harry, I'm going to tell that baby a few things.'

He made to spring out of bed. But de Bahl's hand restrained him. 'You must take a practical view, my dear sir. Why not humour him? For a man of your wealth the sum is not large. Remember, we are miles from anywhere and Grenander is master of the situation. He has fifty men absolutely under his orders — there's a guard outside in the corridor now — and he can make things extremely disagreeable for you, for us all, unless he gets that money.'

'I'll see him in Hades first!'

'Also' — with an apologetic cough he eased his collar with his finger — 'for Miss Melissa. Forgive me for drawing your attention to it, but she's entirely isolated in the Green Turret, surrounded by Grenander's guards.'

For the first time consternation showed in Selmar's face. 'You're not telling me that he'd dare to harm Melissa?' He thrust out his lower jaw. 'How do I come to be here?'

'They brought you over last evening while you were asleep.'

He frowned. 'Asleep? Baloney!' He clenched his fist. 'Gosh, now I know where I got this terrible head. That medicine — it was drugged.' His voice rose angrily. 'By God, Baron, that doctor of yours — he drugged me!'

De Bahl spread his hands. 'Pardon, he was Grenander's friend, not mine. I wouldn't put anything past Grenander, you know.'

Selmar snorted. 'You'd better get this straight, de Bahl. I shall hold you responsible if anything happens to Melissa. You engaged Grenander: you told me he was a qualified engineer. And now I discover he's nothing but a blackmailer, a gangster and a kidnapper. It's an outrage!'

'He deceived me, Mr. Selmar. His qualifications were beyond question. But I do beg of you to use discretion in this matter. If you sign this cheque he will release you and you can join Miss Melissa.'

'I'm signing nothing. And you, get out of here — I want to think.'

The Baron dropped his eyes. Going to the door he signed to someone in the corridor. Boulton came in. 'If you will not listen to me,' de Bahl said to Selmar, 'maybe you will listen to a fellow Anglo-Saxon.'

The Englishman spoke up briskly. 'You sign that cheque, Mr. Selmar, or there'll be trouble. They're a wild lot in this camp and you don't want them to start getting rough with Miss Selmar.'

'You can go plumb to blazes,' said Selmar.

Boulton remained unperturbed. 'Now, don't go losing your shirt, Mr. Selmar. Can't you see we're only trying to help you, the Baron and I? You're in a spot, we're all in a spot. If you're sensible, you'll take the Baron's advice. Trust him, if you won't trust me. He wouldn't lie to you any more than your American baron.'

'What the devil are you talking about? What American baron?'

'Baron Pearl. Jack Pearl,' was the composed answer.

Selmar jerked up his head and surveyed the Englishman sharply. De Bahl smiled deferentially. 'An American baron?' he observed with an amused air. 'This is something I never heard of before. Unless it is a beef or an oil baron...'

Boulton laughed. 'It's just a name the people have given him. Jack Pearl is a celebrated figure in modern America, known for his rugged honesty from coast to coast. They say of him that the Baron cannot tell a lie ——'

'Like George Washington, eh?'

'Exactly.'

He took de Bahl aside. 'Leave me with him,' he said under his breath. 'I'll get that cheque out of him. See, he's calming down already.'

The Baron clapped him on the shoulder. 'Right, my dear boy. Believe me, it'll be better for all of us.' He smiled encouragingly and went out. When his footsteps had died away in the corridor, Selmar said, 'Ouch!' and sat up stiffly. 'What do you know about our American radio?' he demanded of Boulton sternly.

The young man grinned. 'Enough to have had many a good laugh at Jack Pearl. I drove in New York for a bit and I had a radio in my cab. "The Baron" and "Sharlie" were great favourites of mine. Any time they were on the air, I'd switch on.'

Selmar's bright blue eyes searched the Englishman's face. 'You're not so dumb as you look,' he growled. '"Baron Münchausen" — that's what Jack Pearl calls himself on the air, isn't it? So you were trying to tell me that de Bahl's a liar, is that it?'

'He's deceived you from the first,' replied Boulton, cocking his ear towards the door. 'He's neither a Baron nor an antique dealer but a notorious international espionage agent. And what's more, there was never any Pasha's treasure, either. The whole thing was a plant to use you to cover up this ruffian's nefarious activities.'

'What activities?'

'Gun-running. The Castle's full of arms they've smuggled in with your building materials. They're planning a raid into the Ukraine.'

Selmar sat up with a jerk, then clutched at his back with a cry. 'Gosh, it's fearful to be crippled like this. They're going to invade the Ukraine, you say? With fifty men? They're crazy!'

'Not so crazy, Mr. Selmar. They're all in the arms business. At least, Grenander has been for years the secret agent of various international syndicates; you know, interlocking concerns that supply the Powers indiscriminately with arms for use against each other. Von Wahlczek and Frangipani are in the racket, too. Ukrainian Nationalists have been here at the Castle hobnobbing with de Bahl and the others. Actually the chances of a successful Ukrainian rising are about one in a million, I'd say. But de Bahl don't care anything about that. All he cares about is running the stuff across the ice, and for that the force he has here is more than sufficient. What puzzles me is why they should run this risk just for the sake of dumping a comparatively small amount of stuff on the Ukrainians.'

Selmar grunted. 'Well, the boys would sure sell a lot of merchandise if the Ukraine went up in flames.'

'There's not a chance of it. What are the handful of men here and a lot of wild-eyed Ukrainian revolutionaries going to effect against the Red Army?' He shook his head. 'No, Mr. Selmar, there's a link missing somewhere in this business, but I don't seem able to detect it.'

The American grunted. 'There should be a cigar case in my coat on that chair. Thanks!' He took a cigar from the case Boulton brought him, lit it and drew a couple of contemplative puffs. 'You reminded me of something just now. De Bahl was pretty close to Ardza, did you know that?'

'Miss Selmar told me.'

'Ardza was the king-pin of the munitions racket. The old man controlled a whole row of concerns — big corporations like the Mannheimer Arms Factory, that Italian outfit they call the F.E.T.A., the Tourcoing United Chemicals. Well, Ardza died. You didn't know, perhaps, that de Bahl had a call on large blocks of shares in all these companies. He sounded me out once about going in with him — he said with everybody arming all round it was easy money. But I never speculate.' He paused to blow a long spiral of smoke. 'Do you know what I think, son? It's a flutter in armament stocks. As you say, they don't give a damn what happens in the Ukraine. But a first-class war scare will send all armament shares soaring, and these babies will be on velvet.'

The other smote his brow. 'They spoke of a frontier incident. By Jove, sir, I believe you've got it.'

Selmar ground his teeth on his cigar. 'The rats! And to think that we're isolated here! We've got to sic the police or somebody on to them, son, and quickly. When I think of that poor girl of mine...'

'Miss Melissa's all right, sir.'

'You've seen her?'

He nodded. 'It's not very conventional,' he said with a grin, 'but I've found a way of getting to that balcony of hers at night over the roofs. I've no time to tell you more now. What you have to do for the present is to play for time. Don't let de Bahl see that you suspect him. Temporise with Grenander, even if it means signing that cheque; we might be able to stop it. You might even make your own terms; insist, for instance, that they allow Miss Melissa to leave the Castle: as long as they're in their present mood she's in constant danger.'

'They'll never agree to that. She'd give the show away.'

'I know. But it's a talking point. And we must gain time, if I'm to get word to the authorities.' A loud clanging noise invading the room cut across his words. It was the gong for midday dinners. Boulton grabbed his cap. 'I must go. Then I can tell Grenander you'll see him?'

'O.K. Just what's your interest in this man de Bahl?'

The young man's face became mask-like. 'I should have to refer you to the firm I represent for an answer to that question, sir.'

Selmar frowned. 'Munitions, too, is it?'

'In a manner of speaking.'

The American grunted. 'Well, as long as we're both agreed that this damnable conspiracy must be broken up . . . How long have you been trailing him, son?'

'Indirectly ever since Grenander and the others left Trieste.'

There was a glint of humour in the blue eyes. 'You wished yourself on to the big cheese, did you? How did you work it?'

Boulton grinned boyishly. 'Well, it meant drinking his French chauffeur under the table and locking him up in a coal cellar: I had to tamper with the car a little, too. Then, when they found their chauffeur missing and the Isotta apparently busted, I just happened along. That's all! But that's under your hat, remember!'

'O.K.'

'And please to keep on remembering, Mr. Selmar,' said Boulton from the door.

'Dumb as a drum with a hole in it.' He uttered a faint groan. 'This confounded back of mine!' He grasped the young man's hand. 'When do you think you'll see Melissa again?'

'This afternoon, once it's dark, if I can manage it. She's so eager for news of you.'

'My dear love to her!'

'I won't forget.'

Selmar closed his eyes wearily as Boulton hurried out.

The Great Hall, a wilderness of scaffolding and painters' ladders, ran above the room where Selmar lay. Since the men were not working that day the place was deserted, save for a solitary figure that sprawled full length on the floor with ear bent to a square opening disclosed by the removal of a plate covering a heating-flue. The voices having ceased in the room below, a white topknot of hair moved among the litter, and de Bahl hauled himself to his feet. With extreme caution he noiselessly replaced the plate and lingered a moment, listening. When no sound save that of the men trooping to their dinners came from without, he turned and, picking his way on tiptoe through the disorder of the hall, descended the circular stair of the entrance tower and threaded the stone passage that led to his office in the staff wing. As he reached the bottom step there was a movement in the shadow under the stairs, but, immersed in thought, he failed to see it.

Melissa's engaging friend looked a good deal less engaging than usual as, squeezing each hand alternately with a nervous gesture, he made for the office.

The Baron Has a Plan

A BLAST of tobacco smoke rose in de Bahl's face as he entered the office. The windows overlooking the yard were shut, the stove glowed redly. Grenander was there, scowling over a cigar as he straddled a chair and chatted with von Wahlczek, who was warming his long legs before the stove, while Frangipani was at the window, drumming a tattoo on the pane. At the sight of de Bahl, Grenander sprang up so violently that his chair fell over with a thud. With an oath he growled: 'Where vere you? Ve search the whole place for you.'

'Well?' queried the Baron coolly.

'Guido, he's dead. They yoost find him.'

The heavily lidded eyes were averted. 'Where?'

'His cap was hanging on a bush at the foot of the wall near the Boyar Tower. The body was in a snowdrift on the edge of the river. His neck's broken and most of his bones besides. He was t'rown from the girl's balcony, I guess.'

The dark eyes snapped, but the face remained a marble mask. 'How do you know this?'

Von Wahlczek spoke. 'We traced his footsteps on the roof — on the balcony, too, while the girl was at her lunch. There's a rope up there on the battlements — that's the way he climbed down.'

De Bahl drew deeply on his cigarette. 'Get me Boulton!'

Grenander looked at him enquiringly. 'Boulton?'

'He's been seeing the girl secretly.'

Grenander cast him an angry glance. 'Impossible,' he declared, flushing. 'Vithout I know it, no one can pass my guards.'

De Bahl's lip curled. 'Boulton did. I'll tell you something else. It was he who killed Guido.'

'Boulton? That dumb Englishman?'

'Not so dumb as some people I know, Axel. Do you suppose it was our little Miss Melissa who pitched our poor friend off the balcony? Boulton's been seeing her privately, at night in her room. And shall I tell you why he got rid of Guido? Because Guido was smarter than the rest of us, because he found out that this English rat is a spy.'

The other's florid face darkened. 'A spy? Who says so?'

De Bahl sat down heavily at the desk. 'There's a lot that goes on under your nose without your knowing it, my friend. I don't forget that it was you who pushed this nosey Parker, as the English say, on to us — well, it might interest you to hear that he tampered with your car at Trieste, and made your chauffeur drunk in order to be able to report on your movements.'

'It's a lie!' declared Grenander.

'It may be. All I know, he was boasting about it to Selmar just now. Maybe he was only making it up.'

The other growled. 'Who's he working for? Did he tell Selmar that?'

'He said it was for some arms concern, but I believe he's a British Secret Service man. He must tell us himself which it is.' He helped himself to a cigarette from the box on the desk. 'Fetch him, will you, Axel?'

In a sort of blind run Grenander, his eyes suffused with blood, made for the door. It opened outward and as he flung it back, it momentarily hid a figure that flattened itself against the wall. Without looking round Grenander swung the door to behind him, and went scurrying along the passage. At the same instant the eavesdropper stepped swiftly into the doorway and remained there, dividing his attention between the murmur of voices within the office and the sound of Grenander's departing steps. As soon as they had died away he skipped out, and after a preliminary glance had told him that the corridor was deserted, ran lightly along it and up the circular flight leading to the Great Hall. When the bend of the stairs concealed him from view from below, he halted a moment to doff his fur cap and mop his streaming brow. Running his fingers through his fair hair he pursed his lips in a noiseless whistle. 'Plenty trouble,' he murmured. Then the ring of ironshod boots on the flags below sent him flying upstairs.

It was Grenander coming back. 'He's not at mess with the others,' he announced as he re-entered the office. 'I've sent to find him.'

De Bahl gazed at him from under his black eyebrows. 'He hasn't left the Castle?' he questioned sharply.

The other cast him an injured glance. 'I gif an order; it is obeyed,' he declared with an oracular air. 'Nobody can enter or leaf vithout my permission. For the form, I ask at the main gate. No one has passed out, they say.'

The Baron nodded, drew a lungful of smoke, coughed and said: 'This affair has precipitated matters. We shall have to strike at once. Meanwhile, the important thing is to get our orders in' — his glance travelled to the desk clock — 'ready for the stock markets when they open tomorrow.' He drew a

fat wallet from his pocket and from it took a typewritten slip.
'I have here the list of stocks we discussed, with the amount
each of us proposes to take set against his name. The European bourses may be a little slow at first tomorrow, but by the
time New York opens — with the seven hours' difference, that
will be at 5 P.M. here — I fancy things will be livelier.' He
smiled round the circle. 'I've prepared the code message for
Schlesinger at Geneva' — he showed a couple of typewritten
sheets — 'to be despatched as soon as the job at the Ferryman's House is completed.'

'And when will that be?' said Grenander suspiciously.

'But tonight, Axel. I said we should strike at once.'

'Tonight? So soon?'

'Certainly. I shall have the *troika* waiting outside and take
the message to the telegraph myself. Schlesinger will break
the news promptly; it will be in all the newspapers tomorrow,
and then' — he rubbed his hands slowly — 'and then, my
friends, I think you will see the pot begin to bubble. Meanwhile, there's the list. Will each of you kindly initial it so that
there'll be no recriminations after?'

He handed the paper to Grenander. 'And Guido's share?'
he muttered.

'I shall assume that.'

The fat man scowled. 'With twenty points rise you make a
fortune, I t'ink!'

De Bahl laughed. 'Twenty points? Wait until we cross the
river. Twenty points, indeed! A great Power affronted, the
Ukraine in flames — you'll see a jump of a hundred, two
hundred!'

'And I who brought you the idea...?'

'Without me where would you have been? Didn't I produce

Selmar and his castle? I discovered the practical execution of the plan: therefore I'm entitled to the lion's share.'

'The fox's, you mean,' said von Wahlczek.

The Baron blinked indolently. 'If you will. But come, gentlemen, sign! And Frang will run this bunch of telegrams down to the village in the caterpillar.'

The list went round, each man initialling it. De Bahl carefully stowed it in his letter-case, then gave the Italian a sheaf of wires. Frang clumped out on his short legs. The Baron sat at his desk, wreathed in smoke, puffing at his cigarette and thoughtfully contemplating Grenander. 'This Englishman of yours is a problem, Axel,' he remarked mildly. 'When I encounter problems I like to dispose of them.' He paused, eyeing the other. 'Boulton must be disposed of.'

Grenander nodded stolidly. 'I t'ink yes!'

'I believe I have a way — I think you'll admit it's ingenious. It has the advantage of killing two birds with one stone.'

A loud knock at the door interrupted him. Von Wahlczek answered it. A shaggy sheepskin cap was visible in the corridor — one of the overseers was outside. There was an interchange of words, then von Wahlczek swung round to de Bahl. 'Boulton can't be found,' he said. 'They've hunted the whole place for him. They're certain he hasn't left the Castle...'

Grenander clenched his fists. 'If them damned guards let him t'rough, they answer to me, by yimini!'

The Baron laughed softly. 'Bah! You could look for an entire battalion in a rabbit warren like this and never find it.'

'Ask him, did they search the Green Turret, Wally,' Grenander called out.

Von Wahlczek turned to the overseer again. 'He says the Green Turret's out of bounds,' he spoke back. 'But he questioned the sentries, and they swear that no one has been in or out.' The engineer was about to ask another question when the Baron restrained him. 'Let the man go!' he bade von Wahlczek. Then he drew towards him the typewriter that stood on the desk, put in a sheet of paper and, laying his eternal cigarette aside, tapped out a couple of lines, scanned them carefully, then pulled out the sheet. 'A morsel of cheese for the trap,' he told Grenander, handing him the sheet. 'Let Wally see it,' he went on when Grenander had read it. 'This is a job for Wally.'

Grenander's small eyes twinkled behind their glasses. 'If it vorks, it's good,' he declared.

Von Wahlczek glanced over the sheet, then shrugged his shoulders. 'If it works!'

The Baron indulged in one of his velvety laughs. 'We must see that it does work.' He lowered his voice. 'Here's my idea ...'

The Ferryman's House

TWENTY-FOUR hours had elapsed since Stephen's disappearance. No word of him came to the Green Turret isolated behind its guards: the Baron and his companions remained invisible.

To Melissa, devoured with anxiety about her father, the time dragged insufferably. All day long a sense of unreality haunted her. It had started at her first waking. Opening her eyes upon the early morning sunshine streaming in from the balcony, she found herself wondering, as the occurrences of the night came back to her, whether it was not all a dream. Things simply did not happen with such tragic violence. Yet they had happened to her, and there were muddy footmarks on the blue rugs to prove it. It was unbelievable. Before coming to Orghina she had never seen a dead body: now in swift succession two men had been killed under her eyes, not to mention the poor wretch she had seen put to the torture. Yet more incredible even than these experiences, Steve, her natural protector in the midst of the perils surrounding them, had been silently and mysteriously torn from her.

Charles had no news when he brought her breakfast. Neither Ali nor the kitchen boy had turned up, he told her: the day's provisions had been left outside the kitchen door. Rather anxiously the valet asked whether she had been disturbed in

the night: very honestly he admitted that, having lain down
on his truckle bed in the lobby, he had dropped off to sleep
and awakened only to hear the gongs sounding for reveille.
He seemed so contrite that she had not the heart to tell him
the truth: besides, she was not sure how Charles, a Frenchman,
would interpret a young man's nocturnal visits to her room.
She contented herself with warning him that Boulton might
try to communicate with her, and bade him look out for a
message.

To while away the endless morning she devised a series of
tasks for herself, such as shampooing her hair, washing out
gloves and stockings and pressing a frock. When Charles called
her to lunch, the sight of her father's empty chair gave her such
a pang that she asked Charles to bring her a tray to the living-
room. Here, luncheon over, she remained at her old place by
the fire busy with her knitting, while the short afternoon wore
on and the early dusk set in.

It was snowing again. The sentries in the yard powdered in
white suggested the Retreat from Moscow. Her needles flying
in the firelight, Melissa made a brave effort to master her
nerves. She must not worry any more about Steve, she told
herself. If she was to preserve her self-control, life must pro-
ceed as before at the Castle, just as if Steve were there. No
more pigging it with trays: that evening she would change her
frock as usual and dine, if needs be, in solitary state, in the
dining-room. Meanwhile, she fixed her thoughts deliberately
on the approaching night: knowing her great anxiety about her
father, surely Don would try to reach her with news of him.

She announced her decision to Charles when he brought the
tea. Dinner at eight as usual in the dining-room. 'Then if
mademoiselle can spare me,' the servant informed her, 'since

I shall have the dinner to prepare and serve, I will go and change now.' He said this with an air conveying that in the circumstances he might be relieved of the necessity of putting on his evening dress. But Melissa did not take the hint. She meant to see that the normal routine was observed, just as, she felt sure, Steve would have wished. 'Very well, Charles,' she said. 'I don't need you at present. Let me have a cocktail here at a quarter to eight.'

The Frenchman had a room in the rear of the Green Turret above the kitchen. She remembered that it was well out of earshot of their living quarters when, having switched on the lights and drawn the curtains, he padded away. A door slamming in the distance stressed the silence ensuing on his departure: she felt a little nervous as she poured herself a cup of tea. Then a sound behind her brought her round in a panic and she saw von Wahlczek in the doorway leading to the vestibule. His fur cap and short hunting jacket with its deep fur collar were all speckled with snow and he carried a pair of fur gloves.

She was on her feet in a moment. 'Where's my father?' she cried hysterically. 'What have you done with him?'

He motioned her down with his hands. 'Please, I come to take you to him. But you must make no noise. Please, Miss Melissa!'

Her sense of relief was so immense that the tears welled into her eyes and she sank back upon the settee: for the moment she was unable to speak. Von Wahlczek said in a whisper, 'The Englishman, Boulton, sent me. He couldn't fetch you himself, but he gave me a note.' With a cautious glance at the door he drew a folded piece of paper from his sleeve.

The note was typewritten. Melissa read:

I have found your father. He is at the Ferryman's House down along the river. I am with him now. Sorry not to have reached you earlier, but it was impossible. You can trust v. W. He will take you to the place. Go with him, but hurry.

A 'D' scrawled in pencil served as signature.

Von Wahlczek said: 'It's now or never. De Bahl and the others are out of the way for the moment and I've fixed the guards. I've a sleigh waiting outside the Boyar Tower. You'll want to wrap up. Where's your coat?'

'In the hall.' She wavered for an instant. Von Wahlczek was one of the gang and she could not help remembering his sneering remarks about Stephen in the mosque. But the note must be authentic: no one could possibly know that she and Boulton had been seeing one another. Besides, hadn't Boulton told her that he was on friendly terms with von Wahlczek and hoped to make use of him?

She sprang up, the letter fluttering to the ground. 'I'm ready But you must let me tell Charles.'

Her companion stamped his foot imperiously. 'There's no time. If anyone sees that sleigh of mine we're lost. This is your one chance to release your father. Do you want to ruin everything?' So saying, he grabbed her by the arm and fairly ran her into her lobby, helped her into her raccoon coat that lay there, thrust her béret and gloves into her hands. Then he plucked open the heavy, ironbound door. A smother of snow blew into their faces, the door fell to with a bang behind them and they were out in the icy dark all a-flutter with the falling flakes. The sentry was a whitened pillar under the arched entrance: he made no move as they hurried by.

If there was a guard under the Boyar Tower, they did not see him. A horse coughed out of the blackness outside and in the faint radiance of two old-fashioned carriage lamps the graceful lines of a small sleigh were discernible. Melissa had seen a similar sleigh among the royal carriages at Versailles, a narrow affair to hold a single passenger with a saddle-like seat behind for the driver, who straddled his feet on the runners.

It was quite dark but between the snow-clouds spread low in the sky and the whitened fields all about enough lightness survived to show the track cleared between the drifts winding beside the snowy chasm that was the ice-bound river. The horse was fast: the sleigh flew, bells jingling, the snow spouting up on either side. Presently Melissa made out ahead the outline of a crazy shack, its starred wooden walls very black against the whiteness, cocked perilously on piles to overhang the stream.

Melissa knew about the Ferryman's House. She had seen it from her balcony, bleak and forlorn with a ramp descending to the ice. In summer, the Baron had told her, the house, besides accommodating the ferryman and his family, was used as a tavern where the peasants could take a dram while waiting for the ferry. But since the opening of the new bridge some miles downstream the ferry was little used. The Ferryman's House had fallen on evil days and in winter, when the river traffic was suspended, the ferryman closed the place up and retired with his wife and family to the village.

But now as, having tethered the sleigh to a ring in the wall, her companion led the way up a steep flight of dilapidated steps to a tavern door, Melissa perceived a light within the house. Pulling a leather latchstring, von Wahlczek ushered her into a sordid tap. A lighted oil-lamp placed on the little bar revealed a low, smoke-grimed ceiling, crumbling wattle walls, an iron stove glowing almost red-hot in a corner. The place reeked of damp, and a deathly silence reigned. The girl hung back in the doorway. 'But there's nobody here,' she said. 'Where's my father?'

'Ps-st! He's upstairs!' Her escort crossed to a built-in stair that mounted beside the bar and pulled open a door. 'Follow me, please! I take you to him, no?' he said, waiting for her. The tavern door, blowing to behind her in the glacial draught, settled it. She joined von Wahlczek at the foot of the stair. A light shone down from a door at the top. They went up and her companion opened the door. The yellow radiance of a hanging lamp disclosed a typical peasant bedroom, clean enough, with the inevitable ikon in the corner, a dismantled bed and a great tiled stove. Melissa swung to her escort. 'Why have you brought me to this place?' she demanded hotly. 'Where's Mr. Boulton? Where's my father?'

Von Wahlczek had remained at the door. 'Gently, gently,' he said. 'A little moment and I am back. I go to tell them you are here, no?' Before she could speak he was outside, closing the door behind him. The next instant the key was turned.

She hurled herself at the door, frantically rattling the handle. 'Unlock this door at once!' she cried. 'Von Wahlczek, let me out, do you hear?' She hammered at the panels with her fists until the slamming of the front door below told of his departure. A moment later, the faint jingle of sleigh bells drifted in from without.

He had locked her in there and returned to the Castle. Not a mouse stirred as she stood there listening — there was not a soul in the place but herself. In a sudden burst of panic she tried the handle again. At the same moment the lamp trembled and the bare boards under her feet vibrated to a heavy footstep that seemed to come from the adjoining room. The next instant she heard a familiar rasping cough. The blood drained from her face as, turning her back on the door, she gazed in an agony of fear about her. There was a small door beside the bed. The footsteps had stopped on the other side of it: the door handle was slowly turning. Someone coughed. Then the door swung inward.

De Bahl stood gazing at her from the threshold.

'Not of the Lion, but the Fox'

IN THE few seconds in which they silently faced one another, terror swept over her in icy waves. She could neither move nor speak, held in the grip of a cataleptic force that paralysed her body but left her mind unimpaired. Indeed, the shock seemed to quicken her perceptive powers. Unconsciously, she found herself registering the smallest detail about him, as, for instance, the fact that he was smoking a cigarette of normal size instead of one of his customary Brobdingnagian brand or that his heavy fur driving gloves dangled from a cord about his neck.

He was dressed in the garb in which he had met them at the railway on their first arrival at Orghina — in the high-peaked fur cap and long-skirted pelisse with its deep sable collar; he might have been one of Stephen cel Mare's boyars come back to life. The ear flaps of his fur bonnet were down — the fur setting stressed the fine chiselling of his features: now that his hair was concealed, the sternly handsome face had the vigour of a man of thirty. It was a face of alabaster, as bloodless and as unchanging. Only the eyes lived, eyes that had the hard gleam of jade, fixed upon her in a questioning, enigmatic stare. Confronting him there with her heart making wild leaps, she was aware of a subtle change that had come over him. The old indolence was gone. A strange vitality seemed to burn with a cold fire behind the menace of his regard. She remembered the look of ferocity she had surprised on his face in the mosque when they had questioned the Russian spy: it was as though the same expression was permanently stamped on the stony countenance framed in its oval of fur. The thought came to her that the agreeable companion of their Monte Carlo days had never been anything more than a figment of her imagination. Behind the mask of the charming man of the world, the heartless unscrupulous monster Boulton had depicted was lurking; and she was now meeting him face to face.

It was she who broke the tension at last. Pride, and the realisation that to betray her abject fear would be fatal, came to her aid and gave her back her tongue. 'I was told that my father was here,' she said in a voice that sounded to her exceedingly unsteady. 'Where is he?'

'Your father? Ha!' He gave a barking laugh and snapped his strong jaws together. 'As far as I know, your father's back in your quarters at the Castle, waiting for you!' She looked at him curiously. Even his voice had changed. It was fuller, deeper and almost without a trace of its usual huskiness.

He closed the door behind him and came in. He pointed to a chair behind her. 'Sit down!' he ordered brusquely.

She sat down blindly. She was beset with terror about Boulton. He had asked her to meet him there, but there was no sign of him. A dread suspicion seized her and simultaneously hardened into conviction. That note, typewritten with its scrawled signature, was a forgery! It was meant to lure her there — Boulton, too, perhaps. But why? She took hold of herself then. She did not know how much they had found out about Boulton, but she realised she must be careful not to give him away.

De Bahl's first question filled her with dismay. 'You came here to meet your friend, Boulton, didn't you?' he said.

He was standing in front of her, taking the last puffs of his cigarette and drawing the smoke deeply into his lungs, as was his habit. Through the operation of lighting a fresh cigarette from the butt of the old and of stamping the butt out on the uncarpeted boards, his eyes scarcely left her countenance. 'I came to find my father,' she answered stoutly.

Strange, how the light came and went in his eyes! They were like twin lamps burning in a tomb, so cold and white was his face. He ignored her reply. 'People who interfere with me never have any luck, remember that,' he said, and added: 'Have you forgotten Apostolou? He, too, was a spy.'

He spoke with unwavering calm. It only enhanced her fear. The silence of the house pressed in upon her. The dusty, untenanted room, the shuttered windows, a subtle, aromatic fragrance that seemed to spread about her as she sat there — remembering that she was alone with him in that isolated, snow-girt tavern, lapped in the hush of the winter evening, the atmosphere of the place was unbearable to her. She did not know whither she could flee; but she must escape, she told herself. Could she make a dash for the door? It would have to be the small door by which he had come in, since the other was locked. He was between her and the small door. Could she elude him?

The room was intolerably close — a long pipe from the stove in the tap below warmed it. She longed for air: her head was throbbing. Suddenly she was aware that de Bahl was offering her a cigarette from his case. To gain time she took one and let him light it for her. 'Don't make this English rat's mistake,' he told her over the flaming match. 'Those who have dealings with me know the penalty of treachery.' He chuckled. 'Or do they know it? How much do we know in the

next world?' The match burned out and he dropped it. 'Don't
get your fingers burnt, too, little Melissa. Be warned in time!'

He laughed again. It struck her that his laugh had an hysterical ring. Everything about him was odd today. He seemed
bigger and taller than before, looming over her in his long-
skirted overcoat. The aromatic fragrance she had noticed
before was stronger than ever in the heated atmosphere: the
room was swimming about her. Her cigarette tasted vile. She
laid it down in the ash-tray that stood on the table beside her
and pressed her hands to her temples. De Bahl's voice seemed
to come to her out of the distance on a rising note, curiously
gabbling.

'Loud-mouthed imbeciles like this Grenander think that the
world is ruled by bluster and violence,' he declaimed. 'Oh, no,
it isn't — it's ruled by craft. Only when craft fails does violence become necessary; but craft will not fail if under the velvet glove the steel fist is felt. Did you ever read *The Inferno*?'

She felt his eyes drilling her through and through. Against
her will she took her hands from her face. She tried to with-
stand the power of his regard, but it was too strong for her.
Slowly she raised her eyes to him. He repeated his question.
'Some of it, at my finishing school,' she answered at random.

The strange eyes glittered. 'One of those whom Dante met
in hell was Guido de Montefeltro. Ah, there was a man after
my own heart! In his prime he was a mighty *condottiere*, a man
of blood: only in his old age did he repent of his crimes and do
penance for them in the habit of a Franciscan monk. When
Dante asked Montefeltro who he was, the reply was, "When I
was on earth as a man my deeds were not of the lion, but of the
fox." Of the fox!' He laughed wildly. 'That's what they call
me. "The Fox"! Let fools like this Grenander be the lions,

going about roaring and baring their fangs: let me be the little fox, creeping by and never seen.'

The room had stopped revolving: her mind was clearer now: she was noticing things again. She wondered whether he was under the influence of some drug — the brightness of his eyes, his ghastly pallor, the incoherence of his speech, suggested it. She remarked that from time to time he seemed to be listening, his head turned, now towards the windows, now the door, and more than once he glanced at his watch. She had the impression he was expecting someone. Was it Boulton?

Boulton's name struck on her ear. De Bahl had asked her another question. Her mind grappled with it through a fog of renewed fear. 'Who sent Boulton here to spy on me?' he had demanded suddenly.

The imminence of danger helped her to regain her self-control. She was on the alert at once. 'What makes you think I know anything about it?' she retorted disdainfully.

His eyes searched her face. 'I thought you might be in his confidence.'

'Servants aren't in the habit of taking me into their confidence.'

He thrust his head forward. 'Or of visiting you in your bedroom at night?'

She sprang up. 'I don't propose to sit here and let you insult me.'

Again the lodent flame leaped from his eyes. 'Don't play-act with me! I know who killed Miklas and how he was killed.' He seemed to gnash his teeth. 'I ask you for the last time, who sent this Englishman here to spy on us?'

'And I tell you for the last time I don't know anything about it!'

It sounded brave, but inwardly she was quaking, the beating of her heart so loud in her ears that she thought it must be heard in the room. She made a bold effort to brazen it out, but before the deadly menace of his glance, she felt her resolution slipping from her and when she tried to avert her eyes, found she was unable to look away. 'For business reasons,' he said rather thickly, 'it's imperative that I should have this information.' His voice became shriller. 'I'll have it from you or I'll have it from him.' With lightning rapidity his hands shot out, grasping the scarf that she had loosened about her neck and twisting the two ends in his powerful fingers. 'What does this Englishman want here?' he screamed. 'Who are his accomplices? Was Apostolou in his pay? Why did you kill Guido, the pair of you? Answer me, before I choke the life out of you! Answer me, I say!'

'Let me go!' she gasped, beating on his broad chest with her hands. 'Let me go!'

With a high-pitched laugh he suddenly released his grip of her scarf and slipped his arms about her. She struggled frantically, but she was powerless in his embrace. 'What does this English tramp mean to you?' he cried stridently. 'Why should you and I who have been good friends quarrel about him?' Of a sudden his voice grew soft. 'Many women have loved me, my little Melissa,' he murmured in velvety tones. 'Am I so unattractive to you? Come, look into my eyes! Why do you struggle against me? Why not lie quietly in my arms and let me tell you how lovely you are, *ma belle*, so proud and straight and white! Melissa *mia, carissima, bellissima!*'

As he spoke he was drawing her to him. The reek of wet fur was rank in her nostrils: the moisture pearling on his fur collar brushed her cheek damply. His eyes bore down on her with irises oddly dilated: his mouth was a cruel line. Desperately she sought to free her hands. She felt her senses slipping — she must go on struggling if she was not to faint. But her arms were pinioned: do what she would, she could not tug her hands away; and all the time now the full mouth was approaching her lips, while a string of endearing words, the sense of which she had lost the ability to follow, poured from him.

Then she saw his expression change. In a flash he had let her go and had sprung back, swinging round to face the door leading out on the landing: in the second of silence that followed she heard a step on the wooden stairway leading from the room below. De Bahl's air was triumphant. 'Is that you, Wally?' he called.

The door handle turned: she remembered that the door was locked on the outside. 'If the door's locked, come round by the other door,' the Baron ordered, at the same time casting a malicious glance at his companion. The key turned in the lock, the door facing them swung open. But no one appeared. With a muttered exclamation de Bahl took a pace forward, at the same time drawing an automatic from his coat. In the same moment Melissa saw the smaller door behind him silently open. A lightning glance the Baron flung her as he advanced towards the other door to investigate showed her gazing intently behind him. On the instant he whipped round. But he was a fraction too late. As he turned a figure that had noiselessly appeared in the doorway between the two rooms launched itself upon him: de Bahl tried to bring his gun into play but found his hand seized and held high. By leaping backward he broke the grip, but the next moment he was butted by a charging head fair in the middle of the stomach. As he doubled up a flying fist caught him on the point of the jaw with a crack that rang through the room; he tottered, spun half round, then crashed to the floor. He grunted once and collapsed.

'Nine, ten and out!' said a cheerful voice. Through a mist that swam before her eyes Melissa was aware that Don Boulton was grinning at her across the prostrate form.

Frontier Incident

HE CAUGHT her as she fell forward. 'Hullo, hullo, hold up!' he said. But she did not faint: she just clung to him, her head against his coat. He was sniffing, his nose in the air. 'What's been going on here?' he demanded. He dived forward and retrieved de Bahl's cigarette as it lay smoking on the ground, smelled it. 'Reefers!' he snapped. Then his eye fell on the ashtray on the table. He pointed to the smear of lipstick on the butt of the cigarette she had discarded. 'Did he give you one?' he demanded.

She nodded. 'But I couldn't smoke it. It made me ill. My head's still spinning from it.'

He frowned. 'I'm not surprised. It's hasheesh. Drug addicts smoke these cigarettes. They call them "reefers." They're made of marijuana — that's Indian hemp.'

De Bahl, sprawled like a sack at their feet, had not moved. Boulton stooped suddenly and with a brisk tug detached the automatic from the clenched fingers and dropped it in his pocket. 'I thought he was drugged,' said Melissa. 'He talked so wildly and acted so strangely. He'd have killed you, Don, if you hadn't knocked him out.'

He nodded and stuck out his underlip. 'They're wise to me — I only discovered it this morning at lunch-time and promptly went to cover in a hiding-place I've found under the rafters of the Great Hall. A nice sort of idiot you were to walk into their trap. Your old man's given them their cheque, and as per schedule they've let him go back to your quarters and taken off the guards. I had it all set to whisk the pair of you off to the village when you have to go and disappear. If I hadn't found that decoy note on the table in the living-room — hullo, hullo, what's the trouble?'

With a little cry she had fallen against him, covering her face with her hands. He caught her in his arms. She was sobbing convulsively. 'Sorry!' he murmured. 'But I've been almost out of my mind with anxiety about you. When I found that you'd disappeared... what has that brute been saying to you?'

She shook her head. 'It doesn't matter. Nothing matters now that I know you're all right.' She looked up at him through wet lashes. 'Oh, Don, I was so frightened about you!' She clung to him desperately, burying her face against his snow-wet jacket. 'Melissa!' he cried in an anguished voice, then his arms drew her closer and his mouth brushed her hair, her eyes. On that she raised her tear-stained face to his and, her arms about his neck, gave him her lips.

'You don't know the hell I've been through since I discovered you were missing,' he told her. 'It seemed to me that I'd die if anything happened to you.'

Her fingers toyed with a button of his jacket. 'I never thought you cared anything about me.'

'Ever since that first morning I met you in Monte Carlo, I've done nothing but think about you. I've a job to do here, maybe the most important job of my life, but it's you I think of all the time. It's all wrong, I know, but ——'

'All wrong to think of me?'

'To fall in love with you.'

'Do you love me, Don?'

He nodded, sighed and looked away. With gentle hands she turned his face towards her. 'You've made me very happy because — well, because I've never met a man I could care anything about before I met you,' she said with great simplicity.

He shook his head. 'People don't fall in love suddenly like this. We say these things to one another because we're out of the world here, centuries away from today, just the two of us in this forgotten little house clinging to one another because danger has brought us together. When you get back to New York, everything will seem different ——'

'Not to me, darling. I'm not making any mistake. I knew it the first time I saw you.'

He folded her in his arms again. 'You're my girl,' he said, smiling down at her, 'and that's no make-believe, my love. From now on there'll never be any woman in the world for me but you, but I'm telling you now, we can't go on with it. All the same, I'm going to remember this moment, Melissa darling, and bask in its lovely, sunny memories and bless you for them, to the very end of my life.'

The figure on the floor had stirred, breathing stertorously. 'My gracious!' the young man exclaimed; 'I declare I'd forgotten all about him. Well, the quicker we're out of this, the better. But first to get rid of our horizontal champion.' Swiftly his gaze ran round the room. 'Open that cupboard, will you, Melissa?'

There was a vast built-in press in the corner, with door ajar. The press was empty. Boulton had turned de Bahl over and was going through his pockets. From one he took a bulky wallet which he appropriated, from another two typewritten sheets, which he carried to the light. 'By Gad,' Melissa heard him mutter, 'it's the frontier incident.' He held up one of the sheets. 'It's a code message addressed to Geneva all ready to be sent,' he said, 'and here's the message in plain language written in above the code words in the carbon copy. Look!'

The transcription was in French. She read:

> Dr. Gustav Metzger German Vice-Consul Mirapol Ukraine stabbed to death tonight at Ferryman's House Orghina Bessarabian side of frontier by unknown assassins believed to be Soviet emissaries who afterwards set fire to premises and escaped Stop Metzger prominently identified pro-German party Ukraine and crime created greatest sensation throughout region Stop Metzger was in close touch Ukrainian Nationalists and widespread reprisals feared.

The message was signed 'Lhabed.' Boulton showed Melissa the signature. '"De Bahl" spelt backwards,' he pointed out. 'I don't understand this,' he said, 'because they're hand in glove with Metzger — it may interest you to know that those pills he gave your old man were drugged so that they could carry him off more easily. Nevertheless, it's pretty clear what's going to happen. Everything's set for the raid. Up at the Castle Grenander and the boys have been checking arms and ammunition all day and getting sleds packed. What they're waiting for is the frontier incident which is to justify the expedition.'

'And Doctor Metzger is to be murdered to give them their incident, is that it?'

'That seems to be the idea. I don't understand it very well because he's in this conspiracy up to the neck and as thick as thieves with de Bahl and the gang ——'

'That wouldn't worry de Bahl any.'

'I expect you're right. Well, Metzger's to be bumped off, in this very house, tonight, and then the fun starts. The first thing we know there'll be what this telegram calls "reprisals," that's to say, the raid, the object being to set the Nazis and the Bolshies at one another's throats, and there's your war scare. Armament stocks will soar, which is all de Bahl and his pals care about. Your worthy parent says the whole thing is nothing but an attempt to rig the market and, by Jove, he's right.'

His attention drifted to the unconscious figure at their feet. 'He left the troika outside, tucked out of sight in the lane,' he said. 'We'll borrow it and drive to the village and try to ginger up the police, then return with them to the Castle and collect your old man — the rest we can leave to the Rumanians, I guess. But first we'd better dispose of old Beastly here. Lend me a hand with him, will you?' Between them they half lifted, half hauled the dead weight across the floor and lodged it in the deep closet. 'He's not dead, is he?' Melissa questioned rather tremulously, staring down at the frowning, livid face. Boulton shook his head. 'Not on your life.' He grinned across at her. 'A sweet upper-cut, wasn't it? If I knew anything about my job, I'd finish him off. But there...'

He was looking for the closet key. But there was no key, and the bolt was broken. 'No matter,' he said, shutting the door. 'We'll be well out of this before the old devil emerges from dreamland.'

He raised a hand in warning, sprang to the lamp and blew it out. The last glimpse Melissa had of his face showed it watchful and alarmed. A sleigh was approaching the house at a furious pace — they could hear the smothered clip-clop of hoofs on the snow, the sleigh-bells' chime. They heard it stop — in the long silence that ensued Melissa's hand found her companion's in the stuffy darkness, gripped it tightly. Footsteps climbing the stairs to the front door broke the taut suspense. A hinge groaned in the room below and an icy draught whistled through the uneven planking. Von Wahlczek's unmistakable drawl, curiously muted, mounted to their ears. He was speaking German. 'You're sure you've got everything, Herr Doktor?' he said.

Melissa felt Boulton's fingers tighten on her elbow as he held her arm in the dark. The rather snarling voice that answered was Metzger's. It resounded from the foot of the boxed-in stair. 'Had we not better see whether de Bahl is still here?' he said in German. They heard the door at the foot of the flight open and a little light from the room below shone in upon them.

'There's no one here. Can't you see it's all dark upstairs?' von Wahlczek retorted, his voice much nearer now. 'He's gone and taken the girl with him.'

'We didn't meet the troika ——'

'He spoke of going to the village to send that telegram. Hand me that gear of yours.'

The voices drifted away from the staircase. They heard von Wahlzcek say, 'It's the right watch, is it?' and Metzger's answer, 'It's inscribed with my name. If you don't believe me, look inside!'

A long silence then, broken presently by a quiet 'glug-glug-glug' as of liquid being poured. Von Wahlczek's voice came up, 'Give us some more of those shavings.' Silence again, then, 'He wouldn't have come and gone?' It was the doctor speaking.

His companion's strident laugh rang out. 'He hadn't left the Castle when we started out, had he? And if he had, we must have passed him on the road. Come on, he mustn't find us here. Besides, that horse won't stand. Let's join the others.'

'And if he doesn't come?'

'He'll come, all right, now that he's found that note.'

'I'd rather do it here.'

'So would Axel. But you know de Bahl. He won't risk a shindy here on account of the frontier guards, and he's right. The Englishman is tough and likely to put up a fight. It's safer and surer on the road. . . .'

The murmur of their voices was swallowed up in the slamming of the front door. Boulton's hand on Melissa's arm restrained her as they stood in the darkness during the long pause that followed. Then came the sound of a departing sleigh with the jingle of bells receding in the distance.

Boulton stole to the door, opened it, listened. All was deathly still. He raised his head and sniffed. 'Petrol!' he said: as he came back to Melissa she saw in the faint light shining from the room below that his face was set in grim lines. 'Now I get the idea,' he told her. 'I was meant to find that decoy letter. They used you to lure me here. I was never very happy about the guards being taken off and I made up my mind to slip out of the Castle unseen, just in case it was a trap. It's a good job I did, also that I avoided the direct road, or I'd be cold meat by this.' He laughed. 'They certainly meant to have that frontier incident.'

'But that telegram speaks of Doctor Metzger ——'

'They never intended to kill Metzger — I was to take his place. Don't you realise, the plan was to decoy me here to this shack, knock me on the head on the way, dump me here among certain articles belonging to Metzger such as this watch he spoke of and fire the place. Metzger would conveniently disappear and my charred remains would have been claimed as his by de Bahl and the gang. Those fellows below stairs have been laying the train — the whole place reeks of gasoline. The sooner we're out of it, the better.' He tucked the telegrams back into de Bahl's wallet and placed it in Melissa's hands. 'It'll be safer with you than me. Wait there: I'm going to see if the coast is clear. When I whistle, come down, and we'll make a bolt for it.'

He stooped to her lips and for a brief instant they clung together. Then, drawing from his pocket the big automatic he had taken from de Bahl, he cocked it and disappeared down the stairs

She heard the woodwork creak as he crept down. Then suddenly the wind from the floor blew about her feet, a door banged below, there was a shout, a deafening report, another, a crash of glass, a thud.

At the same instant, her ear caught a slight movement behind her. She swung about.

The closet door was open. De Bahl stood in front of it, with blood running down his chin, swaying unsteadily on his feet.

The Pot Begins to Boil

HER first thought was of the wallet in her hand. She paused just long enough to thrust it down the front of her jumper, then darted for the door. The hesitation was fatal. Her feet were on the threshold when she felt herself grasped by the shoulders from behind, pulled violently back and flung against the wall with a violence that shook the breath from her body. As she collapsed in a heap on the floor, she had a fleeting glimpse of de Bahl dashing past her to the staircase.

For an instant she lay there dazed. Then a strange, cracking noise came to her ears and at the same time she smelt smoke. As she struggled to her feet de Bahl reappeared in the doorway, snatched her up in his arms and carried her out to the stairs. She screamed 'Don!' despairingly, but a flabby hand was clamped over her mouth. The air was laden with the acrid fumes of burning wood, wisps of smoke rose to meet them, a lurid light flickered in her eyes, as she was borne swiftly down.

The lower room was on fire. A sheet of flame ran from the shattered fragments of the lamp overturned on its table to the floor, shooting out across the uncarpeted boards. The front door was swinging in the wind and, fanned by the draught, the flames roared and crackled amid dense clouds of smoke that caught them by the throat. Struggling frantically she freed herself from the gag of the imprisoning hand and called 'Don!'

once more. But as far as she could see for smoke the tap-room was empty. Remembering the shots she had heard, 'Boulton,' she cried to de Bahl, 'he's here somewhere. Oh, please, wait — we must rescue him.'

But her captor paid no heed. With lowered head he drove through the growing sea of flame and smoke for the entrance, lurching perilously, colliding with the furniture, gasping, coughing. Halfway across the floor, he tripped and almost fell: as he recovered himself, Melissa perceived a motionless form stretched out at his feet. The tumbled flaxen hair, the rough brown tweeds — 'Stop!' she entreated. 'Stop! It's Boulton! Oh, you can't leave him here to die!'

Inexorably de Bahl stumbled on, and the only result her desperate efforts to liberate herself achieved was to increase the vice-like grip that pinioned her. Out of the flaming house and down the greasy steps into the snowy yard they slithered, and the next thing she knew she was pitched into a pile of furs in a waiting sleigh, her companion scrambled in beside her and they were scudding through the biting dark. Then only did her resistance give out and she slumped among the furs, closing her eyes. By and by the cold revived her. At the sight of de Bahl, his face, dim in the reflected light of their lamps, a mask of dried blood and black smears, she uttered a little cry. As though he read her thoughts he said bluntly, 'The man was already dead.'

'How can you know that when you wouldn't wait to see?'

'I saw him there when I first went down. Was I to risk our lives for a dead man? Another minute and the place would have been a torch. Look back!'

They were dashing along the road beside the river, headed for the Castle. Behind them a smother of flame and smoke crimsoned the surrounding whiteness. In bitter anger she swung to her companion. 'You lured him there to kill him. Even if he did attack you, it was only to defend me. You might have saved him — if you'd a spark of humanity in you, you might have saved him. To leave him there, perhaps to be burnt alive...' She began to sob.

With a hard laugh he lashed the horses. 'The man who lays hand on me may count himself lucky to be dead. I told you I was a bad one to oppose. The law of Moses has always been good enough for me — an eye for an eye, and a tooth for a tooth. *Hold, halt!*'

Tugging at the reins he pulled up the three horses yoked abreast. Round a turn of the road, where a great tree thrust its bare branches into the sky, figures moved in the light of their lamps. Von Wahlczek's little sleigh stood on the road, the horse steaming and panting, a man in furs and shaggy sheepskin busby at its head. Three other men similarly attired stepped with arms outspread in the path of the troika. Then von Wahlczek, smothered from head to foot with snow, emerged into the path of their lights. 'De Bahl!' he cried in astonishment, peering at the other's grim and livid face. 'Man, you're wounded! Your face is covered with blood. Have you come from the Ferryman's House?'

'Quiet!' growled the Baron at his stamping and straining team. 'It's no thanks to you if I have,' he told von Wahlczek, glaring at him oddly.

'But how comes it that the house burns already? The Englishman has not passed.' He turned for confirmation to the men about him, speaking to them in Ukrainian, and they replied in unison.

De Bahl was breathing hard. 'Not only did he pass but he

attacked me, you bungling fool. If this is your idea of carrying out orders ...'

'But we carried out your orders to the letter, and not a quarter of an hour ago,' said von Wahlczek, his eyes on the other's face.

'It didn't occur to you to see if the girl was still there?'

'The place was in darkness. We thought you'd gone to the telegraph in the village and taken the girl with you. How were we to know ...'

'They could have turned out the light, couldn't they, idiot? What's Metzger doing back there?'

Von Wahlczek turned colour. 'There was an accident. When we were coming away, the horse bolted and Metzger got left behind. I couldn't hold the cursed brute — I believe he'd have taken me clear back to the Castle if these fellows hadn't scared him and landed us in a drift. I thought Metzger would have followed on foot. Where is he?'

'Back there on the floor with a bullet through his head. The Englishman, too.'

Von Wahlczek gazed past the speaker toward the reddening sky. 'Good God!' he murmured.

De Bahl veiled his eyes. 'It is the best solution. For now at least we shall have the evidence that a crime has been committed, if the fire leaves any evidence. Is your horse all right?'

'Yes.'

'Then take this wire to the village. It's the code telegram to Schlesinger ...' He was fumbling in his pockets. 'It's gone. My wallet, too! That blasted English rat — I must get back to him before it is too late.' He swung to Melissa, whipping the sleigh robes away, 'Get out! Get out! I'll send that wire myself,' he told von Wahlczek. 'Take the girl back to the

Castle — she can join her father in their quarters in the Green
Turret, but see that no one has access to them. Let two of
these men come with me: the others can return to the Castle.'
Von Wahlczek spoke an order and two of the men clambered
into the troika even as it was turning. De Bahl whipped up
the horses and the sleigh dashed away by the way it had come.

Von Wahlczek had caught Melissa in his arms as she
stumbled from the sleigh. She cried hysterically: 'He's lying!
He didn't have time to see whether he's alive or dead. Follow
him! Take me back! Oh, don't you understand? Boulton's in
that burning house back there. We must try to save him!'

Already the troika had disappeared into the dark. 'Look!'
said von Wahlczek, pointing. Above the curve of the snow-
laden bushes a pillar of orange flame, smoke-tipped, reared itself torch-like against the sky. 'Come,' he told her, slipping
his arm into hers, 'I take you back to your father. If Boulton
is still living, de Bahl will rescue him.' Tears blinded her: she
let von Wahlczek help her into the sleigh. The sleigh moved
off, passing as it went the two remaining men who were trudging through the snow back to the Castle.

They had driven some way in silence when von Wahlczek
said: 'I fear you think badly of me.' A sob was his only answer.
'We're all in the power of this man,' he went on. 'For me there
was no choice. I had my orders and I had to carry them out.'

'You knew it was a trap,' she burst out furiously. 'You
knew they meant to kill him. Yet it was you who used me to
lure him there.'

With a meditative air he laid his whip across the horse. 'It
was Boulton or me. Believe me, I could not help myself. De
Bahl has it in his power to send me to my death. A word from
him to the new government in Austria, for example, about —

about certain matters in my past, would doom me as surely as
if you were to put a bullet through my head. I'm sorry about
Boulton because I like Englishmen. But he was playing a
dangerous game. First Miklas and now, as it would appear,
Metzger. Believe me, Miss Melissa, you waste your sympathy
upon this English spy.'

Her eyes flamed. 'If there's one thing I hate more than a
coward, it's a hypocrite. Please leave me alone — I don't want
ever to speak to you again.'

He shrugged his shoulders and plied his whip once more, for
they were approaching the ramp leading to the Castle gates.
The great doors were closed, but on recognising the sleigh the
guard tugged the bell and they were admitted. The outer yard
was full of movement, with men passing to and fro and figures
silhouetted against the double line of lighted windows marking
the barrack rooms. As they drove through to the inner yard
they were aware of a great bustle under the Boyar Tower. The
sentry outside the Green Turret clanged the bell and brought
Charles running. Behind him Melissa perceived a familiar
figure in a velvet smoking jacket. The next moment she was
in her father's arms.

She was hysterical, incoherent. But in the quiet warmth of
the living-room, with Stephen's arm about her, she blurted out
her story. The high colour slowly ebbed from his face as she
proceeded, but he said no word until she had finished. Then
with icy calm he spoke. 'We're surely in a spot, honey,' he
said. 'But what matters most to me just now is that I've got
you back safe and sound with me, and that's an ace point. For
the time being we're at the mercy of this scoundrel de Bahl and
there's nothing very much we can do about it. But if we come
out of this mess I'll get that big gazeebo, if it means following

him to the ends of the earth and costs me my last dollar. And let me tell you this — the British will help. Did Boulton tell you that he was a Secret Service man?'

She shook her head. 'He used to be an Air Force officer — that's all I know about him. But von Wahlczek says he's a spy.'

'De Bahl's a notorious espionage chief, isn't he? — the thing sticks out a foot. He was a fine young fellow and he gave his life for his country: if it's any consolation to us we can be sure the British will avenge him — they go to the bat for their own people, I'll say that for them.'

She was fumbling in her jumper. 'He took de Bahl's wallet — he gave it to me to look after for him. You'd better have it, Steve.' She drew the wallet from her dress, holding it for an instant as the thought came to her that it was almost the last thing those strong, brown hands had touched before their tragic parting.

Selmar took the wallet. It was full to bursting: money, a wad of English five-pound notes — Stephen counted them: there were sixty of them, three hundred pounds; visiting cards, a mass of letters. Melissa picked out the typewritten slip, the message destined for Geneva, and unfolded it. 'It's the telegram about the frontier incident,' she said. 'He went off to send it — he could write it out again, I guess. It's probably on the way by this.'

Selmar put on his glasses. '"Widespread reprisals feared," eh? That's the raid, of course.' He tapped the paper. 'Here's the fuse and the raid's the charge that's to blow the price of armament stocks sky-high everywhere. Humph!'

He began to turn over the remaining contents of the wallet. 'There's nothing much here,' he muttered disgustedly, glancing through one letter after the other. Then he uttered a sharp

exclamation. 'Gosh, I knew it. It's a market flutter. Look!'
He held up a sheet of note-paper covered with figures. 'Here's
a list of the gang's orders to their brokers in London, Paris,
Amsterdam, New York, mainly New York — de Bahl, Grenander, Frangipani, von Wahlczek. Well, I may not be very
familiar with the European stock exchanges, but the New York
market I do know something about.' He glanced at the paper
again. 'Whew! They've certainly gone a flyer — they're in up
to their necks. The rats! As long as they can start an arms
boom, they think nothing of sending all these boys to their
deaths.' His eyes clouded over. 'And to think that we're
corralled here, that there's nothing we can do to stop it.' He
shook his head. 'It's too tragic about young Boulton. The kid
had guts, and he could use his brains. If only we had him here
with us now — why, Melissa!'

His daughter had fallen into a storm of weeping. 'Why,
honey?' he said and slid his arm about her shoulder. Presently
she dried her eyes on the handkerchief he offered, stood up.
'Come with me to my room, Steve,' she said.

Arm in arm they climbed the turret stair to her bedroom,
where she led him out on the balcony. The snow had left off.
The moon had not yet risen and the stars hung like jewels in
the wide expanse of sky. Far below, where the white trough
of the frozen river curved away, the Ferryman's House was a
dying beacon with sparks that whirled up and little figures
moving against the glow. In the immediate foreground two
discs of light moved rapidly along the river road towards them
to the jingle of sleigh bells — it was the troika being driven
furiously towards the Castle.

But Melissa's eyes were fixed on the burning house. With a
shuddering sigh she spoke. 'It's like a Viking's funeral,' she

murmured, then clung to her father. 'Oh, Daddy!' she sobbed.

He remembered she had not called him that since she was a little child. 'Melissa, darling!' he said, greatly moved.

'It's as though I'd left a part of me down there to die with him,' she faltered through a mist of tears. 'He loved me, Steve, and I loved him. Now he's gone, and I just can't face it.' She shivered. 'Let's go inside. I'm so cold.'

Back in her room, he told her that Charles was getting her some dinner. She didn't want to eat, she protested. When Stephen tried to reason with her, she exclaimed impatiently: 'Oh, won't you please leave me alone? Can't you see I want to cry?'

Seating himself on the bed, he drew her down beside him. 'Listen, Melissa,' he said. 'You say you loved this Englishman. All right. But remember, he was on a job and for that job he gave his life. They got him but we're here to carry on in his place. That's what he'd want us to do, isn't it? Or do you think he'd like us to quit?'

She sniffed forlornly. 'You know he wouldn't.'

'Then chin up, sweetheart! Grieving won't help him, and it certainly won't help us. There's a damnable conspiracy going on here; what we have to do is to put our two heads together and see if we can't stop it, as young Boulton was trying to do. Am I right?' She nodded and groped for his handkerchief. He patted her hand. 'That's the spirit, darling. Now look. For the time being we're isolated here. When I gave Grenander his cheque he promised to take the guards off. But I might have known — the moment he got his hands on the money, he broke his word. The men are still confined to their quarters, Charles said, so that the only ones who can move in and out of the Castle freely are de Bahl and the heads, I guess.

Which means that we've a pretty poor chance of getting a message out. I wonder if one could fix Ali . . . .'

'Bribe him, is it?'

'Sure.'

'He's devoted to the Baron. You could never trust him. But there's von Wahlczek.'

'Von Wahlczek? He's hand and glove with the Big Boy, surely?'

'He hates him, he told me so himself. Besides, he's a rat — I think you might "fix" him, as you call it.'

Her father was radiant. 'Can do. But how are we going to get hold of him?'

For some time they had been conscious of a growing tumult rising faintly to their ears from the interior of the Castle, a medley of shouts and cries. The noise was louder now and Selmar, going to the staircase door, opened it and listened. 'It sounds as if they were holding a meeting,' he remarked as the distant hubbub welled into the quiet room. 'Shut the door,' said Melissa. 'I can't bear to hear it.'

He closed the door and came back to where she sat on the bed. 'Well, they haven't started yet, by the looks of it,' he observed. 'But it's kind of warming up, I guess.' He seated himself beside Melissa again and put his arm about her. She did not speak or look at him, but one tear after the other rolled down her face. So they sat in silence for a long spell as gradually the distant clamour died, and the only signs of life were the long fingers of the Russian searchlights across the river, framed in the balcony window as they restlessly groped in the sky.

A Tap at the Window

UNDER the four-square tower which was the main entrance of the Castle the great doors were shut when the troika came cavorting up the ramp. No guard was visible, and one of the men in sheepskin busby who descended from the sleigh had to ring a series of peals on the bell before a wicket opened in the gate and a gold-tressed monkey-jacket gleamed in the light of the lamps. 'Son of a hundred fathers, child of the pig!' the Baron snarled in his fluent Arabic as he flung aside whip and reins; 'why am I kept waiting? Is there no sentry? And why are the gates closed at nine o'clock?'

As his master clambered to the ground Ali recoiled before the livid face, smeared with blood and grime. With eyeballs that glistened whitely in the dimness, '*Sidi*,' he said in an awed voice, 'they shut the gates an hour before the time by order of the *Mefetish*.' *Mefetish* or Inspector was Ali's Arabic title for Grenander. 'There is trouble among the workers, *Sidi*. The word goes round that the German *Hakim* and the English foreman were murdered tonight and the men are murmuring — there is much disorder.'

With a grunt de Bahl stepped through the wicket, pausing under the archway to contemplate the scene. The outer yard was full of men standing about in groups, arguing, gesticulating. He did not enter the yard but, turning right-handed under the tower, took the stone corridor that led to the staff wing. There were voices in the office, but he passed it and entered his bedroom. Here Ali was waiting to relieve him of his outdoor things. A can of hot water stood in the basin and, stripped to his shirt, he washed the blood and grime from his face.

His mouth was swollen. He lingered for a moment before the glass, examining the bruise and staring sourly at the burning eyes and leaden countenance reflected in the mirror. 'Ali!' he called presently and made a cryptic gesture with his fingers to the servant. The native went to a drawer, and returned in a moment with a tiny hypodermic syringe, which he handed silently to his master. Rolling back his shirtsleeve, de Bahl plunged the syringe deep into his forearm, already marked by a series of tiny punctures, then sank down wearily into a chair. On noiseless feet the servant came forward and, kneeling, drew off his master's wet top boots, replacing them with dry shoes he had brought with him. Sitting back on his heels with his limpid black eyes wistfully regarding the other, he said: 'My lord is tired. Will my lord eat?'

The Baron shook his head. 'A man thwarted me tonight and now he has escaped my vengeance,' he observed sombrely. 'That has never happened to me before, Ali!'

'My lord is all-powerful!' replied the Tunisian, dropping his eyes.

'A woman lured me,' said de Bahl, frowning. 'When a woman steps between a man and his goal, Ali, it is rarely that he attains it.'

'Women, it is well known, will turn a man's bones to water, *Sidi*!' was Ali's humble rejoinder.

'I allowed myself to be diverted from my purpose this evening and I feel it bodes evil.'

The Tunisian threw him a diffident glance. 'I told my lord I was against this undertaking from the start. I read the stars and saw no good there.'

A warmer tint had crept into the Baron's face. 'Bah!' he said. 'I am not guided by the stars. I write my own fate and tell the stars what they shall prophesy. The cigarettes, Ali!'

The servant darted to the bedside table and brought an open box of the big cigarettes. Lighting one and inhaling deeply, his master said, 'Where is that uniform I bought in Bucharest?'

'In the black suitcase, *Sidi*.'

'Unpack it and hang it in the wardrobe. I may have need of it. Wait! It will do presently.' He smoked for a moment in silence. 'Now pay heed to what I say. At seven o'clock to-morrow evening we start off across the river. At six o'clock you will take my smallest suitcase with one suit and a change of linen to that disused outhouse that stands against the Castle wall beyond the Boyar Tower. You know it?'

'Yes, *Sidi*.'

'You will find the caterpillar tractor there. You will place my suitcase in it and wait there for me. Frangipani and I will join you there as soon after seven o'clock as possible. Is it understood?'

'It is understood, *Sidi*.'

'And not a word of this to anyone, is that clear? Neither to the *Mefetish* or von Wahlczek or any of them.'

'My lord's wish is law.'

He leaned forward and pulled the servant's ear. 'It had better be, imp of Shaitan, or I'll tear your black tongue out by the roots.' He stood up. 'Now find me a clean collar! I must go to the office!'

With a firm tread he moved to the mirror, his equanimity quite restored. He was smiling secretively as he ran a comb through his white pompadour of hair and sprayed eau de Cologne on a clean handkerchief. 'At six o'clock tomorrow,' he reminded Ali, and tripped blithely out.

In the office Grenander and von Wahlczek, drinking slivovitz, the local prune brandy, heard his rasping cough as he approached along the corridor. Von Wahlczek was saying: 'You know what he's like when he's been at the smoke. He was high, I tell you — his eyes glittered like fireflies. He's never so violent as when the stuff's cold in him. With the men in this mood we're in for trouble, Axel....'

His companion motioned him to silence as the door opened. 'Man is born to trouble as the sparks fly up,' said de Bahl gaily. 'But I don't see that that is any reason for you two to be glooming here as though the world were coming to an end. *And* getting fuddled on that filthy schnapps. The affair's in train, you know. As Wally has probably told you, Axel, the Englishman did the job for us and our code message is already on its way to Geneva.' He rubbed his hands together cheerfully. 'My friends, by this time tomorrow the pot will be boiling.'

The two men exchanged dumbfounded glances. Except for the bruise on his lower lip, the Baron was his normal self. Behind his old mask of imperturbability his air was as alert, his eyes under their heavy lids as calm and confident, as ever. 'But I thought you told me that Boulton took that code telegram when he stole your wallet?' said von Wahlczek.

'He did. But I could write it out again, couldn't I?'

'Without the code? You didn't telegraph it in plain language, I hope?'

The Baron laughed quietly. 'I sent it in code, of course. Any message I turn into code myself I do not forget. A simple feat of memory. You should cultivate a photographic memory, Wally. It has its uses.' He drew on his cigarette. 'As for my wallet, it has gone up in flames at the Ferryman's House, I'm afraid.'

Grenander's small eyes stirred into life. 'They're both dead, then?'

'Burnt to a crisp, if what's left of Metzger is any proof. They were able to reach him as he was lying just inside the door: they identified him by his watch and the buckle of his belt with his initials, which were found close by. They haven't been able to get in far enough to reach the Englishman — the place is a furnace. I doubt if they'll ever find anything of him — you and the doc made a good job of it, Wally.'

'What about the police?' Grenander demanded.

'The gendarmes and the frontier guards are at the scene, of course, together with every man, woman and child from the village. There's nothing to connect Metzger with us here for the moment, and if they inquire at Mirapol all they'll discover is that he left some days ago to go to Bucharest on business. Meanwhile, the post-mortem will in all probability reveal the fact that he was murdered, and if it doesn't, you can leave it to me to spread sufficient rumours to confirm our message to Geneva. As for the Englishman, they're unlikely to find enough of him to trace him to the Castle, but we must be prepared for a visit from the captain of the frontier guards. Tomorrow, therefore, we resume work on the restoration of the Castle until dark, when we'll issue the arms and despatch the party across the ice.'

The engineer scowled. 'With all the gendarmes and frontier

guards assembled at the fire, better we strike tonight, I t'ink.'

De Bahl shook his head. 'We must give the kettle time, my friend. First the incident to start it simmering, then, at twenty-four hours' interval, the raid to bring it to boiling point, as it was planned. It is all to the good that the attention of the frontier authorities will be focussed for the next twenty-four hours on the investigation into events at the Ferryman's House. For the rest, our original plan developed in agreement with Rypnik and Vassenko must stand. While the first party under young Vassenko makes a feint at crossing the river opposite the Castle, the main body led by us will slip over at the point we selected at the bend of the stream half a mile above the Castle. The Ukrainian leaders will be here this afternoon. I shall tell them I've decided that zero hour is 7 P.M. tomorrow night.'

'If we can vait so long,' Grenander rumbled. 'The men are pretty excited. First they get a rumour that Metzger's been killed by Russian spies, then they hear that Boulton's missing, too, and since then there's been no holding them. The Englishman was pretty popular round the Castle, you know — the boys regarded him almost as one of themselves.' He raised his hand. 'Listen to them outside, how they buzz like a lot of angry vasps!' A growing volume of sound was audible from the yard. 'They're for starting at vunce — tonight,' he explained.

'I'll not have the ship spoiled for a ha'porth of tar,' declared de Bahl crisply. 'This little venture of ours is not going to go off at half-cock if I can help it. On the other hand, we can't risk the gendarmes arriving and finding the place in a turmoil. I'd better speak to them — I can manage Rumanian, if I can't Ukrainian.' So saying he unlocked a drawer of the desk from a key on his bunch and drew out a bundle of greasy papers. 'These are the papers of that Russian spy we dealt with the other night,' he said to von Wahlczek. 'Wally, you know where Boulton bunks. There's no one in the barrack-rooms just now — they're all out in the yard. Plant those papers in Boulton's locker, will you? And if he has any of his own, bring them to me here. But be quick about it while the coast is clear.'

He pitched the bundle to von Wahlczek, who hurried out. 'Open that window, will you?' he bade Grenander.

'They're in a dangerous mood, Alexis,' said the other.

'If that's all that worries you,' retorted the Baron contemptuously. Shouldering him aside the Baron plucked the casement wide. 'Men,' he cried in a clear, rather shrill voice that came echoing back from the battlements. 'Men, listen to me, your leader!'

The hubbub in the quadrangle ceased on the instant. All faces swung towards the figure framed in the lighted window and there was a concerted rush towards the speaker. 'A dastardly crime was committed at the Ferryman's House to-night,' said de Bahl when silence fell. 'Doctor Metzger, German Vice-Consul at Mirapol across the river, was struck down by a Soviet assassin.'

A shout of rage arose from the yard. From the front rank of the crowd massed under the window a man sprang forward. 'And how long shall we idle here at the mercy of the Red scum?' he vociferated furiously. 'What are we waiting for to avenge our German brother?' A chorus of voices answered him. 'Forward! Forward to the Ukraine!'

'Peace!' cried de Bahl. 'It is I who command here. We start when I give the word, and not before!'

'We wait too long!' the spokesman of the rabble shouted back. 'We have the arms, we have the men. Forward tonight!'

The crowd bellowed its approval, shouting in a medley of languages, 'That's it! Forward tonight!'

With unwavering calm the Baron replied. 'So you want to see the inside of a jail, do you?' he trumpeted. 'At any moment the gendarmes may come to the Castle inquiring into this crime. If you don't wish to see your vengeance frustrated, you'll disperse now. Tomorrow evening, maybe ——.'

But fresh protests cut him off. 'Tonight!' they cried. 'Forward across the Dniester tonight!' Others yelled: 'Where's the murderer? Hand the dirty Red over to us! Kill him!' There was a surge of men outside the window.

De Bahl faced them unmoved, waiting for the wave of passion to be shattered out upon his rock-like impassivity. Gradually the air of authority he radiated asserted itself and quiet fell again. 'The murderer perished in the fire at the Ferryman's House,' he announced. 'He is known to you all, a vile bondslave of Moscow who wormed himself into your confidence as into mine.'

'The name,' came a great shout back. 'Give us the name!'

'It is the English foreman, Boulton.'

A howl of execration went up, mingled with defiant shouts and cheers. It was a full minute before the Baron could make himself heard. 'This miserable ruffian has met with his just deserts,' he cried. 'We have long suspected him to be a Soviet emissary, and I should like his comrades of the barrack-room to search his locker for evidence of his association with our enemies. Meanwhile, all I ask of you is a little trust and a little patience. Tomorrow morning let the Castle present once more the spectacle of peaceful industry so that no suspicions may be aroused if the frontier guards come prying, and when night falls, on my faith as your chief, men, I will lead you across the river. Is it agreed?'

A wild cheer came rolling back at him: the men began to disperse to their barrack-rooms. The Baron stepped back and closed the window. 'The curs!' he said to Grenander. 'All they needed was a crack of the whip.'

The engineer looked at him anxiously. 'It's for tomorrow, then?' he said, adjusting his glasses.

'Tomorrow it is. There's no drawing back now.'

'And the full moon?'

'They'll be across before it's up. The moment they knock off work at four, we'll start with the issue of arms and ammunition. You'd better see the foreman about getting the orders out at once.'

Still Grenander lingered. 'They'll be massacred to a man.'

The Baron laughed softly. 'We should worry, Axel.'

His companion grunted. 'You say that, but how do *we* manage?'

'You and I will keep together. We will slip away at the first opportunity. From eight o'clock on Frang will have the tractor waiting for us at the main gate.'

'And the plane?'

'Everything is in order. It will be standing by for us at the Chisinau airport.'

His companion indulged in a throaty chuckle. 'You t'ink of everyt'ing, by yimini!'

De Bahl dropped his eyes. 'I try to, Axel.' He gave his little cough.

But the other still had something on his mind. 'And which of us is to lead the column? This old fool Rypnik will be with the first files: he will expect one of us to accompany him.'

The Baron smothered a yawn. 'Wally's a soldier. His place is in the front line.'

'It will not be so easy for him to get avay.'

'Is it so important?'

'Ve don't vait for him, then?'

'We don't wait for anybody, Axel.'

Von Wahlczek's monocle glittered in the doorway. 'Rypnik and the other delegates are here,' he announced stolidly.

'Where are they?' de Bahl asked.

'At the main gate. And pretty excited.'

'I'll see them here — alone. Send them along, will you?'

Von Wahlczek gave him a quick glance, shrugged his shoulders and disappeared. 'Best I go see about those orders now,' said Grenander, draining his glass. 'You arrange with Frang about the tractor, yes? Eight o'clock outside the main gate.'

'Leave it to me.'

'Best ve stick together vunce ve start tomorrow so there's no slip up, I t'ink.'

'Definitely.'

The Swede clumped out.

'We don't wait for anybody, Axel,' de Bahl said softly, looking after the retreating figure, and smiling.

Up in Melissa's bedroom in the Green Turret Stephen Selmar looked at his watch. 'A quarter to ten. I don't believe they're planning to start tonight,' he said. He patted his daughter's hand. 'Come on, honey. I'm going to take you downstairs and have Charles fix you a sandwich and maybe a glass of wine.'

She stirred unwillingly from her immobile pose. 'I don't want to eat, Steve — truly I don't,' she told him. 'I guess I'll go to bed.' Then he felt her grow rigid in his encircling arm. The balcony window was softly rapped — a shadowy figure was visible outside. With a scream Melissa sprang to her feet. 'It's Don!' she cried, and flew to let him in.

The Cat's Ninth Life

As MELISSA pulled the balcony door open, Boulton swayed towards her and would have fallen if she had not caught him. Her father running to her aid, between them they lifted him on the bed. He was hatless, with hair and eyebrows singed, his face as black as a sweep's, and a very dirty handkerchief was bound round one of his hands. 'Quick, Steve, he's fainted,' she cried, and would have sprung up but for a grimy hand that restrained her. 'I've some brandy in my room,' exclaimed Selmar.

Boulton had opened his eyes. 'Make it a whisky and soda, a large one,' he murmured — though he panted with exhaustion his air was still faintly mocking. Selmar hurried out. The young man smiled through his grime at Melissa's anxious face. 'I'm all right,' he gasped. 'Just petered out, I guess — that last bit over the roofs. It's — extraordinary. Whenever you see me — so grubby!' He closed his eyes wearily.

She laid her face against his. 'Oh, Don, darling, thank God, you've come back to me. When I saw you lying there among the flames . . .'

With a little sigh he snuggled his cheek against hers. 'Now that I've found you again, I feel like never letting you go.'

She held him to her in her arms. 'Don't talk. Rest.'

His hand stroked her hair. 'I was out of my mind with

anxiety about you when I found you'd disappeared tonight.
I thought you were trapped upstairs, but the rooms were
empty.'

'De Bahl carried me off ——'

'I guessed he had when I met the troika coming back and
saw that he was alone: I had just time to duck down behind
the hedge before he spotted me.'

'He thinks you're dead. He said he saw you lying dead on
the floor.'

His laugh was rather hollow. 'They're not so easily rid of
me.' He closed his eyes. 'I thought I'd never get here, through
the snow. But I had to discover what had become of you.
I've been outside the main gate for ages, trying to get in.
Then a party of Ukrainian delegates arrived and I managed to
dodge in behind their sleighs.' His eyes were open again and
smiling up at her. 'By rights I should have gone to the gendarmerie before coming here. But I couldn't rest until I knew
you were safe.' He fondled her hand. 'Now that I know you
are, nothing matters, not even that I've fallen down on my job.'

Selmar bustled in with a tray. 'Here you are, my boy,' he
said, bringing him his drink. 'Down that! No, stay as you are!'

But the young man insisted on struggling up. 'I'm all right,
sir.' He raised his glass. 'Well, here's to the cat's ninth life!'
He drained his drink at a gulp. 'My goodness, I wanted that.'
He grinned through the black smears that streaked his face.
'Don't look so serious, Mr. Selmar. They can't kill me, you
know.'

'They seem to have had a darn good try,' said Stephen.
'Melissa here has been crying her eyes out over you. What
happened? And why aren't you dead?'

He laughed. 'That was the little cherub's doing — you

know, the one that sits up aloft. I expect Melissa has told you
how we tackled that scoundrel — well, when I went downstairs
to investigate, there was this fellow Metzger just coming in at
the front door. I told him to put his hands up, but I didn't
notice he had a gun. He was a game fellow and promptly let
fly at me, missed and then — maybe his gun jammed — he
flung it at me just as I fired. His gun crashed the lamp and
took me on the temple. When I came to, there I was on the
floor with the flames all around me and the doctor lying dead
just inside the door.'

'But weren't you terribly burnt?' said Melissa.

'Only one of my hands. And my boots and gaiters are a bit
singed, but nothing to speak of.'

The girl ran to the travelling medicine chest that had been
her father's gift to her. She returned with alcohol, lint and
adhesive tape. 'Let's see this hand of yours,' she bade Boulton.
He winced as she unwrapped it — it was badly blistered.
'And you climbed over the roofs with a hand like this?' she
demanded as she cleansed it. He nodded, biting his lip. 'It
wasn't so pleasant, but I managed it. The raid's for tomorrow
night,' he told Selmar. 'I heard de Bahl telling the men just
now: he was making a speech to them in the outer yard. There's
been a spot of trouble with the boys over Metzger's death,
apparently. De Bahl denounced me as Metzger's murderer
and said I was a Soviet spy. The chaps didn't half howl for
my blood. It'll make it a bit awkward getting out again.'

Melissa was just completing her bandaging. 'You're not
thinking of leaving the Castle again, surely?' she said anxiously.

He laughed, but rather shortly. 'Ah, but I am. We have
to stop this raid. It'll mean lying doggo for a bit and watching
my chance, but I must get word to the gendarmerie before

nightfall tomorrow, when the fun is due to begin. Indeed, the sooner I can warn them the better, because the frontier guards are pretty scattered and in the village itself there's only a sergeant and a couple of gendarmes. To bring these madmen to their senses, the Castle will have to be surrounded, and that means troops. And with the roads in their present state ——'

'There's no need for you to go,' the girl broke in. 'Can't we find some other way of sending a message?'

He shook his head. 'There's no one I can trust. We can't afford to run any risk.'

'What about von Wahlczek? He hates the Baron — he told me so himself.'

'Melissa thinks he could be squared,' Selmar put in.

'He's yellow,' Boulton agreed sombrely, 'he'll do nothing to imperil his own skin. He may hate de Bahl, but he's scared to death of him. You could try what a bribe would do, but I wouldn't trust our Wally even then. He might serve as a second string, but it'd be a precious weak one. No, there's only one person to take that message to the village, and that's me.'

'But can you get out?' asked Stephen dubiously.

'If I got in, I can get out — it stands to reason,' the young man answered placidly. 'I'll get out all right, although, as I say, I'll probably have to bide my time — maybe, later on in the night, while they're changing the guards before dawn. The main thing is that we know the raid's fixed for tomorrow night. We have to stop it, therefore it will be stopped.'

Selmar nodded. 'I expect you'd like a wash. Charles will take you down to my bedroom and fit you out with clean things of mine. Meanwhile, stay under cover. The Baron thinks you're dead, so see that you stay dead as far as he's concerned.'

There was a knock at the door. The valet's rather woebegone face was thrust in. 'Herr von Wahlczek is below,' he accounced.

'Von Wahlczek?' Selmar echoed, glancing from his daughter to Boulton. 'What does he want?'

'He does not say, monsieur. He asked for monsieur.'

Stephen's face cleared. 'It's in the bag,' he pronounced.

'You intend to see him?' Boulton asked, frowning.

'You bet!'

'Don't trust him, Steve!' cried Melissa.

Her father laughed. 'Not me. I'm going to bribe him.'

'You'll lose your money, sir,' said Boulton crisply.

Selmar stuck out his chin. 'Watch me.' Then he handed the guest over to Charles and went quickly downstairs.

Money Talks

'You asked for me?'

Von Wahlczek, nonchalantly smoking a cigarette in the Green Turret lobby, turned to see Selmar descending the stairs. He dropped his cigarette on the floor and set his foot on it. 'If I'm not intruding...'

'Come in,' said Stephen, ushering him into the living-room. He fetched a box of cigars from the desk. 'Cigar?'

'Thanks.' Von Wahlczek, still elegant, his rough outdoor clothes notwithstanding, gave him an inquiring glance as he helped himself from the proffered box. He seemed a little puzzled by his host's manner, non-committal, bland almost. He lit his cigar at the match Selmar struck for him then, affecting to scrutinise the tip, remarked, 'I was anxious to hear that Miss Selmar is none the worse for her adventure this afternoon.'

'I feel sure my daughter will be grateful for your inquiries,' Stephen replied stolidly.

Said the visitor, looking about him, 'If I might sit down...'

'By all means.'

They found chairs. Von Wahlczek said after a pause: 'I have been your guest, Mr. Selmar: it has been my privilege to break bread with you. I am a gentleman, and I find myself much distressed at having been the unwilling instrument of the occurrences of this afternoon.'

With a detached air his host was carefully piercing his cigar. 'From what Melissa told me,' he observed judicially, 'I gather that you, like ourselves, are not a free agent.'

The other snatched at the olive branch. 'This is very magnanimous and very like your charming daughter, Mr. Selmar.' He cleared his throat. 'It is because I am in this false position, do you see? that I wish to make to you what amends I can.'

Stephen laughed dryly. 'That shouldn't be difficult.'

'Please?'

'I say, you can very easily make amends — by getting us, my daughter and me, out of this place as soon as possible.'

He shook his head firmly. 'That, I fear, I cannot do.'

'It would only mean a wire to the American Legation in Bucharest.'

'Impossible!'

'At a pinch it would probably be sufficient if you rang up the local police.'

He sighed and shook his head again. 'It would be as much as my life is worth.'

Selmar flicked a fragment of ash from his sleeve. 'And if I made it worth your while?' he inquired casually.

'You couldn't — I should be signing my own death warrant. You don't know the man we have to deal with, my dear sir. He has ears everywhere: if I should betray him he would certainly find it out and that would be the end of your poor friend Otto von Wahlczek. And anyway,' he went on confidentially, 'you can take it from me that the present restriction of your liberty will be over very soon. Now that Grenander has his cheque, he will not trouble you further — in fact, between ourselves, I think I can promise you that at this time tomorrow you will once more be master in your own house.'

Selmar's blue eyes rested on him steadily. 'You mean that de Bahl and his friends will have cleared out?'

Von Wahlczek indulged in a series of rapid nods. 'All gone' — he made a gesture with his hands as though shovelling something away — 'Pouf! Like that! You'll have the place to yourselves. But that remains a secret between us, eh?' He laid a well-manicured finger on his lips. 'There is, therefore, as you see, no need to alarm your legation or to summon the police — you would find the Rumanian police very troublesome.' He blew a cloud of smoke. 'Nevertheless,' he went on, 'there is perhaps a small service I can render you — because, as I say, I am a gentleman and anxious to show myself not unworthy of your esteem and Miss Melissa's in spite of the part I was forced to play this afternoon.' He paused. 'Mr. Selmar, I flatter myself I know Americans. I have not yet visited your great country, but I have many American friends and, well, I know you to be a practical people. You appreciate the value of money, *nicht wahr*?'

'When we have any....'

The other laughed extravagantly. 'Excellent, excellent, a millionaire's joke. But it seems to me, my dear sir, that even though you are a millionaire, you would not be averse from making a great deal of money quickly.' He stuck his glass in his eye and surveyed him expectantly.

Stephen shrugged his shoulders. 'Who wouldn't?' His tone was casual, his eyes half-closed against the smoke curling upward from the cigar firmly grasped in his teeth. But between their lids his eyes were very watchful.

'If I were to let you into a secret, a secret that would enable you to realise an immense profit on the Stock Exchange, would it be worth paying for?'

His manner was tense. The American remained unmoved. 'It'd depend on the secret,' he remarked, shifting his cigar round in his mouth.

Von Wahlczek leaned forward in his chair. 'Suppose I gave you the names of certain stocks that will have a colossal rise on the New York market within the next twenty-four hours?'

Selmar shook his head. 'I don't play the markets.'

'You don't understand, Mr. Selmar. This is not speculation: it's certainty.' He moved his hands. 'This murder will be a political sensation. As soon as the news becomes known armament shares will soar. Moreover, as I may tell you in confidence, arising out of this incident, certain events are impending that will lead to an even more sensational rise. As it happens, I'm in a position to know the stocks that will be principally affected. You're a rich man, you have abundant capital. Profiting by my advice you can make what I think you call a killing.' He beamed at him through his monocle.

'Humph.' With a thoughtful air his companion flaked the ash from his cigar. 'And how do you propose that I should avail myself of this tip of yours? The telephone's cut off and I can't reach a cable office.'

Von Wahlczek glanced cautiously around. 'The others must know nothing of it, but I can smuggle a message down to the telegraph office if you wanted to cable your broker.'

Selmar fingered his moustache, contemplating him appraisingly. 'And the price of the information?'

'That I would gladly leave to you, *lieber Herr*, except that I find myself in an unfortunate predicament. Time has hung heavy on our hands here and — well, to be frank, I have allowed myself to be drawn into various games of écarté with

our friend, Grenander — in short, I find myself in immediate
need of — ten thousand dollars.'

The American shook his head. 'Too high.'

Von Wahlczek stiffened. 'I would remind you, Mr. Selmar,
that I am an officer and a gentleman — it's not becoming that
we should haggle like a couple of horse-dealers. The modest
sum I ask will enable me to settle my debt of honour and at
the same time, as I hope, put the ocean between myself and
this abominable ruffian who calls himself the Baron de Bahl.'

'I'll pay you ten thousand dollars to do as I asked you, to
notify the American Legation, and at the same time the local
police.'

The other blanched. 'No,' he said between clenched teeth.
'No! I have told you already, this I dare not do. But a cable
to your broker in New York I will send and for the profit you
will make, ten thousand dollars is not too high a price.'

Selmar rubbed his nose reflectively. Then he took from his
pocket a battered leather portfolio and drew from it a packet
of paper, clean and crisp. 'I tell you what I'll do,' he said
firmly. He held up the wad. 'There's three hundred pounds in
English money here. Five-pound notes — you can change 'em
anywhere. Send off the cable I'll give you for my broker and
the money's yours. You can pay for the cable out of it and
keep the change. Three hundred pounds — fifteen hundred
dollars — isn't a bad tip for a messenger, my friend.'

He spoke with a snap, his manner blithe and keen. Von
Wahlczek had stood up. He stared at the packet of notes in
Selmar's hand. 'All right,' he said at last rather sullenly, and
put out his hand.

'Not so fast!' Selmar observed. 'I shall want proof that my
cable has actually been sent. Half now and half when you

bring me my receipt from the telegraph office.' Wetting his finger, he counted through the notes, making two packets of them. His companion glared at him. 'You don't trust me. *Herr*?'

The other chuckled. 'I'll say not. How do you think I got rich? I never trusted anybody in my life — not in money matters, anyway. That list of securities, please!'

He beckoned with his finger. Glowering still, von Wahlczek eased a slip of paper from his inside pocket and gave it to his companion, who thereupon placed one of the two wads of notes in his hand. 'Now for that cable! Excuse me!' Selmar went to the desk, unlocked a drawer, found a small book and for the next five minutes the tapping of the portable that stood on the desk was the only sound in the room. Then Selmar pulled out the sheet, detached it from its carbon and handed it to the visitor.

Von Wahlczek put in his eyeglass to examine it. 'But it's in code!' he objected.

Stephen laughed. 'I don't want to boast, but my name stands for something on Wall Street. Don't you realise that if I cabled orders of this magnitude in plain language it would immediately affect the price? Use your brains, man!'

The other indulged in a surly nod and buttoned the cable away. 'You shall have your receipt within the hour. In the meantime, not a word to anybody, you understand?'

'Trust me!' said Selmar, and von Wahlczek stalked out. A moment later an indignant voice spoke from the door. 'Steve!'

It was Melissa. 'I was outside and heard every word,' she said. 'I could scarcely believe my ears. Why, Steve, to think that you'd let these gangsters run you into their miserable

speculations! And was it really necessary to pay that horrible
von Wahlczek all that money for something we already know?
Have you gone crazy, or what?'

He chuckled. 'That money wasn't for the tip, sweetness, it
was for acting as messenger.'

'You mean to say you give a man three hundred pounds
just to send off a cable?'

He began to laugh. 'It wasn't my money, honey — it was
our friend the Baron's, those five-pound notes he had in his
wallet. You see,' he went on chuckling heartily, 'that fellow
von Wahlczek gave me an idea. I just had to send that cable.'

'I don't see anything of the kind. Don't you realise you're
every bit as bad as they are, buying these shares for a rise?'

'I'm not buying,' he gasped out.

'Not buying?'

He shook his head, holding his sides and shaking with
laughter. 'That stuffed shirt doesn't know it, because my
cable to Bob Sylvester is in my private code. But I'm going
to sock this bunch of chisellers where it'll hurt them the most,
and that's plunk in the old wad. We're not buying, sweetheart — *we're selling!*'

She stared at him, her eyes shining, her lips breaking into
the tenderest of radiant smiles. 'Oh, Steve, you old devil!'
she exclaimed rapturously. 'You darling, foxy old devil!'

'It's a bear raid!' he cried. 'Watch me force the price back
tomorrow! We may be prisoners here, but your old man still
knows a trick or two. Money talks, they say, but I'm going to
make it holler. Raid or no raid, I can hold these punks, I guess;
but they're relying on this filibustering expedition into the
Ukraine to convulse Europe and send arms stocks rocketing,
and if Don can fetch help in time, whew! the cat'll be right

among the pigeons. Bucharest is seven hours ahead of New York time, so, as the New York market opens at ten, we shan't have any news until some time after five o'clock tomorrow evening. But then, I promise you, you'll see the fur fly. Whoopee, I haven't enjoyed myself so much in years! And what makes it such fun, de Bahl, the big cheese, is footing the bill!'

A Shot in the Dark

SINCE the hammering of the gongs had doused the last light and banished the last burst of sound in the men's quarters, a great stillness had rested over the Castle. For the first time for many nights no stealthy noises under the Boyar Tower broke the silence, no caterpillar treads thumped thunderously up the ramp to the gate, and the chugging of the electric light dynamo in its cellar behind the Green Turret tapped as quietly upon their accustomed ears as the tick of a clock in a sickroom. Boulton remarked upon the stillness. 'They're giving them a good night's rest. It's the calm before the storm,' he observed.

Refreshed with food and in a clean shirt of his host's, though he had resumed his shabby working kit, he seemed to have regained his old spry air, Melissa observed, when, on von Wahlczek's departure, she and her father joined Boulton upstairs. As their living quarters on the ground floor were always exposed to a surprise visit from de Bahl or one of the others, they had decided that Boulton might best remain unobserved in Stephen's bedroom until such time as he had to leave the Castle. The night was dry and clear, and a full moon high in the sky made everything as bright as day. But clouds were coming up, and the young man's plan was to wait on the chance of the moon's being obscured to make his way across the roofs to the main gate. There he would remain in hiding until he saw an opportunity of slipping out.

It was snug in the turret room with the curtains closed and their three chairs drawn up round the great tiled stove. Boulton, pipe in mouth, absorbed in examining the contents of the Baron's wallet, had not spoken for some time. His air was relaxed. It was Selmar who seemed to be on edge, chewing his cigar to rags and continually jumping up to go to the door and listen.

For the sixth time since he and Melissa had come upstairs after von Wahlczek's visit, Stephen consulted his watch. 'Half-past eleven nearly!' he fumed. 'He won't come now.'

'It's a brilliant idea, sir,' said Boulton, holding up one of the letters in the wallet against the light. 'Nemesis striking from across three thousand miles of ocean to rob these callous ruffians of their ill-gotten gains — there's something God-like about it. But' — he wagged his head dubiously — 'I didn't want to dash your hopes when you told me about this cable of yours, but I've a secret feeling that we've seen the last of our dashing friend von Wahlczek.'

'There's a hundred and fifty pounds waiting for him to collect when he brings that receipt.'

'Agreed. But the hundred and fifty he's already had from you will be more than enough to take him out of harm's way — why, it'd pay his passage to South America, which, as old Sam Johnson said about patriotism, seems to be the last refuge of every scoundrel. You know the saying about rats leaving the sinking ship!'

'But, gosh darn it, he's in this flutter up to the ears like the rest of them. Surely to goodness he'd want to stick around and see it through?'

The Englishman shrugged his shoulders. 'You may be right. But if he'd sent off that cable he'd have been back with your receipt long before this. I admire the diabolical ingenuity of your plan to turn the tables on de Bahl and his pals, and I wish you luck with it. But what happens on Wall Street won't affect the position here. The raid's going forward — in fact, when they find the market turning against them, they'll be more determined than ever to push on with it, to keep the pot a-boiling.'

He held up the wallet. 'I'll take charge of this, if you don't mind. There are one or two things here they'd like to look at in London.'

'Go ahead,' said Selmar. 'It's your prize. Or Melissa's.'

Boulton's eye sought out Melissa with a great tenderness. She met his gaze with a brave smile. 'My particular worry just now,' said he, shuffling the papers together and restoring them to the wallet, 'is whether I can get the troops here in time. This place is so out of the way that there are no troops anywhere within easy reach: one point in our favour is that, as soon as it hears about Metzger, the Rumanian Government is likely to start moving troops over to this region of the frontier as a precaution. You see, Soviet Russia has never recognised the Rumanian annexation of Bessarabia, and the Rumanians are always a bit windy about this frontier. Whatever happens, it looks like being a darn close call. Though they have no real chance of success, once the raiders get across the ice they'll find plenty of hotheads among the Ukrainian Nationalists ready to join them and the fat'll be properly in the fire.'

He knocked out his pipe in the wood box beside the stove. 'But that's not my headache, that's up to our Foreign Office,' he remarked cheerfully. 'My particular pigeon was to find out what our old friend, Baron de Bahl, was up to, and that I've accomplished. But I shan't consider my job done until I have him safely under lock and key. If I can pull that off, I shall feel I haven't lived in vain.' With a sombre air he sucked his empty pipe. 'So many better fellows than I have had a go at it and failed. And some of them never came back.'

'The British have been after him for a long time, have they?' Stephen put in.

'Ever since the war. What a run he's had for his money!' He frowned. 'He's a killer, a man-eating tiger, and like a man-eater raiding a peaceful Indian village, wherever he appears he spreads terror, destruction and death.' With mechanical movements he began to fill his pipe from the battered pouch he took from his pocket. 'You know,' he went on, 'the de Bahl type, like the man-eating tiger, used to be an isolated specimen. But today, with the rule of violence spreading throughout the world, it flourishes like the green bay tree. The wild beasts have come out of the jungle in troops to attack the villages, and honest folk can no longer sleep quietly in their beds. Well, you can't handle these people with kid gloves any more than you can a tiger that has tasted human blood. Actually, I never killed a man before but I've killed two since I came to Orghina, and I'd do it again if I had to.' Raising his eyes to Selmar, he went on rather shyly, 'I'm telling you this, sir, because I don't want you to think of me as a sort of gunman, a cold-blooded brute who makes nothing of shooting a man as I had to shoot that poor devil of a doctor this evening, and sitting down calmly to a good dinner after.'

Selmar clapped him on the arm. 'Don't give a thought to it,' he said rather gruffly. 'If I had a chance of putting a bullet into that smug villain, de Bahl, I'd take it, believe me! And that goes for his fat friend the Swede, too.'

Boulton laughed and stood up. 'Let's take a look at the moon,' he said and, going to the window, peered through the curtains. 'It's clouding up nicely,' he announced. 'I'll have to be on my way.'

'I'll just see what Charles has done about that ladder...' Stephen bustled out.

'Ladder?' echoed Boulton, looking at Melissa.

'To reach the battlements from my balcony,' she explained. 'I thought it would spare your poor burnt hand.'

He smiled at her. 'You think of everything.'

'Why did you speak to Steve just now as though you weren't coming back?'

'I wasn't speaking to Steve.' He flushed. 'I wanted *you* to understand.'

'Then it wasn't necessary. All my memories of you are sweet, Don. But you haven't answered my question.'

His eyes fell away. 'I'll come through all right, Melissa.'

'Don't fence with me. Tell me the truth. It's dangerous, isn't it? One of those hit-or-miss things?'

He shrugged his shoulders. 'I shan't fail, because I can't afford to fail.' He paused. 'I have to get out of the Castle now, before it's light. If I fell into the hands of the men, they'd tear me to bits, after what they've been told about me.' His teeth closed doggedly on his pipe. 'But I'll manage somehow.'

She said desperately, 'I've been so happy tonight, sitting with you over the fire. Why do you have to go? What's the Ukraine, what are all their stupid politics, to you and me? You've done enough, Don. Why should you risk your life again?'

'It's my job,' he answered stolidly. 'A man has to stick to his job, whatever the risk, Melissa. It's my job and I have to finish it.'

'Do I mean nothing to you?' she cried passionately. 'Don't you care for me at all?'

He sighed deeply. 'God, and how much!' Then she was in his arms. 'It's madness,' he told her, brushing her brown hair back from her forehead, 'but it's lovely. Because nothing can come of it, you know, my love. An ex-Air Force flight lieutenant on three hundred pounds a year and Stephen Selmar's daughter — it doesn't make sense.'

'Money isn't everything, Don.'

He shook his head. 'Isn't it, though! Look at your father, pulling strings from here. I can only capture old de B. and chuck him in a cell. But your old man can beggar him, and not only him but everybody even remotely connected with this ramp.' He drew her to him and laid his face against hers. 'Don't let's spoil this little moment of happiness by talking of money, darling. Let me just hold you and pretend it's for ever.'

She clung to him desperately. 'Don, I can't let you go. It seems to me that I never began to live until I met you.'

He smiled down at her. 'I've felt that way ever since that first morning at Monte Carlo, but I never dreamed that you did. Since I had to give up flying nothing has seemed to matter particularly. I've been in some tight places in this funny job of mine, but I never seemed to give a damn whether I came through or not, not because I'm especially brave or especially reckless, but because I'd always found existence pretty drab and hardly worth living for. But since I've known you everything's changed. It's as though someone had come along with a damp cloth and rubbed all the dirt and grime off the world, leaving it bright and shining. And I want to live — gosh, how I want to live! It's such a big world and I've seen so much of it, without liking any of it very much. Yet all the time it held someone like you, and I never knew it. God, it's like looking at the sunrise!'

She had listened to him with lips parted, her head thrown back, eyes shining. Now she dropped her eyes and he found himself thinking what long and glossy eyelashes she had. 'And still you want to leave me?' she murmured huskily, fingering a button on his rough tunic.

He nodded. 'And you're going to tell me to go!' he said.

She looked up at that. 'Go then, Don, and God go with you!'

He took her in his arms again. 'I'll be thinking of you every minute of the time,' he whispered, 'and the memory of this moment will be like a light to guide me.' He stooped to her lips. 'Now I must be on my way and you must go to bed.'

A garden ladder was reared on Melissa's balcony. Ragged brown masses of cloud had drifted across the face of the moon, but beyond their edges the sky was full of light. Charles had come up with a flask and a packet of sandwiches: Stephen and Melissa watched silently as he helped the Englishman on with the suède jacket Stephen had lent him. Charles himself had contributed a béret and a dark scarf — muffled up to the eyes Boulton held out his hand to his host. 'Good night, sir, and thanks for everything,' he said. 'With any luck you'll see me back before dark this evening.'

'Take care of yourself, son. You'll be a sight for sore eyes.'

'*A tantôt*, Charles, *et merci!*'

'*A tantôt, monsieur, et bonne chance!*'

He took Melissa's hand and held it for a moment without speaking. 'Come back safe, Don,' she said. 'Don't make me go through another night like this is going to be.'

He gave her his vagrant smile. 'I'm the bad sixpence —
I always turn up. *Éteignez*, Charles!'

The light went out and plunged the room in darkness.
They saw him for an instant framed in silver in the doorway,
then he lifted his arm in salute and was gone. Charles was
visible for a moment peering out, then he in turn disappeared.
Sundry bumping noises followed and the end of the ladder protruded into the room. Stephen and Melissa helped to bring
it inside. The light went on again.

'*Ça y est!*' said Charles, shutting the door and drawing the
curtains. 'He was up the ladder like a squirrel, that one. A
chic type!' He shouldered the ladder. 'With monsieur's permission, I go to bed. Monsieur and mademoiselle will be
wise to follow my example, for it seems we may have an exciting day tomorrow.'

'Good night, Charles!'

'Good night, monsieur; good night, mademoiselle!' With
Stephen holding the door for him, he edged out with his burden.

Melissa had not spoken. Lost in a reverie she was staring
at the window as though her eyes could penetrate the curtains
into the night beyond. Her father put his arm about her.
'I like your young man. He gives me a good feeling. He's
reliable. He'll be back — you see if he isn't.'

'I want to marry him, Steve,' she said.

He bent his keen gaze at her. 'What does he say?'

'He says it's impossible.'

'Hitched up already, is he?'

She shook her head. 'No. But he hasn't any money, and
he thinks I've too much.'

He grinned. 'So you have. Never mind, sweetheart —
it's a better reason for turning you down than if you had none.'

She squeezed his arm. 'Darling Steve, you always think of such consoling things to say.'

Then they heard the shot.

It was a single shot fired in the distance. It shattered the silence of the night and died away, to be succeeded by the deathly stillness reigning about them, so absolute now that they could hear the ring of the sentry's feet on the frozen path far below.

Von Wahlczek Comes Back

IN THE early morning sunshine the Castle hummed with activity. Hammers rang and saws whirred, and there was the metallic scrape of shovels from the courtyards where lines of men were clearing the snow away and dumping it into wheelbarrows. To Melissa after a sleepless night of torturing anxiety all this busy stir was sheer agony. It took her mind back to their first days at Orghina when life was pleasantly enlivened by the fascinating prospect of a treasure hunt, the Baron's pleasant companionship and the propinquity of a not too unpresentable young man.

The blank silence following upon that solitary shot ringing out of the night was hardest to bear. She would have run down to the yard to find out what it portended had not Stephen forcibly restrained her. If anything had happened to Don, they would learn of it soon enough, was his argument: if he had survived the shot but had been recognised on escaping, any curiosity they displayed might reveal the fact that they had harboured him and jeopardise the success of his mission. So they had remained upstairs in Stephen's bedroom, crouched in the window with the light out, gazing down upon the black quadrangle at their feet, their ears strained for any sound from the massive pile about them.

But no sound came. Little solace the silence brought to

Melissa, realising as she did that they were too far removed from the main gate for their ears to detect any noises less penetrating than a shot, the shrilling of whistles or the clanging of the great Castle bell. She had visions of guards with lanterns sallying forth into the snow and picking up a poor broken body lying at the foot of the battlements.

She was forced to play a part to induce her father to leave her and go to bed. She let him think she was pacified by his declaration that the unbroken hush was a sure sign that Don had got away; but her heart was heavy as she climbed the winding stair to her room. Lying in bed with the vast expanse of moonlit firmament framed before her eyes in the open door-way of her balcony, she fancied she saw him there again, alert and imperturbable in his fur cap and stained working clothes. The whole of their adventure at Castle Orghina was so fantastic it might have been a dream. Must it be that he was merely a part of it, an unsubstantial figure melting into nothing with the coming of day? Day appeared in the sky as she lay there tossing, the last grey shadows of the night dissolving into an angry dawn that flooded her chamber with crimson fire. At long last the clash of iron on iron gonged the Castle into reluctant life and she knew that another day had begun. A critical day for them all, for her in particular, feeling as she did that on its outcome her whole happiness depended.

At breakfast with her father, she saw through the dining-room window a procession of men emerging from the Boyar Tower carrying planks, bags of cement and the like. Most of the men seemed to be engaged on such menial tasks. She remembered that Don had told her that there were not ten skilled hands among the remaining working force, and mentioned it to Stephen. 'Camouflage, in case the police come

nosing around,' he growled. 'But wait till it's dark and they'll
be goose-stepping, the whole pack of 'em!'

There was no news, he told her. Charles had questioned the
orderly who had brought the day's supplies, but the man pro-
fessed ignorance of any untoward happening in the night.

Suspense was everywhere. Soon after breakfast they had a
glimpse of Grenander disappearing under the archway of the
Boyar Tower, and a little later the Baron picked his way delicately across the inner yard among the busy snow-shovellers.
He did not so much as cast a glance in the direction of the Green
Turret but with preoccupied mien bobbed out of sight under
the tower.

Stephen was nervous. He paced up and down the living-
room champing on his cigar. He was halfway through his
second cigar of the morning when he called Melissa to the
window. 'Hell's begun to pop!' he exclaimed. 'Look at Frang,
will you?'

She put down her knitting and joined her father at the
window. The stocky figure of the Italian was visible scudding
across the quadrangle, his hands full of telegrams. His dark
eye rolled and the perspiration glistened on his swarthy face
in the dazzling sunshine. He, too, vanished under the Boyar
Tower. Stephen glanced at his watch. 'London and Paris
are open by this,' he remarked, 'and these are the first re-
actions, I guess. New York doesn't open till 5 P.M. our time.
I wonder if we shall hear anything before the balloon goes up.'
He ground his teeth together. 'That pill, von Wahlczek!
And I thought I had those ruffians where I wanted them!
Gosh, how I hate to miss the fun!' Melissa tried to pacify him.
But he would not be pacified, fretting and fuming and stamping
up and down.

Lunch was a listless affair, with Stephen frowning down at his plate and his daughter starting every time Charles came in with the dishes and making the merest pretence of eating. And then the miracle occurred. They were at coffee in the living-room when without warning von Wahlczek stood before them. 'Not a word,' he said impressively, closing the door behind him. 'I couldn't get here before. De Bahl has gone to the telegraph in the tractor and Grenander's snoring like a pig in the mess ...'

Selmar had jumped up. At the sight of his irate contenance von Wahlczek laughed softly. 'You thought I'd run out on you, didn't you? You tell yourself you kiss good-bye to your hundred and fifty pounds, no?'

'Did you send off that cable?'

'But of course. At about ten-thirty last night.'

'And the receipt?'

'*Voilà!*' He placed a printed slip of paper on the coffee tray. 'My messenger was shut out of the Castle on returning and couldn't get in till this morning.'

Stephen had snatched up the receipt and was scrutinising it eagerly. 'Good!' he exclaimed. He was radiant. He drew an envelope from his pocket and dropped it on the table. 'There's the balance of your fee. The other hundred and fifty pounds — count 'em!'

Swiftly von Wahlczek ran his eye over the wad of notes, smiled seraphically and stuck them in his tunic pocket. 'Thanks,' was his languid acknowledgment. 'You know,' he went on, 'you could have safely made it the ten thousand dollars I asked and never missed it. Our friend Metzger is on all the front pages this morning: the worthy Doctor dead has kicked up a fuss he'd never have achieved in life. The bourses are in a turmoil, government bonds dropping, munition stocks shooting up. Hitler has flown from Berchtesgaden to consult with his generals, all Rumanian troops are confined to barracks, the Russians are reinforcing the Ukraine garrisons.' He laughed triumphantly. 'And it only begins! Wait till New York opens this evening, wait especially for the latter part of the session, because before the market closes there'll be news that'll send all arms securities soaring like a firework display.'

His voice rang exultant, his rabbit mouth was curved in a gleeful smile. Without warning his listeners saw his face change. His eyeglass rattled against his jacket, his eyes widened with fear, his chin dropped. At the same instant a slim hand swooping down between Melissa and her father as they stood with their backs to the fire snatched up the cable receipt where Stephen had laid it down among the coffee cups.

It was de Bahl. He had entered unperceived from the dining-room. In a tense silence he scrutinised the receipt. 'New York, *hein*?' he rasped in a choking voice, tapping the paper with his finger. 'The sentry on the main gate reported that a man tried to get out last night, but the lying hound declared he scared him back with a shot. Who took this telegram?'

His gaze rested on Selmar, then shifted, when the American remained silent, to von Wahlczek, who had lost all his normal poise. The perspiration pearled on his high forehead and ran down his livid cheeks: under the neat moustache his lower lip dangled vacuously. De Bahl's countenance darkened. 'It was you, was it?'

'No, no, I swear...'

'Who took this telegram?'

The shifty eyes dropped away. 'One of the Ukrainians.'

'The name?'

'Starenki.'

The heavy brows came down. 'I might have known you wouldn't have had the guts yourself. What did this telegram contain?'

Von Wahlczek seemed past speech. He made a feeble gesture towards Selmar, who took it as an invitation to speak. 'It was to my broker,' he said calmly.

The Baron's eyes returned to the paper. '"Robsyl New-york,"' he read out and nodded. 'Yes. I recall the address now. I remember you have sent cables to this address before. Well?'

Stephen shrugged his shoulders. 'Herr von Wahlczek thought that, as a business man, I might be interested in making a little money in the market.' He outlined a vague movement of the hands. 'He was good enough to give me a quiet tip...'

De Bahl's glance swung suspiciously from one to the other. 'In which, I'm bound to say,' Selmar went on, 'he showed a greater sense of loyalty than you've displayed, seeing that we've been partners since the start.'

The other seemed nonplussed. 'Do you mean to say...' he began.

Stephen nodded briskly. 'Just that. After all, a flutter's a flutter — why be selfish about it?'

'Then this cable of yours?'

'Following your lead, Baron, I'm in this operation of yours for all the traffic'll stand.'

The Baron made one of his wheezing noises. 'A true American, eh? Business first, and all that! So your high sentiments melt away when there is a profit to be made, my friend?'

Stephen moved his shoulders. 'I don't see why I should turn down the chance of making a little easy money,' he retorted, assuming a sulky air. 'Von Wahlczek tipped me off and I've gone banco on his information. I hope you're not going to tell me I've slipped up?'

De Bahl's good humour seemed to be restored. 'On the contrary,' he said amiably. 'I'm in for as much as I can afford myself, but if you'd care to carry me, say, for another hundred thousand dollars.... There's still time to get New York on the telephone before the market opens.'

Selmar shook his head. 'Sorry, Baron, but I've gone my limit.'

'And how much does *he* get out of it?' He jerked his head contemptuously in von Wahlczek's direction.

By this von Wahlczek had regained some of his composure. 'If a gentleman cannot reimburse a debt of hospitality by disinterested service...' he began, mopping his brow.

The Baron tittered. 'Sure, sure.' He swung to Selmar. 'What did you have to pay the weasel?'

Stephen drew himself up. 'I wouldn't have insulted a man in von Wahlczek's position...'

A dry laugh answered him. 'All right. But if you won't tell me, he will!' Plunging forward in a lightning movement he grabbed von Wahlczek by the collar. 'To the office, rat! You and I and the good Axel must have a little conference!' Brushing past Melissa and driving his captive before him, he swept out.

Left alone with Melissa, Stephen said, 'How was my act?' She smiled at him lovingly. 'It was swell, Steve.'

He blew out his cheeks. 'It was a close call. I wonder what's going to happen to the poor devil if they find that money I gave him just now. I bet old de B. has the numbers of those notes.'

By way of response, Melissa opened her fingers. The wad of notes was reposing there. 'They were in his outside pocket, sticking out — I was terrified the Baron would spot them, so I fished them out as they pushed past me. It seemed safer.'

Her father clapped his arms about her. 'Bully for you!' he cried. 'Just wait till New York opens, sweetheart! We're going to town!'

She drew a deep sigh. 'I don't give a damn where we're going until I know what's happened to Don,' she answered brokenly.

Monsters out of the Night

THE clock on the mantelpiece chimed five times. Selmar took out his watch. 'There we go!' he remarked. 'New York's opening now. Your throw, sweetheart!'

It was quite dark outside now, the evening wild and blustery, though dry. As they sat at the backgammon board in the living-room, they heard the wind go romping through the quadrangle. An hour before the gongs had called the men from work. Normally to the trample of feet and the clatter of tools being laid aside as the men trooped off to their barrack rooms a period of peace succeeded. But on this evening the whole Castle seemed to be astir with noises vague and undefined.

Suddenly Charles slid into the circle of light cast by the table lamp. 'Monsieur!'

'Well, Charles?'

'They've taken off the guards.'

'Ah!' said Selmar, his eye on the board. 'Then they're preparing to start. Do you suppose one can go as far as the outer courtyard and take a look?'

'Monsieur had better wait while I reconnoitre.' He glided away. Melissa put down the dice-box. 'It's no good, Steve. I can't go on. Oh, why hasn't Don showed up? I can't stand this suspense.'

Stephen continued to study the pieces. 'Chin up, honey!' he said composedly. 'My money's on Don and it's your throw!'

Notwithstanding her distress, Melissa found herself studying her father. His fresh, good-humoured face was untroubled as he bent over the board in the strong light. There was an inch-long ash on the end of his cigar, which he smoked with evident enjoyment and unruffled calm: he seemed to have no difficulty in concentrating on the game. Looking at him, she realised that this was the sort of strain familiar to him in his business career. Imperceptibly he had slipped back into the groove of his old life in which courage, the ability to take lightning decisions and nerves of steel had laid the foundations of his fortune.

She cast the dice. Stephen said: 'I'm banking on Don arriving with the marines in time to stop this raid. It's either that or they get off before de Bahl discovers that another kind of raid is on in New York: otherwise, the old devil is apt to come nosing around to find out just what was in that code cable of mine and we're in for a spot of trouble.' He threw and restored the dice to the box. 'I can't move. It's your turn, Melly.'

Melissa uttered a little cry. 'Charles, how you frightened me!'

The valet had come back. 'I go as far as the outer yard,' he announced tersely. 'They are distributing arms in the barrack-rooms. There are men in steel helmets in the yard, and mitrailleuses on little carriages and bombs which they hand out, two to each man.' He smote the back of the settee violently with his hand. 'Shall we do nothing to stop them? Poor deluded fools, the free Russian proletariat will rise as one man in its might and blast them out of existence.'

Selmar had his eye on the clock. 'I didn't realise that you were a Communist, Charles,' he observed absently.

'All the dead of the World War are Communists,' was the passionate reply. 'I count myself among them, for, if my body survived, my soul lies there with my three brothers under their wooden crosses. Can we not prevent this crime? Are we to stand by and see these unfortunates butchered to make a profit for this de Bahl and his *canaille*?'

'Profit, Charles?' His employer shook his head. 'You can take it from me, they'll make no profit. For the rest...' He shrugged his shoulders. 'How long will it be before they start, do you think?'

'Some time yet. The men are not yet formed up. They wait for their leaders.' His air was sullen.

'Where are the Baron and the rest of them?'

'In the office. They telephone.'

Stephen's eye lit up. 'I wonder whether New York has come through yet. Is there any way of finding out? If von Wahlczek were anywhere around, he might tell you, if you said I was inquiring.'

Charles nodded sombrely. 'I go. Meanwhile, let me thank monsieur for the great consideration he has shown me while I was in his service...'

'But, Charles, you're not leaving us?'

A shadow seemed to fall across his face. 'If all other means fail,' the lanky figure spoke from the threshold, 'I shall know how to act.' So saying he opened his hand, showed a flat, black object that lay there and vanished into the lobby, shutting the door behind him. Stephen jumped up. 'Charles, come back!' He swung to Melissa in consternation. 'My gracious, did you see what he had? It was a bomb.'

But Melissa, rigid in every line, was staring past him at the door beside the fireplace, the door that led to the dining-

room, and beyond it to the staff wing. There was a step outside, a throaty cough, then the door was violently flung back.

The Baron was dressed for out-of-doors in his fur cap and
pelisse. Leather leggings protruded from under his long overcoat. He walked up to Selmar and fairly hissed at him, 'So
you'd trick me, would you?'

Selmar's glance, keen and very cool, took in the glittering
eyes, the leaden pallor of the face, the fluttering hands, of the
man confronting him. With a challenging air he stuck his
cigar in his mouth. 'So what?' he enunciated clearly.

De Bahl seemed to struggle for words. His chalky countenance was distorted with fury: like a fox's mask it seemed to
snarl, with nose ruffled and mouth dragged down in a grimace
that bared the teeth. 'They're forcing the price back in New
York,' he chattered. 'It's a bear raid. That code message you
bribed this treacherous rat to send for you, where is it? I
mean to see it, and I want to see it in plain language.'

With elaborate nonchalance the American shook the ash
from his cigar. 'I'm afraid you're out of luck — I didn't keep
a copy.'

The Baron's clenched fist whirled above his head. 'Don't
lie!' He seized the other by the shoulder. 'You're coming to
the telephone with me now to call your New York broker and
cancel those orders. And you'll tell him to buy, d'you hear?'

Selmar shook him off. 'I'll see you in hell first. And keep
your hands to yourself!'

A demented flame appeared in de Bahl's face. He ground
his teeth together and snarled. 'So you'd defy me, would you?
You poor fool, I'll show you who's master here. I'll make
sausage meat of you and feed you to the Castle dogs, you and
your daughter too. But first you'll give those orders to your
broker, d'you understand?'

'Not on your life,' said Stephen. 'And now get out!' His hand dived into his pocket, but quick as a flash a pistol was thrust in his face.

'Steve!' Melissa screamed, and flung herself on her father, dragging him back.

'Stay where you are, both of you!' the Baron shouted.

At that moment heavy footsteps reverberated on the flags of the lobby. A figure in a steel helmet loomed up in the doorway. It was Grenander, his pudgy face crimson, his pig-like eyes under the steel visor distraught with fear. 'Frontier guards,' he cried, 'two sleighs of them, approaching along the river road!'

De Bahl lowered his weapon. 'Tell them at the main gate to parley with them but not to admit them. Their commander may be permitted to enter as far as the guard-room: I will see him there. Are the men ready?'

'Ready and standing by!'

'Warn them to be prepared to move off at a moment's notice. Jump to it, and quickly.'

Grenander stormed out. The Baron looked at his watch. 'Are you coming to the telephone with me?' he said to Selmar.

The latter shook his head. 'The jig's up, you know. This is only the start of it.'

Footsteps thundered without. Grenander poked a panic-stricken face in the door. 'Tanks!' he gibbered. 'They're approaching from all sides!' He did not wait, but flung out. The Baron, with a face of death, elbowed Melissa and her father from his path, and rushed out after him. Rapturously, Melissa gazed at Stephen. 'Oh, Daddy, he's done it!' she murmured in a dying voice.

Her father laughed gaily. 'Didn't I tell you?' He caught her arm. 'Let's go to your room. There's a view from there.'

The wind was savage on the balcony. Beyond the river the Russian military posts explored the sky with long pencils of light from their searchlights, but in the plain below their observation post the night lay like a black mantle with only the faint pallor of the snow to lighten it. Out of the darkness eerie noises, a great awe-inspiring clanking and chugging, came rumbling, and presently they made out bizarre objects, swart against the ubiquitous whiteness, lurching rapidly from several convergent directions towards the Castle. Suddenly without warning the balcony was bathed in blinding light. A projector mounted on one of the crawling monsters blazed full upon the Castle, and turret, buttress and pinnacle, every lichen-encrusted stone, was revealed in its dazzling beam. Stephen was staring in fascination at the scene when his sleeve was violently plucked. 'What are we waiting for?' cried Melissa. 'Don't you realise that Don must be back? Come on down!'

Under the Boyar Gate

As THEY crossed the inner quadrangle they perceived through the dividing arch the redness of torches on the age-worn masonry of the enclosure beyond. The wind blew the flames out like plumes: in the ragged glare the yard with its heaps of dirty snow was seen to be a jostling mass of helmeted figures. Overhead the oblong of sky was criss-crossed with the wheeling beams of the searchlights, picking out details of buttress and chimney-stack as they swung. The air was loud with the crepitation of the advancing tanks.

They went as far as the central arch and scanned the crowd for any sign of Boulton. But it was evident that the Castle was still inviolate — the lines of men in steel helmets, with rifles slung on their backs, the little sleds strapped down with canvas, proclaimed as much, and here was Grenander, his red face streaming with perspiration, pushing his way through the press: if Don Boulton had arrived he must be still outside. De Bahl was nowhere to be seen, but they had a glimpse of Ali running from group to group, as though in search of him.

There was much confusion and noise. But as they stood there in the shadows under the arch the tumult began to abate and they were aware that here and there in the rabble heads were turned and fingers pointed aloft. From somewhere outside the Castle — probably from the high ground beside the

river — a searchlight had come to rest on the roof of the Great
Hall. Between roof and parapet a solitary figure stood bathed
in silvery radiance. Melissa clutched her father's arm. 'Steve,'
she whispered ecstatically, 'it's Don!'

With hands planted on the coping stone he calmly surveyed
the scene. Then the searchlight swung on and he was lost to
view. But the crowd below had recognised him and a medley
of angry cries went up. When the travelling beam wheeled
round once more, halted for a spell and caught him in its glare
again, he was no longer alone. A tall figure was beside him.
The Englishman raised his hand, then in ringing tones spoke a
phrase. Melissa could not understand the language — it was
Rumanian or Russian, she supposed.

The quadrangle was in a ferment. Rifles were unslung, fists
brandished, infuriated shouts hurled back. Then Boulton's
companion stepped forward and with his first few words quiet
was restored — it was von Wahlczek. He spoke and turned to
Boulton, who cried in English: 'Tell them I don't know enough
of their language to make a speech in it: tell them that I'm not
a Bolshevik spy but their friend who has come to warn them.
The Castle is surrounded with machine guns trained on every
gate: tell them if they don't want to be massacred to lay down
their arms.'

He paused while von Wahlczek translated in a growing din.
There was a sudden scuffle in the crowd. Beside a man who
held a blazing pine torch aloft a rifle was pointed, then struck
down, and from their post under the arch Stephen and Melissa
saw Grenander, rifle in hand, struggling with the crowd who
were trying to disarm him. Boulton was speaking again.
'Your leaders have betrayed you,' he proclaimed. 'They told
you you were to free the Ukraine — comrades, it's a lie. These

men are speculators in armament stocks, whose only object is to make money on the Stock Exchange at the expense of your lives. Tell them what I say, von Wahlczek!'

The searchlight had circled on again by this, and von Wahlczek's voice resounded out of the dark. The light came back as Boulton resumed, 'The Castle is surrounded and the Soviet frontier guards are everywhere on the alert. Don't be less clever than your leaders, who are looking for the first chance to abandon you and save their skins. If you don't believe me, find if you can the Baron de Bahl!'

He uttered the last words gaily with hand upraised to shield his eyes from the glare, and stepped back to make way for von Wahlczek to interpret. At that moment a detonation rang out from below and a bullet screamed in the air. Grenander had broken away from the group about him and stood out in the light of the guttering torches, a smoking rifle in his hand. High up on the roof, von Wahlczek, fully revealed in the blazing beam, was seen to clutch violently at his chest, fall half forward and collapse upon the parapet. But the parapet was low and his fall carried him over: he went crashing down to the flagged yard below, even as the light swung on and darkness once more enveloped the battlements. Simultaneously a tremendous uproar started outside, with the bell at the main gate pealing and a vast hammering at the doors. Panic seized the crowd. On all sides men were flinging down their rifles and scrambling for safety. Now the very atmosphere trembled to the thunder of the tanks and presently, with shattering suddenness, the whole interior of the Castle, the inner and outer quadrangle alike, was bathed in blinding light as the searchlights sent their beams through the main gate on the one side, and under the archway of the Boyar Tower on the other. With arms upraised men were seen scudding this way and that in the brightness, fleeing before lines of steel-helmeted soldiers in unfamiliar uniforms pouring in from two directions.

Melissa, her mind numbed by the tragedy she had witnessed on the roof, felt her arm clutched as Stephen rushed her back to the shelter of the Green Turret. From the entrance they watched the soldiers driving the men who had bolted into the inner court back to the outer yard. The gates of the Boyar Tower hung from their hinges where they had been battered in, and the projector on the tank outside, blazing like a great eye, shot its long beam under the vaulted entrance, lighting up the groined roof and below it the moss-grown flags of the carriage-way, where a wooden hatch marked the cellar entrance. A party of soldiers directed by an officer was trying to lift the flap.

Then Melissa saw Don. He came running to them across the quadrangle, a jaunty, lithe figure. 'The nightmare's over,' he said when he stood before them. 'Mr. Selmar, you're master of Castle Orghina once more.' But his eyes were on Melissa.

'Are you all right, Don?' she said.

He nodded, but rather bleakly. 'I should feel happier if I could put my hands on that ruffian de Bahl. He seems to have vanished into thin air. Grenander, too. With that poor devil von Wahlczek dead, it looks as if all the heads had escaped us.' He broke off. 'But wait! I think I speak too soon.'

He was looking towards the mosque with its low porch. The door was open: lights and figures moved about inside. A party of soldiers was emerging, dragging a rotund, protesting figure in a steel helmet. 'Grenander!' the Englishman exclaimed, and darted forward.

The engineer was almost apoplectic with rage. 'You find

dot de Bahl and I settle him for you, the dirty, double-crossing rat!' he roared. 'He and dot no-good Italian were to take me with them in the tractor to Chisinau, where de Bahl has an airplane chartered, and they ran out on me, by heck. You call the airport at Chisinau and you'll catch him, Don: he's not gone above the hour. And tell the Rumanians that it was I what gif you the tip. Maybe they make it easier for me, yes? You vant information about the famous Baron de Bahl, you kom to me and I tell you plenty.'

Boulton laughed. 'Where did you find him?' he asked the officer in French.

'Hiding in the cellars under the mosque.'

'You didn't come across anybody else down there?'

'No, monsieur.'

The prisoner was hustled away. Boulton rejoined Stephen and Melissa. 'De Bahl's bolted,' he said. 'Apparently he's making for Chisinau, where he has a plane waiting — I'll have to phone the airport at once and get them to hold him.' He was staring out across the courtyard to the Boyar Tower. 'I wonder if those fellows realise that there's enough explosive in that cellar to blow the Castle sky-high,' he observed.

The party they had remarked before investigating the cellar entrance under the Boyar Tower had successfully removed the hatch, and the last of them was just disappearing down the trap. Just then a Rumanian officer emerged from the shadow of the wall and strolled unconcernedly towards the gateway. 'I really think they should be told,' said Boulton, and called to the officer, 'Hey, monsieur!'

But the officer paid no attention. He walked resolutely on into the path of light under the arch until he found his way blocked by the yawning cellar entrance. He paused an instant and his wheezing cough, echoing under the vault, came back to them. 'God!' cried Boulton suddenly. 'It's de Bahl!' Even as he spoke a figure stepped out of a small doorway under the gateway and stood silhouetted in the bright light between the officer and the gate.

It was Charles. '*Halte!*' he cried, and flung up his hand. A pistol roared thunderously under the arch. Charles was swallowed up in the shadow lying black along the edges of the lighted path, but something flat and black, something that smoked and hissed, fell on the carriageway and, ricochetting off the stones, rolled down the open hatch. Boulton flung his arms about Melissa. 'Back!' he shouted, driving her and Selmar across the threshold of the lobby. 'On your faces! It's a bomb!' Crouching there, they saw de Bahl spring forward. Then there was an ear-splitting roar, the air rocked and the earth trembled, and their ears were filled with the crash of falling masonry and the clang of broken glass.

Epilogue in the Fog

'POTTS, my old salt!'

'Blow me down if it ain't Mr. Boulton! Lord love a duck, sir, it's quite the stranger you are!'

'What a stinking day! Do you never see the sun in this cursed town?'

'We 'ad it fine over Christmas, sir. But it's been nothing but fog ever since the Noo Year.' He closed the front door and shut out the blurred vista of the square and the raw January air. The warmth and light of the hall surrounded them. The doorman helped the visitor out of his heavy ulster. 'Miss 'Ancock was jest askin' if you 'ad arrived,' he confided. 'You know the way, sir?'

Miss Hancock was seated at her desk typing with flying fingers. She wore mittens and a grey wool sweater. There was fog in the room. An electric fire glowed redly. 'So it's you, is it?' she remarked, and typed to the end of the line. 'Why haven't we had your expense account? How do you suppose we can run this office when people like you are two months behind with their expense sheets?' She whipped the sheet out of the machine, ran her eye over it rapidly, dropped it in a tray and, in the act of inserting another sheet in the typewriter, looked up. Her expression softened. 'Why, Don, what's happened to you?'

He made a wistful grimace. 'It's a fearful suit, I know. I had to buy it off the peg in Bucharest. The only clothes I had when I left Orghina were those I stood up in, and they made me look like Robinson Crusoe dressed in skins. There was this damned investigation by the Rumanian War Ministry — I couldn't go before the board looking like an Arctic explorer.'

She said, 'It isn't your clothes, silly.' She leaned back in her chair and surveyed him critically. 'You're not ill, are you? The old shoulder hasn't gone back on you?'

He had helped himself to a cigarette from the open packet on the table and was turning it over in his fingers, staring down at it with a brooding air. He shook his head. 'You look — well, different,' she proclaimed. 'Older, or something.' She paused. 'Don,' she said, 'it's not by any chance that you've grown up?'

Very deliberately he tore the cigarette across and dropped the bits in the waste-paper basket. 'It might be that,' he answered glumly. He raised his eyes to her appealingly. 'Hanky,' he said, 'life's gone sour on me. I want to get away. Away from telephones and wireless, away from palace hotels and a pack of painted women. Can't you persuade the Chief to find me another assignment like that one I had in the Sudan?'

'But you're only just back!'

'I don't give a damn. I'll leave tomorrow — tonight, if you like. Now I know what those fellows feel like when their girl chucks them and they go out shooting big game in wildest Africa. I'd grab three months' leave and go on safari myself, if I had the money.'

She smiled at him indulgently. 'Haven't you had all the big-game hunting you want lately? After all, de Bahl was a pretty good specimen to bag. I suppose he's really dead?'

'I guess so. The explosion wrecked the whole of that wing of the Castle, the mosque as well as the Boyar Tower — the Selmars and I would have been for it, too, if we hadn't had a fifteen-foot wall of solid masonry to protect us.'

'And that Frenchman who threw the bomb?'

'We never found him, either. But for him de Bahl would have got away. We discovered in the ruins of the wall outside the Castle the remains of the caterpillar tractor with Frangipani, one of the gang, and Ali, de Bahl's Arab servant, dead inside. Like de Bahl, Frangipani was wearing Rumanian uniform — I guess it would have taken them clear through to Chisinau, where they had a plane waiting.'

She had picked up a file from the pen tray and was using it on her nails. 'You did a good job, Don. The old man's really pleased. He has someone with him for the moment, but as soon as he's free, in you go and collect your laurels. Doesn't that set you up?'

'If you only knew how cold all these things leave me.'

She sighed. 'My gracious, you *have* got the blues.' She glanced at him narrowly. 'By the way, that Miss Selmar's been ringing you up!'

He swung to her eagerly. 'Miss Selmar? From where?'

'From all over Europe, it seems to me. First, from Bucharest ...'

He nodded. 'I know. Immediately after the explosion Selmar insisted on whisking her off, that very night. She called me at Orghina, but I was away, at military headquarters at Chisinau, and when I reached Bucharest, she and her father had already left for Paris.'

'She's telephoned two or three times from Paris. How do you suppose she got this number? Did you give it to her?'

'No, but Peregrine Dyson of Belgrade was in Bucharest when she was there and she probably wormed it out of him. She's rather a determined person.'

'You're telling me! She's been on the telephone already twice today.'

'Are they still in Paris?'

'She's here in London.'

'In London?' His air was dismayed. 'Hanky, what did you tell her?'

'That you'd be here at five-thirty!'

'Oh, my gracious. Where is she staying?'

'At Claridge's. She wants you to call her up.'

'At Claridge's! Oh, my goodness!'

She laughed rather acidly. 'You sound as though she scared you. Don't you want to meet her?'

'Want to meet her? Oh, Hanky, you don't know how much.' He planted his two hands on the desk and leaned towards her. 'Tell me, Hanky, what do you think of a poor man who marries millions?'

'A man who marries for money is a louse.'

'Suppose he's in love, not with the money, but with the girl?'

'Then he's a fool if he doesn't marry her. But if you must get married, why not choose a nice, sensible English girl?'

He slipped his arm about her. 'Because the only nice, sensible English girl I'd ever want to marry is wedded to her work. And she wouldn't have me, anyway!'

'How right you are!' she retorted feelingly. But she did not remove his arm. The buzzer sounded twice. 'That's for you!' she said. 'And it's not a minute too soon. You've held up my work quite long enough.' He stooped and planted a kiss on the top of her head and ran out. Mechanically, her hand went to her hair, restoring it to its pristine smoothness. Then she sniffed, looked for her handkerchief, found it and blew her nose. Turning to the sheet of paper in the typewriter, with rather unnecessary force she typed the date, then reached for her handkerchief again.

The fog had thickened when Boulton left the office: he could no longer make out the outline of the square railings. The side-lamps of a coupé drawn up at the kerb thrust feeble pencils of light into the brown murk.

The young man halted under the porch. Melissa had not telephoned again. Should he ring her? It was no more than common manners, she had called him so often. Besides, knowing that he was in London, she and her father would expect him at least to inquire for them after the vicissitudes the three of them had undergone together — maybe he ought to send Melissa some flowers: American girls expected such attentions. He turned back towards the door: he would call Claridge's from the telephone in the hall. But on the instant he changed his mind — he would go to his club and see how he felt after having a drink: he could telephone from the club.

Once more he faced the fog, stepping out on the pavement and peering through the clinging mist. Not a cab in sight, not a sign of any vehicle, indeed, except the coupé parked there. The Chief's car, he surmised — a pretty snappy-looking bus for the old man to drive, he reflected, running his eye over it. Then he started. That bold streamlining, the coquettish rake of the radiator, seemed familiar — gosh, it was a Selmar Eight. And the door was opening. He caught a glimpse of a small hand, an expanse of silk stocking, and a familiar voice said, 'Are you coming quietly, or do I have to get out and grab you?'

He went to the door. 'Melissa!' he exclaimed incredulously.

'Do you realise I've been sitting here for nearly an hour and a half waiting for you?' she cried. 'I'm frozen to the bone. Hop in! Steve wants to see you. He has a cheque for you.'

He drew back suspiciously. 'A cheque?'

'Will you please get in and shut that door, or do you want me to get pneumonia?' With a slightly dazed air he obeyed. 'You needn't be stuffy about it,' she went on. 'It's your commission on that bear raid of his. He cleaned up a packet and this is your whack — fifty thousand dollars!'

'Fifty thousand dollars! I couldn't possibly accept it. Why, it's a fortune!'

'He's going to offer you a job, too.'

'A job?'

'Uh-huh. Which way do we go from here to get to Claridge's?'

'Straight to the end of the square and turn left.' The engine sprang into life and they drew away. He rubbed the screen with his hand. 'Can you see where you're going? It's as thick as the devil.'

'I can manage.'

'Then follow the kerb.'

'O.K. It's a job in the Selmar works. They're going to manufacture planes and they'll want someone to take charge of the experimental department. Wow, we were almost on the sidewalk then!'

'Hadn't you better let me drive?'

'Certainly not. Are we going right?'

'Yes. This'll bring us into the main road. Hey, mind that car!'

Head lamps bore down on them. The girl pulled out and

stalled the engine. 'How'd you like to go to work for my old man?' she said, setting the automatic starter in action. When he did not answer, she turned her head to look at him. 'Melissa!' he said hoarsely. Then, 'Watch out!' he cried, there was a crash, a jangle of glass, a crunching sound and the car came to an abrupt halt, wedged against a post on the pavement. The young man was about to spring out, but she laid a hand on his arm. 'Don!' she pleaded.

The car lights had gone out, shattered by the impact: the fog swirled about them. 'Why did you run away from me?' she questioned reproachfully.

He gazed at her hungrily. 'I told you — too much money.'

'Was that the only reason?'

'You know it was.'

With a little sigh she drew him to her and laid her head on his shoulder. 'Then that's all right. You can marry me now since you're a millionaire.'

'A millionaire?'

'Certainly. You have fifty thousand dollars. At two hundred lei to the dollar it puts you way up in the class of millionaires — in Rumania. The only difference between you and Steve is that he's a dollar millionaire and you're a Rumanian one. If one millionaire can't marry another millionaire's daughter, I ask you! Aren't you going to kiss me, Don? Wait, I'll put out the light.' Her hand moved to the instrument panel and clicked off the little dash light that cast a feeble radiance on their faces. As the darkness closed in upon them all the sweetness and softness of her was in his arms, and their lips met.

THE END

www.ingramcontent.com/pod-product-compliance
Lightning Source LLC
Chambersburg PA
CBHW031002260626
47169CB00002B/666